ABBIE'S COWBOY CARE

WITNESS PROTECTION - RANCHER STYLE: THATCHER'S STORY

SWEET MONTANA BRIDE SERIES

BOOK FIVE

KIMBERLY KREY

Candle House Publishing

Abbie's Cowboy Care: Witness Protection - Rancher Style: Feel-Good, Christian Cowboy Romance; Thatcher's Story

This is a work of fiction. Names, characters, businesses, places, events, locales, and incidents are either the products of the author's imagination or used in a fictitious manner. Any resemblance to actual persons, living or dead, or actual events is purely coincidental.

❀ Created with Vellum

CHAPTER 1

5 *Years Ago*

Abbie's hand shook as she stared at the test results. A small control panel centered in the white wand showed two pink lines. Shockwaves of horror pulsed through her as she stared at it, blinked, then stared some more.

With a shaky hand, Abbie tipped the pregnancy test to the light, tilting it up, then down to see if that second line might fade.

It didn't.

She was pregnant. Pregnant at eighteen years old, with Thatcher Copeland's baby.

That final thought sidetracked the fear racing through her. *Maybe I really can have a life with Thatcher. This is something Mom can't take away from me.*

But who was she kidding? Abigail Carrington had a role to play. Perfect daughter to Spencer Carrington, highly-renowned hedge fund manager, and Eloise Benedict Carrington, one of only two heirs to the generational wealth of New Hampshire's famous Benedicts.

They were public figures held in high regard. The couple rarely missed a benefit auction, concert, or banquet that let them flash their generosity in spades. *"Can you believe the Carringtons bid 3.4 million dollars on one painting? They have big hearts, that's why. They truly care about the underprivileged youth in America...or the endangered species of the world or..."* Whatever made them look good.

Now it was Abbie's turn to make them look good.

All she had to do was marry Quinten Bromley, one of America's most recognizable contemporary composers. Famous for pieces performed by the world's top orchestras as well as his recent Grammy award-winning album, *Darkest Affair.*

Quinten met Mom and Dad's strict criteria for matrimony. He was filthy rich, devilishly handsome, and adored by the nation's elite. Quinten took a liking to Abbie when they met at his *Strings for Starlight* event—meant to raise awareness of the city's pollution problem. Abbie's parents insisted she accept his advances despite the ten year difference in age. Despite the fact she was already in love with someone else. Not that she'd dared tell Mom and Dad about Thatcher.

Abbie shook her head at the recollection. It didn't matter that she'd been a mere seventeen years old; Mom was set on introducing them—as if she'd *known* the man couldn't resist a name so prestigious. Or a face that looked so much like her own. *"You're a spitting image of me,"* Mom would often say, smoothing the locks of her blonde hair while batting lashes over her matching blue eyes.

Quinten was used to getting what he wanted. The man had the nerve to ask her father for Abbie's hand in marriage just three weeks after her eighteenth birthday. Her parents hadn't told Abbie, but she'd overheard Mom bragging about it during her bridge party the night before Abbie flew to Grandma's for one last summer.

A summer she'd never forget. Abbie looked forward to those Montana ranch trips every year while her parents vacationed in one of the many properties they owned around the world. Her great-grandparents were the reason Abbie didn't see the world the way her parents did. The reason she craved a different life than the one her parents had mapped out for her. Of course, having Thatcher around was icing on the cake. She'd been smitten since they met at the fishbait stand when she was eight years old. And as each summer came and went, Abbie's feelings for the cute boy with the cowboy hat bloomed into something beyond schoolgirl crushes and childhood dreams. She had fallen thoroughly in love with him.

And now she was going to have Thatcher's baby.

Abbie pictured the summer nights they'd spent by the firepit. The many times she'd watched him dig a match out of the matchbox and strike it along the rough, sandpaper edge. She always loved the sound of that sharp crack as the flame sparked to life. Many times, the wind would blow the flame out before Thatcher could lower it to the kindling he'd prepared.

It became habit for him to cup the flame with his large palm. Abbie would help too, positioning her outstretched hands around the fragile flame to keep it alive.

That's what this felt like—this delicious secret she now kept. New life that was half her, half him, and wholly against her parents' plan for her.

A deep ache rippled through her at the thought of them trying to stop this somehow. Reputation was everything to the Carringtons, and they would *not* allow theirs to be sullied by Abbie's actions. Abbie had seen it firsthand as an early teen, seen the way Mom's niece Dorothy —Abbie's older cousin on the Benedict side—had gone wild, acting out against her parents' wishes, winding up in tabloids and media posts worldwide.

If there was one thing they'd drilled thoroughly into Abbie's head, it was that she did not want to end up like Dorothy. And that meant she'd need to toe the line her parents had mapped out for her whether she liked it or not.

At once, she was on her feet and pacing beyond the clawfoot tub, past the enclosed steam shower she had running to keep Mom at bay, and toward the white velvet chaise lounge chair at the far end of her bathroom where a vase of fresh roses stood perfectly in place. She spun on one heel, gaze shifting to the steam-filled enclosure. Not so much as a wisp of vapor had escaped the glass case—just what Mom paid for.

Abbie kept an even pace along the length of the bathroom, but her eyes kept getting drawn back to the great, white trails of steam where they drifted and swirled within the tightly confined space. One thick plume darted toward the upper corner beside the window, looking as if it might somehow escape. She slowed her pace so she could watch, inwardly hoping it might break free.

Her heart thudded out of beat as she studied the gold-lined frame, steam licking its way up the glass. *Come on, just do it. Seep out of that thing.* But just as it looked as if it might push past the tightly-sealed seams, the cloudy trail curled in on itself, bloating, swelling, filling the box with its counterparts from every inward angle.

How could something so weightless and free be trapped in such a way?

Easy. Put a price on it.

Well, Abbie did not have a price. And she was eighteen years old now. Her parents couldn't keep ruling her life, right?

She gulped, rushed back to the latrine—as Mom insisted on calling it—and plopped onto the closed seat. She leaned over the pregnancy wand once more, shaking her head at the sight of those two brazen lines.

Maybe she could run. Catch a bus from New Hampshire all the way to Montana. Would Grandma Dottie let her stay there for good? Her parents would kill Abbie if she left without telling, but if she wanted her life to be her own—if she didn't want to be as trapped as the steam in that shower—Abbie would have to break free.

A sudden knock rapped at the door. "Abigail?"

Abbie stiffened, lowered her gaze to the exposed test,

then snatched the small wand off the counter and clutched it to her chest. "Yeah?"

"Your father and I would like to speak with you, please. Meet us in the entrance hall, will you?"

Abbie shot a side-eyed glance toward the door. Mom had used her formal name—Abigail instead of Abbie. That in itself wasn't much of a red flag; Mom had warned Abbie she'd need to go by that once she turned eighteen. As it was, Dad had refused to call her anything *but* her full name since Abbie was born. Still, when her parents called her to the entrance hall, it meant they had company. She could see it then, Quinten standing before the grand staircase in his pressed suit, one hand in his pocket cupping a ring box.

A torrent of nausea rose like a tide in her gut.

"Did you hear me?" Hints of desperation clung to Mom's tone.

Abbie shot to her feet, ripped open the door to the glass case, and twisted the gold, cross-handled knob, silencing the buffering hiss. She stepped back, stomach churning as she watched the steam break beyond its cage at last.

"I think," she started to say, cringing as acid pooled up the back of her throat. Abbie barely made it to the toilet in time to lift the lid, drop to her knees, and hover over the bowl as her body retched. Blindly, she spun the toilet paper roll, tore off a long strip, and used it to wipe off her chin. "I'm sick," she hollered before another gag started a second round.

"Gracious, Abigail. What have you been eating?"

Abbie only shook her head. "The same thing you guys did." They'd eaten dinner together, after all.

"Well, this isn't going to do." She didn't sound concerned; she sounded put out. Quinten was *definitely* there. Tonight was the night, and Abbie would bet Grandma Dottie's horse that everyone in their circle of friends knew it too.

Throat burning, body weak, and mind darting in a dozen directions at once, Abbie flushed the toilet and reached for a Kleenex off the back of the seat. She wiped her face once more. "Don't worry about me, Mother," she said, sarcasm thick in her tone. "I'm fine."

"*Are* you?" Mom asked frantically. "Are you feeling better now?"

Was she kidding?

"Do you feel good enough to join us for just a moment? Then I can have Sylvia care for you."

This was rich. And the perfect demonstration of the vast difference between Grandma Dottie and her own parents. Abbie's wellbeing came second to her parents' agenda. Always. But Abbie did know one thing that her mom would listen to.

"I look terrible," she warned. "I'm all red and blotchy from the steam bath."

"Then apply makeup. Quickly."

"It won't help. I broke out in a cold sore, and I have this rash on my chin..."

It went silent for a beat, and Abbie could practically hear Mom's wheels turning. "It can wait," she snapped. "I'll, um...I'll send Sylvia to your room."

Abbie spotted the empty pregnancy test box beside the abandoned grocery sack, its receipt curled into a roll just inside. She shoved the box and test in with the receipt, wadded it as tightly as she could, and tugged one of the plush towels off the rack. She bent in half and prepared to wrap the towel around her head.

After two failed attempts to stuff the sack and its contents into the wrapped towel around her hair, Abbie finally got it to stick. She bit at her bottom lip to redden it, scratched her chin to do the same, then sighed at the sight of herself in the mirror.

How was she going to get out of this?

CHAPTER 2

 *resent Day*

Thatcher stared at the dwindling flames in the fireplace, rotating the phone in his palm from front to back, back to front, and over again. Just where in the Hades was she?

The others in the house had long since gone to bed, exhausted from the eventful day. His brother Wes had gotten married no more than twelve hours ago. And though the ceremony had gone off without a hitch, life as Thatcher knew it had come to a screeching halt shortly after the bride and groom said *I do.*

All from a phone call.

He hadn't recognized the number, of course, but the East Coast area code caused an image of Abbie to flicker to mind even then, as if he'd sensed her need for him in that moment. Still, he dismissed the notion and let the call go to voicemail—he was at a wedding celebration, after all.

A message was left, and then his phone rang again. Thatcher dodged that one too, opting to check the voicemail instead. What could be so important? A soon-to-expire warranty? A killer deal on a loan for a new truck? Only, even as he'd lifted the phone to his ear in the crowded space, *oohs* and *ahs* sounding as the photographer snapped photos of the bride and her daughter on the chapel's porch, Thatcher had a feeling it was something more. Something big.

"This is Abbie," she'd nearly panted on the voicemail.

Those three words alone were enough to send shockwaves through his every limb.

"If you never want to talk to me again, that's fine, I understand. I'm just...I don't know where else..." A long pause. And then his phone had started to buzz again.

Thatcher had lowered the device to glance at the screen—same number—then rushed down the steps and toward the shoveled walkway. Stark afternoon sunlight blasted off the chapel's snowy yard as he lifted the phone back to his ear, heart ticking like a timebomb in his chest.

"This is Thatcher."

"Can I come out there for a while?" she'd asked frantically.

His mind spun. *"What?"*

"Quinten's trying to kill me," she'd breathed. *"No one believes me, but he is* crazy."

Panicked, Thatcher had fired off questions as quickly as they came to him. Had she called the police? Did her parents know? *Who* didn't believe her? And most importantly, where was she?

She hadn't answered a one of them with certainty. Just kept insisting that if Quinten found her now that she'd left, he'd kill her. *"I might come out there if it's okay. Grandma Dottie's dead, so he'll never suspect—"*

"Of course," he'd blurted without thinking. Who needed to think? Sure, Abbie had wronged him, but the woman needed a safe place to stay. And hadn't his family just brought on a woman in need with Wes's new bride? And Taja had a daughter to boot.

"I don't know for sure if I will," Abbie had said. *"I'll see."* And then she'd hung up, leaving Thatcher sick, terrified, and drowning in the dark sea of his memories. Memories of Abbie's declaration of love for Thatcher and her conflicting resignation to follow the path her parents had laid out for her.

The sound of a beeping microwave pulled Thatcher from his musings. He sniffed, recognizing the hearty aroma flooded with a rich, buttery scent. *Just who's popping popcorn at this hour?*

He stared at the walkway leading to the kitchen, dark until the microwave popped open, and then dark again once it shut. A clatter sounded, followed by muted thuds that had Thatcher picturing popcorn tumbling into a bowl. Moments later, Nash waltzed into the room, past the colorfully lit Christmas tree, hair mussed, biceps bulging beyond his ribbed tank top. Thatcher and Nash had spent a lot of time building definition like that, and he'd be danged if the two weren't close to the same size now.

"'Sup, brother?" Nash dug a hand into the bowl, slid it onto the coffee table toward Thatcher, and sank into the couch. A soda bottle landed on the table next.

Nash started out as Thatcher's favorite cousin when they were kids; when Nash and his brother Wyatt's parents were killed close to thirteen years ago, the boys had become brothers instead, moving in where they'd lived ever since.

If there was anyone Thatcher would open up to about his torment, it'd be his ride or die, Nash. Of course, he already knew the crux of it. The glaring reality of what Abbie Carrington—the woman who still owned way too much of Thatcher's heart—faced in this moment.

Thatcher shuddered. "Can't believe her idiot parents insisted she marry this..." He bit back a curse, shook his head, then indulged himself by growling the word with a vengeance. "Look what they did. They insist she marry this jackhole because he fits the bill, and the guy ends up trying to *kill* her." Another shock of fear ruptured through him.

Nash crunched on his popcorn. "It's messed up, man. No doubt. Her parents wouldn't know a good guy if it hit them in the face."

Thatcher's brow furrowed, the off comment causing thoughts of abuse Abbie might have endured over the years. Had he been violent all along?

It wasn't a new question to run through his mind in the last twelve hours, but it filled him with enough venom to rival a pit of vipers. Thatcher's fists tightened, his veins bulged, and a volcano of fire erupted in his chest.

"Dude," Nash said. "You should probably go pound the punching bag for a while. You're not going to sleep anytime soon. I'll go with you if you want."

But Thatcher only shook his head. "I feel helpless. What can I do—call the police? Abbie could have done that herself. Instead, she called *me*—an ex-boyfriend from five freaking years ago."

"Well," Nash corrected. "You guys were a *thing*, but she wasn't exactly your girlfriend unless it was summertime."

Thatcher rolled his eyes. Nash was right. Forget the fact that she lived on the other side of the country; Thatcher would never be someone she could bring home to Mom and Dad. They had other plans for Abbie, and for the life of him, Thatcher couldn't understand why she refused to stand up to them.

The fire crackled on. Nash crunched into another handful of popcorn, then tipped back his drink. Thatcher merely stared at the flames, recalling the day Abbie's wedding announcement came. Talk about pretentious. Between the oversized envelope lined in gold, the waxed moniker over the second seal inside, and the other dozen ridiculous embellishments, they'd no doubt spent a small fortune on the invites alone. *Look at us, New Hampshire's newest, hottest, wealthiest couple.*

It had been a dagger to the heart—that smile Thatcher knew all too well.Wide, beautiful, sexy. Only by then it looked cruel as well. *You thought you could have me? You thought I'd really leave all of this behind? You thought what we shared meant something?*

Not something. It had meant *everything* to him.

Thatcher clenched a fist around his phone, wanting to crush it, throw it into the flickering embers or, most of all, use it to call that number back and see exactly where Abbie was in that moment.

"So you're *really* going to let her stay here if she shows up?" Nash asked after a long pause.

Thatcher sensed the meaning behind that question. He and Nash were all but joined at the hip. And in the times they *weren't,* they were off wining and dining the handful of women they were each interested in respectively.

Thatcher had three women he was casually dating: Pageant queen Camille was most like Thatcher of the three; she was loud, fun, and she loved going out for a good time. Leah, whose quiet nature and sharp intellect intimidated lesser men, preferred staying in and binging documentaries she could talk about for hours. Just being with her made him feel more intelligent. Just ask Wyatt, who also liked Leah but hadn't been able to keep her attention since he traveled so often with rodeos and whatnot.

And then there was Deborah Springfield, a savvy real estate investor who texted Thatcher each time she came through town. The two would go out, swap stories, laughter, kisses…

Thatcher had been up-front with each woman, letting them know he wasn't ready for any sort of commitment. He'd found a way, it seemed, to fill the void in his life. Not to a satisfactory degree—only Abbie could do that—but enough that he was happy. Healed. Or so he thought. Abbie hadn't even arrived yet, and already Thatcher felt himself unraveling.

Which brought him back to Nash's question. It seemed he was *really* asking if the party was about to end.

Nash likely sensed the metaphorical wrench plummeting toward his perfectly balanced life. And in a way, Thatcher sensed it too. It was selfish to think of how this would affect them, but just as Thatcher had been there for Nash when he lost his parents, Nash had been there to help Thatcher pick up the pieces when Abbie went and got married mere months after she and Thatcher's intimate rendezvous.

And the fact was, there'd always been an unspoken fear, as lame as it might be, that when either Thatcher or Nash decided to finally get serious about his future, the other would be left behind. Thatcher had always secretly hoped it would happen at the same time. Perhaps a pair of hot twins would move into town and fall in love with the two youngest and best-looking Copeland brothers.

"I don't know what's going to happen, man," Thatcher finally said. "Mama and Pops said she could stay. Said that Abbie and I can move into the bunkhouse once Belle and Scott fly back to Texas." Thatcher's only sister Belle and her husband planned to leave the day after Christmas.

"So you'll be right across the hall from her?" Nash asked. "In that big, empty house?" Insinuation coated his words.

"Yep," Thatcher said blankly. "Not that the circumstances would allow much to happen. She's a married woman, Nash."

"Doesn't the fact that he tried to kill her sort of…void all that out?"

Thatcher only shrugged. If he were honest, he'd dreamed about the day Abbie might call and say things were through between her and Quinten. But never in all his days had he imagined it'd be like this.

Under different circumstances, Thatcher might have an I-told-you-so air about him. But that would be unfair for a whole lot of reasons, the least of which being that Abbie had never *wanted* to marry the guy. She'd simply resigned herself to marrying whomever her parents desired from the time she was young. And that's just what she had done, no matter how much it broke Thatcher's heart. No matter how much, or so she said, it broke her own heart.

And now she was leaving him. Thatcher could barely get past the fact that she was running for her life, but for the brief seconds that he did manage to glimpse beyond that daunting detail, sparks of excitement kindled hot within him. He wanted Abbie more than anything in this world, and soon, she'd actually be there with him.

"She's the one, you know?" Thatcher said, the words drifting from his lips like an afterthought. "The one who keeps haunting me like some long-lost ghost. I can see her face, hear her laugh, and though I haven't pinned down what the scent is, I can smell her sometimes too."

"Do you think she's done with this guy forever?" Nash asked. "Or do you think she'll…I mean…some women go back. This might not even be the first time something like this has happened."

Thatcher winced. He could tell Nash was trying to speak delicately, but the words still scraped against Thatcher's ears like an abrasive wad of steel wool. He gritted his teeth and groaned.

"Sorry," Nash said. "Hey, if you want to get your mind off this, come up to the den. I'm going to put on a movie."

"Dude," Thatcher hissed as Nash headed up the steps with his bowl and drink. "It's four a.m."

Nash spoke over a mouthful of popcorn. "Can't sleep either."

Yep, that's how it had always been with him and Nash. If one of them suffered, they both did.

Thatcher pressed at his forehead as he remembered the list of upcoming events involving Nash—like the double date they were supposed to go on once evening rolled back around. Plus, Deborah was coming through town over New Year's; Nash planned on securing a date of his own so the four could hit a club in the next town over.

Now those plans, and any others in his near future, were mere particles, tossing and turning in the sloshing waves and rising currents. Currents that had Thatcher floundering and gasping for air.

A storm was coming through. And though she hadn't arrived yet, she was already making waves. Still, no matter how destructive it might be, Thatcher would never let it pass him by. No, come hades or high water, Abbie Carrington was one storm Thatcher would run to each and every time.

CHAPTER 3

Streetlights made streaks across the bus window in the dark night.

Abbie's eyelids grew heavy as she took in the passing city. Colorful Christmas lights glowed from several establishments, reminding her of how close the holiday was. She shifted in her seat while hugging the backpack on her lap.

She'd made it from Manchester to Boston, Boston to Chicago, and Chicago to St Paul. Three major cities, four different transfers, and thirty-six hours away from her old life.

Abbie gave into a yawn as her body released another level of tension. During the last transfer, she'd worked up the nerve to call Thatcher Copeland—a man whose name, even in thought, sent a thrill straight through her core. She hadn't planned out what to say, only meant to tell him she might show up at his door.

Already, she was rethinking that plan. Abbie didn't want to force herself into Thatcher's life. As it was, it had taken a lot of nerve to reach out to a man she'd hurt so deeply. He could have disconnected the line at the first sound of her voice or told her off and then hung up.

She'd been prepared for the worst, yet even as Abbie began to ramble about her desperate circumstance, Thatcher piped up with his reply.

"Of course," he'd said, as if it hadn't taken a thought in the world.

Her heart basked in that warm recollection, but she did her best not to overthink it. Thatcher was a gentleman, after all, like Grandpa Buck. His protective nature, especially where women were concerned, wouldn't let him turn her or anyone else down in their time of need. It didn't mean he *wanted* to help or that he was even in a position to do so. Heck, he could be married with kids by now.

That realization was razor-sharp. Abbie closed her eyes until the burning it caused subsided. Images of what might have been played through her mind. What if she *hadn't* gone along with her parents' plan? What if she hadn't lost the baby? What if she'd married Thatcher instead?

They could have it all by now. A cozy home, a growing family, and the lifestyle Abbie knew she'd never get no matter how badly she wanted it.

But that hadn't stopped her from dreaming. Especially once the severity of her situation with Quinten started to sink in.

Abbie had always pitied women trapped in abusive relationships. And she, like so many, caught herself asking why. Why did they stick around? Why didn't they just leave?

Like it was *that* easy. That simple.

She knew better now. Even after Quinten became violent, having choked her on one occasion, kicked and beat her on several others, Abbie hadn't believed she was one of those women—trapped in an abusive relationship.

Abigail Carrington Bromley was helping her emotionally wounded husband work through the unresolved issues of his past. She was a warrior willing to stand on the front lines if it meant helping the man who cherished her above all else. One of America's most beloved musical prodigies—a man with countless candidates among the world's elite—had picked *her.*

He always made a point to tell her as much after his outbursts, often through sobs. He was so sorry they fought; he loved her, and she was everything to him—his entire world would crumble without her.

After Abbie earned her Dartmouth degree in Studio Arts, with an emphasis on photography, she put her aspirations on hold because Quinten didn't want her to work outside the home. Unless, of course, it meant photographing him as he traveled the globe for special events. How could she complain? He had a face worth photographing. Several ads, magazine articles, and billboards featured her photos of him, always earning steady streams of praise, which felt good.

Until it didn't.

And while he was skilled at verbally professing his love for Abbie and even apologizing after his blowups, Quinten never fessed up to his abusive nature. The closest he'd come was during a predictable spell of guilt that shadowed most of his outbursts.

"I'm sorry we argued," he'd say to her. *"You know how intense I get. How madly in love I am with you. With a passion like mine...well, you can't choose which end of the stick you're going to get. I'm a package deal. Just like when I married you, though you were pregnant with some other guy's baby. I looked past it. That's what couples in love do."*

Abbie never had loved him the way he loved her. She'd grown to care for Quinten, to worry about him and, on some levels, respect him too. But playing the role of Quinten Bromley's wife was a job, a coveted one at that, even if it did have its downsides. Acting as a proper wife in high society is what she'd been born and bred to do.

By the time she identified the abuse for what it was, Abbie was convinced that Quinten would never let her leave. That his love—as flawed as he was in showing it—was too consuming. He was possessive and, Abbie believed, unwaveringly loyal. He claimed he'd never love another as long as he lived.

That idea was vanquished when Abbie found out about his many illicit affairs. It turned out Quinten didn't cherish her the way he claimed to. How could he? He was too in love with himself. Quinten hadn't loved, cherished, or protected Abbie. But he *had* tried to keep her as his own—that was the vow he was willing to fulfill—until death do them part.

That's when her awakening began. Quinten didn't care as much about her as he did his reputation. A man like him would do *anything* to keep his dark side hidden from the world.

At the library, where Quinten couldn't track her history, Abbie feverishly searched the topic of domestic abuse. She'd studied countless articles, watched dozens of videos, and read of how others escaped. Eventually, she quietly retained Leona Petrelli, one of the state's top-rated divorce attorneys—a woman who offered to meet her at the library where Abbie worked part-time.

Through Leona, Abbie learned that most domestic abuse homicides take place *after* the victim leaves. But if she was correct about his priorities, he wouldn't care so much if Abbie was gone, so long as she didn't shatter the picture-perfect image he'd maintained throughout his impressive career.

So, hoping he might allow her to cut ties under certain conditions, Abbie had picked her time wisely and approached him. *"I want a divorce. I won't tell anyone about your...our arguments,"* she'd told him carefully, calmly, as if speaking to a lion in a cage. A cage she was trapped in too.

"We can say it's mutual," she'd assured. *"That we simply had too many differences. You can sleep with as many women as you want, and I'll slip quietly out of your life."*

Quinten's face spoke before he could. The angular corners of his jaw popped. His Adam's apple bobbed. *"That's not how it works when you're married to someone like me,"* he told her through gritted teeth. *"Everyone—and I mean everyone—will want a piece of our story. A sliver of the crème de la crème pie. They'll do anything to get you to talk."* He lowered his chin and glared at her beneath his manicured brows, nostrils flaring like a wild bull's. *"And one day,"* he warned while his hand twitched, *"one day you'll* crack!"

He'd accentuated that final word with one of his backhanded blows—or at least, he'd tried to—but Abbie had seen it coming and ducked. Big mistake. One that almost cost Abbie her life. *"You'll slip quietly out of my life, all right, at my command,"* he'd assured, thick hands tightening around her throat.

It was all the incentive she'd needed to follow through with Plan B the very next morning. A plan she'd been plotting for over a year.

Abbie tugged a granola bar from her bag and studied the train schedule as she ate. In about six hours, they'd have a stopover. Then, after a few more city stops, she'd board her final train for a nineteen-hour trip from Minneapolis to Billings, Montana.

Since donning the disguise, it had taken Abbie a while to recognize her own reflection, which was a good sign. It meant that Quinten or one of his paid cronies wouldn't recognize her either. But now, as she stared down at her own crossed leg where it bounced, the ripped tights, combat boots, and black, denim skirt were affectionately familiar. Not quite *her* but belonging to a friend of hers maybe. A strong friend. One with actions as bold as her punk rock fashion.

The transformation took place in a gas station bathroom after she left her library shift early. Quinten had been in one of his moods that morning. Not the silent, angry type, since he'd thoroughly lashed out the night before. It was the common air he assumed after beating her, as if *he* was the wounded one for having done what he did. As the cycle went, he'd become more needy, using a toddler-like voice even to say what he wanted—usually a surprisingly long list of comfort items. *"I want a chocolate torte tonight,"* he'd said, tone pouty as he buried his face in the crook of her neck. *"And I want your breakfast special this morning, with extra capers."* Meanwhile, Quinten petted her hair with the same hands he'd tried to choke her with the night before. *"No one makes foody as good as my wifey,"* he'd added, reaching for the buttons of her pajama blouse. And though Abbie was willing to play along that morning—for the sake of keeping him in the dark about her plan to escape—she drew the line at intimacy.

"Well then I better get cooking," she'd said, slipping out from under him and sliding off the bed.

Quinten groaned. *"Fine, but you'll make it up to me tonight,"* he'd assured.

Not this time, she'd mused. *"You bet I will,"* she'd said anyway.

After preparing his breakfast of smoked salmon, poached eggs with hollandaise sauce, and extra capers on toast, Abbie started the prep work for his favorite triple-layer chocolate torte, which she'd promised to make that night. She melted chocolate, poured it onto the marble slab, and then slid it carefully into the freezer so it could make the perfect chocolate curls. She wouldn't be there to finish the job this time, but the prep work would give Quinten an added layer of security.

"Tonight after dinner," she'd said.

"That's my Benedict bride," he'd said in that stupid baby voice. Quinten loved pointing out the fact that he'd scored one of the coveted Benedict girls; they were a dying breed since Mom had only one sibling—a sister—who had two daughters of her own.

And that was that. Quinten had actually believed, after everything he'd done, that all was well with the world. She should have guessed he'd think so, but she hadn't. She'd spent the entire night worried he'd wake up in a panic and attempt to finish the job so she couldn't report him. At the very least, she'd almost *known* he'd insist she give up her shift at the library that day. She was only part-time, and since she'd taken extra time off for the holiday, it would be her final shift until after the new year.

"I was thinking," Abbie had said while gliding his breakfast plate across the counter. *"I think I'll wear that cashmere turtleneck today. The one you got me last year?"*

Quinten glanced up from his food, eyed the marks on her neck, then nodded. *"I like that one on you,"* he'd said before cutting into his breakfast with a knife and fork. *"You're not really going to their boring party afterward, are you?"*

Abbie feigned a grimace. *"I won't stay too long, but I've got to show up—there's a gift exchange. I can't leave someone high and dry."*

She watched carefully as he scooped capers onto his knife before transferring them atop his next bite. *"Fine,"* he mumbled around his food. *"Take them each a framed copy of my Grammy-winning album, why don't you? I'm feeling generous this Christmas."* And there she had it—Quinten had managed to bring the conversation back to himself again. Sure, some of her coworkers were slightly starstruck by Quinten, but that didn't mean any of them would take up precious wall space to display one of his albums.

Still, Abbie was free to go. He really had bought her everything's-just-fine performance. To him, this was just another day. His *Benedict Bride* would simply adapt to his escalated outburst of rage and abuse like she had for the last five years. The man was as happy and clueless as a clam.

During her shift at the library, Abbie had spoken privately with her boss, Anita, a rather serious-natured woman who—unlike everyone else Abbie knew—didn't gush about Quinten Bromley. In fact, Abbie dared say the woman had spotted the bruises, seen the signs, and suspected that Quinten wasn't all he was cracked up to be.

When Abbie told Anita that she needed to leave the shift early, that she'd miss the party as well, and she wasn't sure about returning after the new year, a flicker of understanding flashed in the woman's eyes. *"We'll have a place for you if you decide to come back,"* she'd said.

"The dump truck comes tonight, right?" Abbie asked. *"Seven o'clock?"*

Anita nodded.

Abbie handed the woman her cell phone and gave her a slow, pointed nod. *"This needs to be in there by then."*

Anita's eyes widened, as if her silent suspicions had been confirmed. She took the phone and slid it into her work apron. "*You'll be okay?*"

Abbie had no idea if she'd be okay. That all depended on how this played out. She nodded. "*Yes. I'm going someplace safe.*"

She thanked Anita, donned her lapel collar overcoat, knowing she'd soon kiss it goodbye forever, and slid on her shades. With a large Gucci bag over her shoulder—another item she'd soon part with—Abbie walked twenty-three festively decorated blocks in the winter cold to the bus station. She passed three other stations along the way before heading to a private, less-frequented restroom in the back corner of the station.

There, she pulled a ratty backpack filled with everything she needed for the transformation from the Gucci bag. She took the items belonging to her old life, carefully tacked them beneath mounds of discarded trash, and walked out a new woman. *Girl* might be more like it.

To top off her punk look, Abbie had styled a pale pink wig into low pigtails, donned a knitted beanie and scarf, then clasped a faux nose piercing around one nostril. She looked just like a teenager.

She'd even switched out her ear buds for a pair of retro wireless headphones that hung around her neck when they weren't in use. The look was a stark contrast to the teenager she'd really been. Proper and poised, not so much as a run in her stockings. That made her disguise all the better.

Her phone let out a buzz. Abbie currently had only

two contacts in her new phone: Thatcher and her attorney. She tugged the phone from the side pocket of her backpack and felt her heart thud out of rhythm at the sight of the screen.

Leona Petrelli: *Quinten has officially been served.*

Elation and panic warred within her. Abbie was thrilled they'd actually been able to serve Quinten with papers; that was a hurdle in itself. She gave the attorney's comment a thumbs up, adding the words *thank you* before hitting send. As understated as Abbie's response was, Leona had to know how grateful Abbie was. Her phone buzzed once more.

Leona Petrelli: *You bet. Here's to hoping he cooperates. Maybe there'll be a Christmas miracle.*

Abbie only wished. She replaced the phone and pulled her water bottle from her backpack next. She unscrewed the cap, took a swig, then stuffed it back in place as well. *A Christmas miracle, huh?*

She hadn't confided in her parents about the abuse in years, but that didn't mean they were ignorant of it. On one occasion, her mother had spotted the bruising through Abbie's makeup. *"Heavens, child, are you running into walls these days?"*

Abbie must have looked like a deer in the headlights. She'd barely been able to choke out a *"no...I umm"* when enlightenment flashed over Mom's eyes.

Her lips hardened into a straight line. *"Well, it's none of my business."*

A year later, Abbie attempted to tell her mother just what was happening at home, but she hadn't gotten far.

"All men have their problems, dear," Mom had blurted with a dismissive hand wave. *"He'll grow out of it, mark my words."*

"Thanks, Mother."

Benedict Financial, the source of Mom's multi-generational wealth, owned several vacation homes on the East Coast alone, each vacant in case the mood struck. For that reason, Mom and Dad would assume Abbie was hiding out in one of those when she went missing. Possibly making a statement of sorts or hoping to draw the line once and for all.

To keep them from panicking or starting a search party, Abbie penned a short letter and sent it from a postbox in Boston: *I'm not missing—I'm escaping, and you know why. If you want me to live, don't help him look for me.*

Her parents would do one of two things:

A: Lie and say the letter was stamped in the Maldives or one of the other dozens of faraway properties they owned, hoping to throw Quinten off their daughter's trail, or B: Cave and show him the Boston postage stamp because they favored Quinten over her. Because they didn't want people talking and Abigail should know better than to go around causing such a fuss. What was poor Quinten supposed to say when suddenly his devoted wife of five years failed to show for one important event after the next?

What they *wouldn't* do is share the contents of the letter with authorities. And since Quinten would call her parents about her disappearance first, they'd tell Quinten not to worry, she'd be back soon. Still...if Quinten was *really* out of sorts, Mom would tell him to check the nearest vacation homes—he was bound to find her in one of them. Christmas was just days away, after all.

Abbie had learned to stop expecting better behavior from her parents. They say that when someone repeatedly shows you who they are you're supposed to believe them. It had taken a whole lot of time for her to do that, but Abbie could finally say that she'd abandoned the misguided faith she'd once placed in them. Their priorities were as warped as Quinten's, which meant they weren't safe to confide in.

But there was one person, outside of Great-Grandpa and Grandma, that had proven to be safe: Thatcher Copeland.

A deep sense of longing burrowed into her chest. It was hard to believe she might actually get to see him soon. Neither he nor his family would be happy with her, Abbie knew that much, but she could say one thing for herself where her relationship with Thatcher was concerned: Abbie had never deceived him. She'd always made it clear that her parents would never let her marry a man from the country, and she wasn't the rebellious type.

Still, when Abbie found herself in the fresh country air beneath the blue Montana sky, she became someone new. Wild, free, daring, and adventurous.

Of course, Abbie had never thrown caution to the wind like she had during her final evening with Thatcher. She'd been the one to initiate new levels of intimacy that night. It may not have been the right thing to do, but the impending separation from Thatcher had sparked a fierce desperation in her, igniting thoughts and desires she hadn't entertained before.

She'd known even then that Quinten Bromley had already staked his claim on her. He wanted Abbie to be his wife, her parents had given their okay, and unless she wanted to become the next Dorothy of the family, earning the public disgrace Mom always warned her about, she needed to go along with it.

Looking back on it, Abbie sometimes wondered if she hadn't subconsciously wanted to get pregnant with Thatcher's baby. Ignorantly hoping, perhaps, that her parents would send her right back to Montana. *"Here,"* they'd say to Great-Grandma Dottie, *"you let this happen. She's your problem now."*

Whether passion, unidentified motives, or sheer desperation for the man she wasn't ready to give up—Abbie had done what she'd done. And as the train sped closer and closer toward the town where it all took place, she relived the moments in vivid detail.

When she first gripped hold of Thatcher's buckle, the two locked in a passionate kiss, Thatcher had kissed her with increased determination, and then come to his senses and stopped her.

"We can't, Abbie," he'd rasped. But she'd persisted. If she was going to endure heartache over losing Thatcher, her eighteen-year-old mind reasoned, she may as well take all she could that night, let herself see what it'd be like to really belong to the cowboy who'd stolen her heart one summer at a time.

She often wondered if he regretted that night. It

bonded the two in a way Abbie wasn't prepared for, as young and naïve as she'd been. Had it been the same for Thatcher?

Abbie held onto that question as she placed the headphones over her ears, cued a song on the phone she'd bought from her co-worker weeks ago, and hugged her backpack like it was her only friend. She closed her eyes then and let herself relive those final moments with Thatcher one last time.

Soon, Abbie would send him a text with her estimated time of arrival. If he was willing to harbor her for a time, he could find her at the downtown train station then. And if he wasn't willing, if he wanted nothing to do with her for the rest of his days, Abbie would get along. Either way, it was time to start her new life now that she'd left her old one behind.

CHAPTER 4

Thatcher shook his head at the sight of the blizzard ahead. He'd thought the storm was bad before; soon, he wouldn't be able to see a thing. He flicked the knob for the windshield wipers until they were going full blast. White, puffy flakes splatted against the glass before getting shoved against the growing mound of slush on the hood of his truck.

As it was, daylight was fading fast. If it got any worse, Thatcher would have to pull over.

But could he really afford to do that? Abbie—whose psychotic husband was trying to kill her, apparently—would pull into the station whether Thatcher was there or not. What if that crazy man was on her trail? He couldn't leave her waiting there like a sitting duck. So it was settled. He'd crash and burn—or in this case, freeze—before pulling over. Good thing he'd activated the navigation system on his phone and connected to the truck. Without it, he may just miss his exit completely.

Abbie's text had come in at six that morning. She'd given him an arrival place and time, adding that if he decided not to pick her up, she'd understand and make other arrangements. *"I'll be there,"* he'd assured, and then fallen fast asleep until noon.

Having Abbie resurface after all this time had set Thatcher back exactly five years, four months, and three days. September nineteenth—that date was forever seared into his brain. Since high school, Thatcher hadn't kept close track of what day it was in which month, but since he spent his days out on the field, he could tell just how far they were into each season by the placement of the sun.

Still, there was something deep within him that sensed the anniversary date as it neared. One moment he'd be focused on the task of herding cattle or mending a fence, the next he was recalling the way Abbie tugged the tucked hem of his shirt from his jeans.

He cleared his throat and gripped the wheel tighter, blinking to chase the recollection away. *Too late for that*—flames of heat had already kindled low in his belly. Dang, that night had been something. And as much as the impending farewell had nearly destroyed him, as much as he'd known he shouldn't have done what he did, Thatcher couldn't get himself to fully regret it. At least, not consistently.

Sure, he'd prayed for forgiveness more times than he

could count, but inwardly, Thatcher knew he'd do it all again if he could.

Gusts of relentless wind whistled and pushed against the seams of his windows, determined to sneak through. It was symbolic of the impending entourage he was about to face. Heck, already he could sense the physical distance between them dwindling. Abbie was a life force of her own, one Thatcher had been perpetually drawn to from the day they first met at the Bait Shack on Main. Buck and Dottie's great-granddaughter, with her golden hair, blue eyes, and that bright smile, had captured his heart at first sight.

He'd heard a lot about crushes the week prior when, on yearbook day after the third grade, Becky Milton confessed that she *like-liked* him. To top it off, she'd drawn pink hearts around her signature on his yearbook. His older brothers said it was only a matter of time before he started crushing on girls in return.

He'd doubted that, which is why he hadn't been able to put words to the odd feelings swirling through him when he first spotted Abbie. All he knew was that his heart beat faster when he looked at her, and he wanted very badly to see her again. He didn't know it then, but he was hooked.

Buck said she was there for the whole summer and needed to make some friends. If she liked it in Montana, she might come back for the following summers too. Pops said she was welcome over anytime, even if he did have a houseful of rowdy boys and one girl who was much older and into things like makeup and boys.

Pops' comment made Abbie giggle and look at

Thatcher while her cheeks went pink. The hook wriggled in deeper. It was one of the strongest sensations he'd felt up to that point, and it only grew greater over time.

The AI voice from his navigator spoke up, pulling Thatcher from his musings. His exit was approaching. It took effort to spot the break in the road, but once he caught sight of it, Thatcher veered onto the offramp. The snow blew in from the side now, giving Thatcher a better view through the windshield as the wipers swooshed and squeaked.

A quick glance at the automated map on the dash said he was minutes from his destination. Anticipation flared so hot in his gut and chest that it shot right up his neck. At the intersection, Thatcher flicked on the AC and aimed the vents at his face.

Most of his family members knew right where Thatcher was in that moment—headed to pick up the woman who'd broken his heart five years ago. She was married, in danger, and needing a place to hide away. And while none wanted Thatcher to turn Abbie down, they'd given words of warning all the same. *"You'd better guard your heart,"* Mama had said. *"Best be careful, son,"* Pops offered. *"The feelings are going to come rushing back,"* his oldest brother Rem had warned.

Nash, who hadn't yet recovered from the sleepless night, said through a yawn, *"What are you talking about, Rem? His feelings for her never left."*

That hot flare of chaos rippled through Thatcher anew, causing his pulse to spike. He hadn't admitted it to the group, of course, but he hadn't denied it either, because what Nash had said was true. He'd never stopped loving Abbie Carrington, and he couldn't help but fear that this time…this time she would ruin him completely.

A blessed break in the storm made the remainder of his drive clear, and soon he was pulling in front of the red log train station. The train was there, pulled along the boarding station while passengers unloaded or climbed aboard.

Thatcher backed into a slushy parking stall, shut off the engine, and gripped hold of the wheel. Heart pounding, temples pulsating, he peered through the snowfall to watch the trail of passengers approach the overpass. A couple came first, a tall man wheeling luggage over the sloppy ground while shouldering a mound of tote bags. The woman at his side clutched a pamphlet with both fists, using it as a shield to block the snow. Sadly, she was blocking her vision as well.

No wonder she wasn't carting so much as a handbag. It took everything in her to stay upright. Which reminded him…"Luggage," he blurted. "I better help her." He tugged the keys from the ignition, pushed the door open, and flinched as wet globs of snow pelted his face.

With an outward palm facing the storm, doing little to shield him from the onslaught, Thatcher glanced between the ground at his boots and the walkway he was headed to. He'd never seen Abbie during the winter months, but on social media he had, and boy did she look like money. Preppy trench coats, jockey-looking boots, and scarves that were probably made of some rare, imported cashmere. For someone who said she wouldn't have chosen such a lifestyle, she sure wore it well.

His mind tortured him with a memory of how well she'd worn his flannel shirts on summer nights by the lake, or his cowboy hat when they'd gone riding on crisp, early mornings, but Thatcher stopped himself cold with one sobering line. "She's been wearing another man's ring for the last five years," he grumbled, the sound swallowed up in the storm.

More passengers filtered onto the overpass as Thatcher approached it from the opposite end. He picked up his pace, not wanting Abbie to be weighed down by a bundle of bags in a blizzard. Yet just as he climbed the short staircase, shielding his face as best he could, he sensed that she was already on the walkway, her energy somehow pushing its way through the storm to reach him.

Pulse quickening, he scanned the growing crowd for signs of that khaki trench coat, those tall boots, and the crimson-colored scarves she tended to favor. *Not her, not her, not her, not—*

"Thatcher!"

Thatcher stopped short, eyes widening as he spun in place. The woman who'd called his name—the voice that was unmistakably Abbie's—was someone he'd just passed. She was walking toward him now, the wisp of a woman wearing a grunge band sweater with a miniskirt and tattered tights. Her hair was pink, unless that was a wig, topped by a beanie that read *Dope.*

It took a moment to get to her face, as distracted as he

was by her outfit, but once his eyes met hers, Abbie Carrington ducked her chin and blushed like she had when they first met.

"I'm…I know I look different," she said, teeth chattering as a puff of smoke trailed from her parted lips. "Let's go." She spun around and began leading the way to the parking lot.

Thatcher hurried to catch up, eyeing the small, fuzzy pink backpack on her shoulder.

"Where are your bags?" he asked, squinting as the snow fell harder from this angle.

Abbie forged on, marching through the mounding snow in combat boots fit for a soldier. "Right here." She popped her elbow to better reveal the ratty thing. What, had she pulled it out of a dumpster?

He could ask questions once they got in the truck, he decided. As they took the stairs, Thatcher resisted the urge to brace her lower back with the palm of his hand.

"This way," he said at the base of the steps. "Stand behind me if you want to take cover," he hollered.

To his surprise, Abbie shuffled up behind him, grabbed a fistful of his flannel shirt to keep up with his pace, and fell right into step at his back. "Thanks!"

His heart missed its next beat. Thatcher pulled in a shaky breath as he kept his eyes on the truck through the snow. Just how in tarnation was he going to do this?

CHAPTER 5

"I feel terrible," Abbie groaned into her cupped hands.

"What's wrong?" Thatcher asked through a grunt as he worked to close the cheap motel door. This, after he'd spent five whole minutes sanitizing his hands.

"This is what's wrong." She waved a hand over the dimly lit room. "It's a few days before Christmas, we haven't spoken in five years—"

"We did more than speak five years ago," he interjected, causing her face to flush with heat.

Good thing it was still hidden by her hands. "And suddenly I swoop in, make you drive through a freaking blizzard to get me, and now you're stuck in some raunchy motel for the night."

"Raunchy?" he repeated, attempting to slam the door once more. This time it clicked. "Got it," he said proudly.

Abbie pried her face away from her hands to see Thatcher spin around and dust his palms in satisfaction.

"Now," he said, "I'll drag a chair over here and—"

His words were cut short when the door burst open and smacked him square in the back with a thud.

Thatcher spun reflexively and swung, landing a punch on the unforgiving edge of the door. He gritted his teeth over a curse, glared at the wind-blown landing, and gave the door a solid kick with his boot. "Piece of crap," he mumbled while shaking out his hand.

Using his other hand, Thatcher secured the chain before dragging a chair to the door and propping it beneath the knob. "What kind of place doesn't have dead-bolts?" He sucked air through his teeth as he straightened up.

"Is your back okay?" she asked, her gaze drifting to his red knuckles. "And your fist? Sheesh, I'm ruining your life."

But Thatcher only shook his head. "I'm fine." He shuffled over to the bed and raked fingers through the wet strands of his hair. It was closer to blond than brown now, and he'd grown it out again. Or perhaps he'd kept it that length from his teenage days. It suited him even still. And so did that short facial hair accenting his jaw. In the cab of his truck, once they were free from the pelting snow and ripping wind, Abbie had checked Thatcher's ring finger. No ring. No tan line either, though she wasn't sure there'd be one in the winter.

Of course, maybe he'd given up on the idea of matrimony by this point. Many men did, though she hoped someone as good and decent as Thatcher Copeland never would.

"Do you want some ice for your hand?" she asked.

Thatcher stared at her, his eyes drifting up to her beanie, where he seemed to inspect it. "Sure." He climbed off the bed, walked to where she sat perched on the edge of the corner chair, and nudged her knit hat.

Abbie ducked. "What are you—" But then she noticed the small cluster of snow he'd scooped from, apparently, the top of her beanie.

"Thanks." He walked back over to the bed, resting his knuckles in the already melting snow mound in his palm. Steady drips of water slipped through his fingers and onto the short, industrial carpet.

Holy smokes, he was handsome. She'd watched him grow over the years, and each summer, Abbie mused he couldn't possibly get any better looking. Each year, he had. And now, this man-sized version of the rather muscled, even back then teenager, was a sight to behold indeed. Which led her thoughts back to his relationship status. If he was *with* somebody, Thatcher would have a hard time explaining this one—some overnight stop at a dive motel on the way home from the train station.

Abbie pulled the beanie off her head, then reached up to smooth the strands of her wig. "Are you, um…is there *anyone in particular* waiting for you back home?"

He lifted his gaze to meet hers.

"Anyone you need to call or text or something?"

Enlightenment flashed in his narrowed eyes as he

scrutinized her. "You mean my wife and kids or my mistress?"

Abbie's brow furrowed. "Stop it."

"Oh, or my *other* mistress—I have two. But only one was expecting to see me tonight." He cleared his throat, lowered his elbows to rest on his knees, and looked at her through his dark lashes. "Guess she'll be crying herself to sleep tonight."

Jealous irritation flared hot in her gut. Abbie lifted her shoulders and chin proudly. "I'm going to take a shower." She assumed he was joking about the mistresses, but the mere mention of him sleeping with other women made her heart hurt. Sure, she'd slept beside Quinten almost every night—minus the nights he was out of town—for the last five years. But not one of their intimate encounters had measured up to that night with Thatcher; he'd been the only one to capture her heart.

She started to move past him, but Thatcher reached out to grab her hand. "When you come back," he said, "I want to hear all about what this guy's doing."

Dread burned through her insides, spreading from her center to her limbs like a disease. Talking about things made them more real, and Abbie wasn't ready to accept the severity of her plight. Still, she'd known it was coming. In fact, had their drive from the station to the motel not been impacted by a raging blizzard, Thatcher would have probably already probed her about the abusive man who wanted her dead.

At last, she nodded. "Yeah, okay."

He gave her hand an affectionate squeeze before releasing it. "Okay."

Thatcher's sweet gesture, as small as it was, worked wonders on Abbie's nerves. He always did have a calming presence. Probably because, unlike her parents, he didn't take life too seriously. In the Carrington/Benedict home, a mere speck of bad gossip was a deadly virus, capable of wiping out the family and its entire legacy in one fell swoop.

And Thatcher wondered why rebellion wasn't an option.

In the tiny bathroom, Abbie reached an arm into the shower and twisted the faucet until water shot from the crusty-looking showerhead. She toyed with the temperature while reservations poured in with more pressure than the water. Dad had embraced Quinten like the son he always wanted. He'd even brought him on as a side partner in the company, a fact that inspired a pricey ad campaign with footage of Quinten composing his work while Carrington Financial "*makes a masterpiece of his investments.*" It was one more way the family would be negatively impacted by such a scandal. No matter how Abbie cut it, *this* was not good press for her family.

Score one more point for the disappearing act. Abbie would happily never speak to any of them again if she could just be left alone. Yet even as that thought ran through her mind, a familiar melody sounded from the other side of the cheap wall. Someone in the unit beside them was listening to Christmas music, or perhaps watching a holiday movie.

Nostalgia washed over her, a cocktail of select memories—the good ones. Like when Mom arranged for a snowball fight photoshoot. The photographer played carols to get everyone in the mood. Mom and Abbie wore matching scarves and gloves, and Dad became the target as his daughter and wife exuberantly tossed snowballs in his direction. Abbie had known it was staged, of course, but even still, the rare sounds of her parents' laughter felt like a gift.

She sighed at the recollection. In some ways, it would be hard not having them in her life. They were the only family she had left. If only Great-Grandma and Grandpa could have lived forever.

That final thought was all it took to trigger a downpour of emotion that begged for release. But Abbie shook her head and put her guard up. This wasn't a time to cry and fall apart over the things she might miss. This was a time to build herself up, to thank the Lord she was finally free, and pray Quinten would grant her the divorce while she was in hiding.

With her wig propped over a spare toilet paper roll on the counter, Abbie climbed into the shower. She took less time than she'd planned to, mainly because the water temperature teetered between lukewarm and outright cold. She was quick to dry off, slip into a pair of thermal PJs, and towel dry her hair. The bruises had gotten darker, she realized, spotting the purple fingerprint bruises where he'd choked her.

"Can't believe he did that," she whispered to herself, still somewhat shocked that he'd gotten so out of control. Her mind attempted to replay the terrifying moments, but she stopped it short. *Never again.* It was enough to know she'd gotten away. Quinten would never lay hands on her again.

Besides, she told herself while hanging the towel, unlike the memories of what he'd done to her, the bruises would fade soon.

Abbie mused on that as she combed through her damp hair with a pick—the only hair-related item she'd brought aside from the wig.

Abbie had never before used the provided soaps or hair products in hotels, but today, she was grateful for them. The matching shampoo, conditioner, and body soap had a fresh scent. One she'd never pick out herself since Abbie typically favored floral or fruit, and this was more herbal. Mint and lavender, she realized, glancing at the label.

And then it hit her: Grandma Dottie grew mint leaves in the front yard. She'd pinch the leaves and drop them into Abbie's lemonade or iced tea. And lavender—that reminded her of Grandma too. Dottie had lavender lotion and lavender soap. She had bunches of dried lavender dangling from the pot holder in her kitchen, strands of string knotted into a bowtie holding them in place.

A world of inner warmth bloomed in her heart. It was a sign. It had to be. *"Coincidence is God's way of remaining anonymous,"* as Albert Einstein once said. Grandma Dottie was with her in this, and that thought gave Abbie a fresh sense of hope.

She decided then to seek other products with the same scent. The refreshing fragrance would symbolize the army in heaven who stood behind her, helping Abbie to break free and start a new life, apart from her captor in her past.

Abbie sucked in a deep breath and said it again. Quentin was a part of her past now. And so were all the belongings she'd left behind—gladly so. Soon, she'd leave the great state of Montana behind as well. Of course, Abbie doubted she'd be so glad about that trip—her final journey out of this country and into her future permanent home in Melbourne, Australia—but she couldn't stay here forever.

Once Quinten and her parents exhausted all the obvious options, they'd start digging deeper. It might take time, but through the process of elimination, Mom would one day recall the pained desperation in Abbie's plea to live the life she'd always dreamed of—a life out in the country like Great-Grandma Dottie and Grandpa Buck.

By that time, the coast outside of the US should be clearer. Abbie could hide in plain sight down under—one of only three continents where the Benedicts didn't own real estate. The fact that she was leaving was reason enough to not indulge her feelings where Thatcher was concerned. Even if Thatcher was available, and even if he somehow forgave her and wanted her back in his life, Abbie's circumstances still wouldn't allow them to be together.

Her shoulders drooped as she set her eyes on the brass doorknob. *Thatcher Copeland is on the other side of that door.* The thought filled her with anxious anticipation.

Leona Petrelli, familiar with cases like Abbie's, had connections and could hide Abbie for a time if needed.

She could have taken the offer instead of reaching out to Thatcher, but she felt it'd be safer to accept accommodations through the attorney after the deal was done. Abbie was fooling herself, of course, because what she *really* wanted was one last chance to see Thatcher, the only man she'd ever loved. Still, she shouldn't lose sight of one simple fact: Abbie wouldn't be at Copeland Brothers Ranch for long, so it was best not to get caught up in the old feelings.

With that detail at the back of her mind, Abbie twisted the knob, swung open the door, and spotted Thatcher exactly where she'd left him, on the edge of the bed, head cradled in his hands.

Slowly, he angled his head to face her. With narrowed eyes, his gaze moved up the length of her until his eyes locked on hers. Abbie may have missed out on the hot water during her shower, but the heat that simmered through her when their eyes met nearly set her ablaze.

Heaven help her, but Abbie wasn't sure how she'd walk away from him a second time.

CHAPTER 6

A soft, familiar fragrance wafted from the bathroom as Abbie stood in the doorway, eyes fixed on Thatcher. She pinned the hem of her shirt between her finger and thumb and toyed with the fabric. Her gaze dropped to the floor.

Thatcher straightened and patted the spot beside him at the foot of the bed. "Come on in," he said. "I won't bite you."

A nervous laugh escaped her lips as she flipped off the bathroom light and began walking his way. Without the lighting at her back, Thatcher could see her face better. Flushed cheeks, damp hair, and eyes that narrowed as she scrutinized the bed.

Thatcher scooted away from the center to give her more room.

Abbie stopped in front of the bed, turned her back to

it, and then leaned against the edge. Not quite sitting, but not standing either. She folded her arms over her chest, a shaky breath making its way through her pursed lips.

"Abbie?"

"Yes?" she whispered, gaze set decidedly on her bare feet.

"You *do* remember me, right?" he asked.

A small V formed between her brows. "Excuse me?" She tore her gaze from the floor and glanced over.

"I know it's been over five years since we've been together…" His choice of wording nearly derailed him, but he cleared his throat and kept the course. "But I'm still *me*, okay? I'm not going to cross any lines—"

"I *know* you'd never do that," she blurted.

"And I won't pressure you to share anything you're not ready to share."

She searched his face, hints of doubt sprouting behind those blue eyes.

"Not tonight, anyway," he amended.

She nodded. "Okay."

"But if you're going to walk around here like some mummy—"

"Mummy?"

"Yes, mummy. You're all balled-up and stiff."

"I am *not."*

Thatcher huffed out a breath and tipped his head to one side. Slowly then, he reached out with his pointer finger, rested it against her upper arm, and gave it a nudge.

Abbie's body swayed enough to knock her off balance.

She unfolded her arms to catch herself on the bed. "Geez," she said. "Okay, okay, I'll sit down."

She climbed grumpily onto the bed, the bright red long johns making her appear childlike as she crawled a few paces, then plunked right onto the center. She folded her arms again and gave him a heated look. "Happy?"

No, he wasn't happy. The sight of Abbie's mini tantrum had given new life to a trail of long-forgotten memories that were now playing out in his mind. Like the time he'd won a bet skipping rocks. Abbie had gotten so riled she pushed him off the dock. The water was dang cold that day, but the sound of her laughter had made it all worth it.

"What are you thinking about?" she asked.

Here in the lamp's light, her fair skin appeared angelic somehow, complimenting the features he'd come to know and love. The soft bridge of her nose, the rounded, rosy tip. He'd expected her to lose some of the fullness in her cheeks, but she hadn't. The rounded shape kept her looking young and…innocent in a way. Or perhaps it was those wide eyes that did that, made her look like someone he wanted to protect if his dying breath depended on it.

At last Thatcher shook his head. "Nothing."

"You were smiling," she pointed out.

Was he that transparent or was Abbie just good at reading him?

"Okay," Thatcher started. If she wanted candor, he'd give it to her. "I was remembering the time you pushed me off the dock because I won a bet."

He watched as her face turned wistful. An echo of the

laugh he used to know got caught in her throat. She seemed to be fighting back a grin. "That's not why I pushed you. I pushed you in because you were spiking the football."

"What? There *was* no football," he teased.

"Don't play dumb. You were doing the most obnoxious celebration dance I've ever seen. Strutting along the dock like the cockiest peacock in town, singing that *we are the champions* song but with your name in it. 'Thatcher's the champion, my friends…'"

He liked how she remembered the details. Familiar heat flared low in his belly. "That sounds like me," he admitted.

"Right. I had to dampen your feathers."

"Yeah, you were good at that." Sparks seemed to ignite as she held his gaze.

This was dangerous ground. Sitting beside Abbie Carrington, reliving fond memories from their past, it might feel warm and cozy at first, like sitting next to a bonfire on a chilly night. But soon Thatcher would realize he wasn't beside the flames—he was smack in the midst of the fire, and Abbie was pouring on the gas.

Good thing he knew how to douse out the blaze. Thatcher knew what Abbie was capable of—lows he couldn't imagine sinking to. That was enough to keep him from flying like a moth to the glowing flame.

Abbie yawned, reached for one of the gross-looking throw pillows, and cuddled the thing like it was a stuffed teddy bear. "I don't even know where to start."

Thatcher tried not to think about all the nasty germs

living in the fibers of the pillow, though the mere thought made him shiver. His gaze wandered to the odd pattern of shadows along her throat. He'd barely paid notice when they first caught his eye, figuring that the dim lighting was playing tricks with his mind. But as he paid mind to the size and places of the dark blotches, a deep and aching chill rumbled up his back.

"Abbie!" he boomed, spinning to face her on the bed. "Did he do that to you?"

Her wide eyes said the question caught her off guard. Or perhaps his sheer volume had done that. Abbie lifted a hand to her neck. "I had it covered earlier. I'll cover it up again when we go back." She looked...*ashamed*? He couldn't be sure. His head was going light, his vision becoming spotty.

Hot adrenaline pumped furiously through his veins, making it impossible to hold still. Thatcher climbed off the bed and broke into a pace. "I cannot *freaking* believe that he put his hands on you like that." His heart raged like a storm of its own, bolts of lightning-like heat, rocking jolts of thunder, and the threat of something far worse than a winter storm looming in the distance.

"What do you *mean* you can't believe it? I told you he tried to—"

"Yeah, I know. But I pictured he...waved a gun at you or something." He sounded ridiculous, Thatcher realized, but he couldn't explain his stunned reaction to the sight of those marks. The obscene amount of fury and fire it flushed through his system.

"What difference does it make?" Abbie asked, pitch high and incredulous.

Thatcher stopped pacing and shot her a look. What *was* the difference? "I mean," he started to say. "The intent's the same, but…" Images of Quinten tightening a strained grip around Abbie's delicate neck made him nauseous. It *was* different. More violent, if that was possible. It felt like his chest was on fire, and it was spreading to his neck and face. He wouldn't be surprised if his upper half spontaneously combusted. "I want to kill him," Thatcher spat.

"Stop," Abbie said evenly.

"No," he cried, pacing once again. Tsunami-sized torrents of rage swelled within him, demanding some sort of escape. "How could he *do that* to you?" Fists trembling, he stared at her, keenly aware of the vast difference between him and her. Sure, Abbie stayed fit. It was easy to see she was toned, muscular even, but compared to him? There was no contest. Thatcher was built for hard labor. Life on the ranch demanded it. But even if Thatcher sat at a desk all day, composing music like that pathetic excuse for a man she'd married, Abbie still wouldn't compare to him in strength.

Another angry crash rippled through him. "That's just a whole new level of messed up."

"I know. That's why I left." Abbie sounded defensive, not that he could blame her. She probably sensed the question sitting on the tip of his tongue. The one he was aching to ask even if it wasn't fair. He picked a different one instead.

"He hurt you like that a lot?" His muscles tensed in preparation for her answer.

"Yes," she said.

Thatcher was half tempted to kick the chair from the door, tear into the storm, and scream at the top of his lungs. He brought a fisted hand to his mouth, clenched his eyes shut, and worked to quell the fury within him.

"I don't know how this is so surprising to you," Abbie said. "I told you he tried to kill me. He's capable of…"

Thatcher's lids pried open. He looked at her through narrowed eyes, not sure if he could handle hearing one more thing.

She shrugged and held onto the pillow tighter. "Of *anything*, I'm afraid."

"*Obviously*," Thatcher grumbled.

Abbie moved further to the head of the bed and began pulling back the blankets and sheet. He watched as she proceeded to climb between the sheets and plunk her head on the pillow.

"I'm exhausted," she said weakly, still cradling that nasty pillow like it was her only friend.

Thatcher wasn't tired in the least. In fact, he couldn't remember a time he'd been more hyped up. If he was home, he'd take to the punching bag and release the relentless, pent-up adrenaline with Quinten Bromley's stupid face egging him on for hours.

"So, what's the deal?" he asked, recalling Nash's comment about women who return to their abuser. "Are you going to try and divorce him or what? *Can* you even do that without having to come face-to-face with him?"

"He's already been served," she said through a yawn.

Thatcher furrowed his brow, figuring he hadn't heard correctly. "Divorce papers? You mean, before you left?"

"After."

Abbie went on to explain that she'd found an attorney months ago. She'd hoped to present Quinten with what she felt was an appealing offer, but before the conversation went far, Quinten had lashed out and attempted to choke her. She was quick to breeze past that part and move on to the details of her escape the following day, but even then, Thatcher felt the blood drain from his head and face.

"So, what's the offer you mentioned, in the divorce papers? And what do you think the likelihood is that he'll sign them?"

"Well," Abbie said softly, "as incentive to get him to sign, I preemptively signed a nondisclosure agreement, swearing to not expose the..." She lifted a hand to make finger quotes. *"Nature* and *extent* of our differences. Plus, I went with the no-fault divorce. It's the quickest, and it basically means no one person carries the blame. If he chooses to, Quinten can sign the papers and publicly announce that we got divorced due to irreconcilable differences. He'd be smart to go that route and avoid the potential scandal surrounding his *missing wife."* She used a dramatic voice for that last part, as if she could already see the headlines.

"Yeah. If he was smart that's what he'd do," Thatcher agreed, pacing at the foot of the bed some more. He tuned in to the sound of Abbie's soft, slowing breaths, in and out. She was here. She was alive. She'd survived, escaped, and chosen Thatcher to turn to. Confide in. Trust with her life. The enormity of those facts settled over him in layers as Abbie's breaths came and went.

Eventually, Thatcher slowed his breaths to match her pace, grateful for the rhythmic pattern of rise and fall.

More walking. More breathing. Slower, then slower still.

At last, Thatcher shuffled to the window, pulled back a corner of the curtain, and eyed the snow-covered lot. Not so much as a fresh footprint or tire track in the drifted snow. If he kept the bathroom door open, he could cool off in the shower before hitting the sack. A quick glance at Abbie said she was sound asleep. He eyed the chair propped beneath the door once more, nodding in satisfaction, and hurried into the bathroom.

The mirror pulled open to reveal a shallow medicine cabinet. Thatcher angled the mirror so that, from the shower, he had a view of the front door.

It didn't take long to strip down, wash off with a bar of soap beneath the less-than warm stream, and snatch a towel off the rack. Once dry, he stepped back into his boxer briefs and shut out the bathroom light.

Abbie lay in the shadow of lamplight. It was a queen bed, big enough for him to sleep there as well, but he reckoned that wasn't such a great idea. He grabbed the rather thin knit blanket draped along the foot of the bed and moved to the corner chair instead. The tin trash can, turned upside down, would serve as a footstool, he decided. Once that was positioned before the chair, Thatcher fixed his gaze on the grimy upholstery. Grease spots, crusty stains, and pet hair coated the burgundy surface. He shivered, yanked the blanket from around his shoulders, and tossed it over the chair. Who cared if he froze to death? It was better than having all that crud against his bare skin...

Abbie was different that way. As pampered as she was, she had a higher tolerance for germs and such. Once, she even picked up a wad of chewed-up gum, brought it close to her lips and said, *"dare me to chew this."*

Heck no, he wasn't going to dare her. He'd stared at it, too horrified to speak, disgusted that she'd have even touched it. And then she did the unthinkable: popped it right into her mouth and started to chew, gritty sand grains be danged.

Thatcher started gagging instantly. When they got home, he demanded she swish with mouthwash to kill all the germs. He'd threatened to tell Buck and Dottie if she didn't. Abbie caved, but she'd laughed at the way Thatcher had been so grossed out.

He chuckled lightly at the recollection as he plopped into the chair, propped his feet on the trash can, and folded his arms over his chest. A moment later, the severity of their stark reality sank back into place. That spunky, fearless girl had grown into a beautiful woman. She could have gone on to do anything, be anything. Instead, she became wife to a man who abused her. And she'd stayed.

That was the question he'd kept himself from asking. The *how in tarnation could you stay with a guy like that? And why?* It never had made sense to him, but then again, Thatcher had never been in such a predicament. Still, it seemed like things like this happened to different types of women. Women who didn't have an ounce of self-esteem to their name. Or maybe women who were destitute without their abuser.

But a strong, vibrant, intelligent woman like Abbie Carrington? It didn't make sense. They'd been married for five years. Had he abused her the entire time, or had something triggered that violent side of him?

Thatcher cringed each time he pictured someone laying so much as a hand on Abbie. If he wasn't careful, the adrenaline would pick back up with a vengeance and he'd be wide awake all night.

She's here now, he reminded himself. *She's safe.* And if Thatcher's life depended on it, he'd see to it that she remained that way—safe and sound and free of further harm.

In his dreams, Thatcher was on the hunt. One minute he was on his motorcycle, trailing after Quinten up a mountain hill, the next he was jumping out of a plane because Quinten had thrown himself off a cliff to escape. Thatcher was running through a cave next, chasing after Quinten to the flickering light of a lantern dangling before him.

Once he finally got to the pit of the cave, a fire-breathing dragon opened its massive jaws and expelled flames big enough to turn Thatcher to ash.

As the dream played on, Abbie strutted onto the scene in a sparkling evening gown and stiletto heels. She walked right over the rubble, grinding the ash beneath her steps, and threw herself into the arms of the beast.

CHAPTER 7

Abbie stared at the unwrapped granola bar, guessed at where the center was, and broke the thing in two. Thatcher would never eat his half if she didn't place it back in the wrapper, so she rested hers on a motel scratch pad and tucked his back into the foil.

As cheap as the room might be, one thing the motel didn't scrimp on was the drapes. If it weren't for the sliver of light surrounding the edge, Abbie might think it was still nighttime. She stepped toward the glowing edge and pried back one of the lower corners. The brightness from the sight made her squint in reflex and drop the edge.

It took a moment for her eyes to adjust once more, but soon she spotted the contraption to open the drapes. She gave it a pull, watching as the heavy curtains split down the center, one inch, then two. Bright sunlight spilled into the center of the room, catching a corner of the linoleum landing and the brown carpet beyond.

She used the sparse light in the quiet moment to observe Thatcher where he slept. Since the back of the chair was along the same wall as the window—just on the other side of the door—he remained in the shadows, unaware that it was well past nine.

He was far too big for the small chair, which must be why he attempted to create a footstool with the upturned garbage can. One heel rested solidly on the center of the base where it ought to be. He'd tucked his other foot beneath the base of the chair, his long, muscled leg bent at the knee while his torso balanced precariously over the edge of the seat. One arm was tucked beneath his head while the other extended over the opposite side of the chair.

How a guy this manly and gorgeous could summon the word *cute* was beyond Abbie, but that's just what the image before her did. It had more to do with the person he was on the inside, she supposed.

A burst of warmth circled her heart. Thatcher Copeland was a good man. He hadn't even asked to share the bed—simply camped out on the stuffy little chair in the corner. After removing most of his clothes, she reminded herself. There wasn't enough light to ogle his muscled torso since that part was shaded most of all, but Abbie was sure they were more impressive than ever.

As it was, the shadows were deeper along the outline of his muscled legs and extended arm. She had the sudden impulse to lean in and run her fingers through his hair, the way she'd done years ago. What would life be like for them now if they had wound up together?

She closed her eyes as a painful layer of heat burned through her chest. It was funny how one simple question could cause physical pain, especially that pesky, two-worded question: *what if?* Somehow that one stung the most.

Yet just then, a new *what-if* question came to mind: What if Quinten found her out here in Montana? A trail of horrific events played out in her mind—Thatcher getting involved, the rest of his family defending him, and the backlash that might befall them.

The images caused bolts of anxiety to shoot through her center, and soon, Abbie's whole body felt charged somehow, electric. She began pacing the floor the way Thatcher had the night before, inwardly willing the thoughts out of her head.

Quinten wouldn't look here. He'd check out all the places on the East Coast, head to the ones on the West Coast, and then set his aim on the vacant properties outside the US. But eventually, when they failed to locate Abbie in all the obvious places, they *might* start to suspect this place. By then, Abbie would be gone.

"You got a singing gig today?"

The sound of Thatcher's voice startled Abbie so much she squealed. She spun around to glare at him. "You scared me."

He dragged a hand over his face and sniffed. "Sorry, but you didn't answer my question. Is there a marquee someplace with your name on it?" He splayed his hands out before him. *"Pink Punk Princess, live at the amphitheater."*

"Yeah," she said, "and under that it says, *with special opening guest—the rock-skipping weasel."*

Thatcher's eyes went wide. "Hey, hey, hey—*weasel?* Why can't you remember that it's a badger? I liked big, buff badgers, not wimpy weasels."

She chuckled, loving that all these years later, he still got riled by that one. "I know."

Thatcher shook his head. "Well," he said, halfway through a yawn, "I'm about to walk across this room mostly naked. If you don't want to see that, I suggest you go look out the window or something."

"Thanks for the warning." Her cheeks flushed as she hurried over to the window, peeking into the lot at first, and then fully opening the drapes to let in more light. "How'd you sleep?" she asked, daring to barely glance over her shoulder.

"Awful," Thatcher said as the bathroom door closed.

Guilt sliced through her as she glanced over her shoulder. Here it was just days before Christmas, and Abbie was intruding on him and his family. Perhaps she should have asked Liona about the shelters when she reached out yesterday.

She caught hints of her reflection in the window and smiled as she considered the way Thatcher teased her about the disguise. He was so good at lightening her mood, and selfishly, Abbie wished she could stay in Montana with him forever.

It didn't take long to get back onto the road. Thatcher, after taking Abbie up on the offered remains of her granola bar, pulled up to a burrito joint and ordered each of them breakfast burritos with extra green sauce for Abbie.

"You still like the green?" he asked, turning to her while ordering at the window.

A spot of warmth sank into her heart. "Yes, thank you." The sad fact was, Abbie hadn't had a breakfast burrito from Rancheros since she'd eaten one with Thatcher during her last summer there. He parked in a sunny spot in the lot so they could eat in the truck.

The storm had passed, and the bright glistening snow seemed to symbolize new beginnings and fresh starts.

"Is your family going to be waiting for us when we get back?" Abbie asked as she peeled back the wax wrapper around one end of the burrito. She popped open the sauce cup, poured on a generous drizzle of green sauce, and took her first bite.

Talk about a tasty dose of nostalgia. Thick, smoky bacon, savory potatoes and eggs, complemented by that tangy sauce and stringy cheddar cheese. Abbie sank against the seat and put a hand to her heart as she savored the first bite. "Mmm. That was amazing."

She opened her eyes to see a satisfied grin on Thatcher's face. "It's been a while?"

She nodded. "A *long* while."

Thatcher took a few bites of his own before dabbing his lips with a napkin and lifting a finger as if he were about to speak. "My family will be serving up in a soup kitchen today," he said. "It's the twelve days of Christmas, Jacki style, which means there's excitement at every turn."

The sales-pitch tone he'd used while saying that last part sparked a memory.

"Remember we used to do that radio show thing? We'd take turns being the caller, and no matter how crazy the issue was, we had to answer professionally."

Thatcher tipped his head back. "Aw, man. Those were hilarious. Like the time I called up complaining about itches in strange places?"

"Or the time I called in and said I found my neighbor's corpse and didn't know what to do?" she said with a laugh.

"You always were a morbid little thing," Thatcher said.

Abbie grinned ruefully. "You were supposed to tell me to call 911, not to bury the body in shallow mud and plant a garden."

"Yeah, but how entertaining would that have been?"

She shrugged. "True. Let's do it right now. Call me."

Thatcher paused in bringing the burrito to his lips, glanced around the cab for a blink, then shook his head. "Nah."

"Oh, come on," she urged. "For old time's sake."

Thatcher bit into his burrito instead.

She cleared her throat and summoned her richest, smoothest vocals in an Australian accent. "This is one-oh-one-point-two with *Abigail Tell Your Tale,* where you at home can call in, share your woes, and get professional help. Who out there is looking for answers on this snowy day?"

Thatcher finished chewing as he locked eyes with her.

Abbie's heart did a flip. Her face warmed, and anticipation tingled at the surface of her mind. Would he play along?

Thatcher dabbed his mouth with a napkin, then made a loop in the air with his finger. "Turn around, remember?"

"Oh, that's right." Abbie balanced her breakfast on her lap while shifting to gaze out the passenger window. It was part of the rules. Callers and DJs couldn't see one another. Now it was her turn to give the caller a name. "Looks like we've got a call waiting on line five by the name of Biff. How can I help you today, Biff?"

She stared out the window, a broad smile on her face, and waited for his reply.

"I think my boss has a crush on me," he said in a raspy voice.

Abbie arched a brow. "Oh, yeah? What gives you that impression?"

"She has me do all these personal favors for her. I pick up her laundry, her groceries, even her prescriptions."

"Are you her secretary?"

"I'm her personal assistant," he explained.

"Well then, those things sound fairly natural, if you ask me."

"Yeah, but last night, she asked me to follow her home from work so that I could draw a bath for her."

Abbie knew this story was make-believe, but her eyes still bulged. "And what was *she* doing at the time?"

"Shoveling the snow."

"Wouldn't it have made more sense to have *you* shovel the snow while she ran the bath?"

"Exactly," Thatcher said. "But here's where it gets weird."

"Okay." Abbie snuck a bite of her burrito.

"While I was trying to find the bubble bath she said was on the edge of the tub—it wasn't—I opened the closet and stumbled onto this…shrine."

Abbie gulped down her food. "Shrine?"

"Dedicated to me," he added gravely.

"Oh, Biff. This is frightening, indeed. Can you explain what exactly you saw?"

"Candles, printed pictures of me. Spells, crystals, a voodoo doll with red frizzy hair like mine."

A laugh snuck past Abbie's lips. "And what did you do when you discovered this?"

"I, um…I don't want to say."

"You can tell me. This is a safe space, remember?"

Silence. A wrapper sounded, indicating Thatcher was taking another bite of his burrito. Abbie did the same, allowing the delicious suspense to swell and fill the cab.

"I freaked out, you know?" he continued. "So I left the water running, snuck out the window, and made a run for it in the snow."

She nodded. "Sounds…practical, actually. Running was the right thing to do, Biffy boy. Good on you, mate."

"Yeah, but I didn't stop there."

"No?"

"No. I found a sled in her backyard, so I dragged it behind me as I raced into the front. Then, I came up behind her while she was shoveling, rammed the back of her heels with the sled, making her fall backward and plop onto it. Then, while she was flat on her back, arms and legs flailing like a beetle's, I pulled her over to the hill by her house and sent her flying down the steep slope—*fast*."

Abbie gave in to a huge grin as she stared out the window, the glistening snow adding a nice effect to the tale. "Oh, my."

"It leads to an icy pond," he explained.

"Goodness. And it was dark out?"

"Pitch black, save the full moon."

"Full moons do bring out our wild side."

"True."

"So her tub was running. Do you think her house flooded while she worked her way off the frozen pond and climbed back up the hill?"

"No. I went back and turned it off because I felt bad about that part."

"That was kind of you. So what now?"

"Now, I get back to my question. Should I give my two weeks?"

"Definitely." Abbie chuckled and spun back around. How had she known it was still there? The camaraderie, the chemistry, that unmistakable connection that had drawn them together from day one.

His eyes held hers as a wry grin pulled at one corner of his lips. Pleasant waves of tingling heat pulsed and swelled in the space between them, bathing over her like a soft breeze on a hot day.

"I miss you," she blurted clumsily.

Thatcher's eyes widened, then narrowed as he looked down at what was left of his burrito.

"I loved you, Abbie," he said, shifting his gaze out the window. "I thought you loved me too. Thought that when you…when *we*…that everything would change. That you'd come back to me."

Slivers of discomfort pierced through the magical bubble they'd formed just moments ago, something that used to be impenetrable when they were together. She'd wanted to. Oh, how she'd wanted to.

"For me," Thatcher continued, "what we shared that night was a promise. I didn't know that, to you, it was goodbye." He took in the final two bites at once and wadded up the wax paper.

That's all it took to light the fuse—the hot, agitating sparks that would domino through her body and mind for hours. She felt the reality of her situation slithering back into her consciousness in the dull ache that burrowed into her gut. She wanted to rid herself of that part of her past somehow.

Still, all she could do was move on. "I'm sorry."

Thatcher put his hands on the wheel and nodded toward her food.

"Oh," Abbie said, glancing at the half-eaten burrito in her lap. "I'll keep working on it as we go. You can drive now."

He did just that, pulling first onto the main road, and then onto the interstate. Abbie counted down the seconds for the discomfort to fade.

It didn't. In fact, as they picked up speed, the slight hum of the engine gave way to a piercing, unwelcome silence as the fast-burning fuse lit regrets that had haunted her since she said *I do*.

Her stomach ached and clenched. Abbie wrapped up the burrito, stuffed it in the bag, and rested it on the seat between them.

"I said I wouldn't press you for details last night..."

Thatcher's voice was a welcome distraction from the bombs in her head. She kept her eyes on the snow-covered land out her window, squinting as the sun made millions of gleaming crystals on the surface.

"But I think I should have a better understanding of what brought you here, me being with another man's wife and all."

She nodded. "Yeah, that's fair." Whenever the *where-it-all-began* question came to mind, Abbie recalled a handful of memories. Very specific events that had shaped an eighteen-year-old Abbie into the perfect mold for a man like Quinten. She pushed those aside and tried to think of the best way to sum up their years of marriage without getting in too deep.

"When was the first time he laid hands on you?" Thatcher asked, voice low and even.

Her shoulders fell. She wasn't ready to admit that it happened so soon into their relationship. It would be better if she could ease into it, but what was the point? She was here now, and Abbie wanted to be honest with Thatcher.

"It was, um...shortly after the engagement party."

"*Before* you were married?" he growled.

Abbie pinned her earlobe between two fingers and

nodded. “He claimed I humiliated him in front of everyone.”

“By doing *what?”* Thatcher boomed. “Using the wrong freaking dinner fork?”

She stared in his direction for a blink, wondering if calling him had been a big mistake. Thatcher Copeland had always been untouchable somehow—proof, in her mind, that good men existed. They were out there; she just hadn’t married one of them. Yet now, as the sound of Thatcher’s angry tone rang dully in her ears, Abbie worried he might prove that notion wrong.

“I’m sorry if I’m yelling,” Thatcher said as if sensing the source of her reluctance. “I’m just pissed, and I want to rip his head off, but I’ll…hold it together.” He cleared his throat and nodded for her to continue.

Abbie’s lips parted as she went to say more, but Thatcher spoke up again.

“I don’t want you to think I’m upset with *you,”* he explained. “I *am* furious, of course, but at *him,* not you.” He huffed out a breath and gripped the wheel like his life depended on it. “What did he say you did wrong at the party?”

“He said I was flirting with one of his friends, which is false. The second offense was that I got the title of one of his songs wrong. Once everyone left, he grabbed me hard by the arms, pinned me against the wall, and told me I must *never* embarrass him like that again.” Abbie shook her head as she relived the shock and terror of it all. And confusion too.

“It took me off guard,” she said. “At first, I didn’t think

he knew how strong his grip was, so I told him it was hurting me. But he only tightened his grip, pushing his thumbs in deeper while the veins in his neck throbbed. His voice was trembling, his eyes were crazed. I was stunned—it felt like he hated me in that moment. And suddenly my dad came whistling into the foyer. Quinten let go of me, straightened his shoulders, and grinned that famous grin. 'What a night, eh?' he said like nothing had happened. My dad said something like, ' you can say that again.'

"I remember looking back and forth between them, questioning myself, even then, as to why I wasn't saying something. But I didn't. I kept his secret, and soon it became my secret too."

A strangled groan sounded from low in Thatcher's chest.

"Late at night sometimes, I'd consider telling my parents, but…" She pressed her lips closed and shook her head, unwilling to speak the words aloud.

"But, what?" Thatcher prodded.

Abbie tested the line playing out in her mind, daring herself to share it. "I worried they might pick sides. The *wrong* side, I mean. And I don't know how I would have taken that."

"You think they would have condoned his actions? Why in all of tarnation would they have done that?"

Abbie shrugged. "You have to realize that I didn't measure up to their standards in a lot of ways. When I married Quinten, they washed their hands of me. 'She's your problem now.' And since he was so much older…

since he was so respected—practically worshiped by so many people, including my parents—they might have figured I was getting what I deserved. Someone had to whip me into shape."

Her mother had all but confirmed it, but Abbie didn't say so. She felt bad enough for saying what she had. She hated that her feelings for them were so complicated. Hated that she had any love for them at all. But she did. For whatever reason, Abbie chose to believe they were merely a product of the society they longed to please.

"You married the guy they wanted you to marry—that wasn't good enough for them?"

"You're right," Abbie said. What she didn't say is that she'd first gotten pregnant with another man's baby, but she couldn't tell Thatcher that now. She might not ever work up the nerve to tell him. "They just know that I'm more of a free spirit, and they've never liked that about me."

"Well, I *love* that about you," Thatcher snapped.

Abbie fought back a grin. "Thanks."

A sign ahead listed the upcoming exits. The sight alone brought memories of the small town. Trips she'd taken with Grandma Dottie and Grandpa Buck. She'd dreamed of seeing the place at Christmastime, but her parents never had let her come outside of summer. Abbie only wished she was seeing it under different circumstances now.

The thought had her realizing, once again, how close to Christmas it was. She hated that she was imposing on Thatcher's family at a time like this. Perhaps if she'd given it more thought, Abbie might have planned something different. Just what could she do to make up for the disturbance?

As she considered that, another thought came to her. "Oh, do you mind if we stop at a department store so I can—"

"Look less like a punk chick about to perform on stage?" Thatcher finished for her.

"No," she answered smartly. "I'm going to look *more* like one. I'm incognito, remember?"

"Ah." Thatcher tipped his head back as the smile drifted off his face. "Actually," he said, his tone turning somber, "you really shouldn't be seen at all. Dottie and Buck were a big part of the community. People around here will remember you. Some have probably kept track of where you are now, who you're with." He waved a finger from her wig to her boots. "I'm not sure all of that...will be enough."

Abbie considered that, shoulders slumping as she realized he had a point. "Well then, what am I supposed to do?"

CHAPTER 8

Thatcher swung the rather hefty shopping bag in his grip as he made his way through the slushy parking lot. He'd parked the truck beside one of the massive snow mounds for added coverage, but he was glad to see that Abbie had remained out of sight in the cab of the truck.

As they'd neared the town, Thatcher had suggested she climb into the back seat and lay low so as not to be seen by any of the townsfolk. Luckily, she hadn't argued. He was glad to find out that Abbie had done one thing right when marrying Quinten—she'd kept her own separate bank account. Mainly, she'd said, because she started inheriting properties on her twenty-first birthday. Properties she could either rent out, vacation in, or both. Through leasing those properties, she'd added to her already sweet balance, which meant at least money wasn't an issue.

Thatcher unlocked the truck and opened the driver's side door. After tossing the sack on the passenger seat and climbing inside, he pulled the door closed. "You, little missy, are going to look like the cutest country bumpkin this side of the Mississippi."

"Oh no," Abbie grumbled from behind. "You better not have gotten me anything crazy."

"I didn't," he assured. "I got you a dress for square dancing, an outfit for banjo-strumming, and some boots for cattle-mucking. You'll fit right in."

Abbie groaned. "Great."

"Not that anyone outside of my family will see you."

"I can't believe I'm going to see your family soon," she said, her muffled voice turning wistful. "Tell me what everyone's up to before we get there."

He decided to start with the oldest in the family and go from there. "My sister, Belle, and her husband are in town for Christmas. Oh, and for Wes's wedding. He got married last week."

"To anyone I know?" Abbie asked.

"No," Thatcher said. "Taja's a single mom from Oregon. She has a seven-year-old daughter named Rosie who's smart as a whip. Spend a day with her, and you'll know more about animals than you ever thought you could."

"Aw, that's cute. So Belle and Wes are married now. What about the others?"

"Nope," Thatcher said. "Rem is the county lieutenant. Wade and Wyatt, they've been chasing bull-riding comps most of the year, and Nash and I…well, you know."

"You and Nash have been breaking hearts."

"Pretty much," Thatcher said through a laugh.

It went quiet for a while before Abbie finally spoke up again. "I think I want to stay in the truck when we get there."

"Huh? For how long?"

"Just for…forever."

Thatcher furrowed his brow. He couldn't help but glance at his rearview though he knew she was lying across the bench and out of sight.

"How come?"

"I don't think I can face your family. They'll probably think I deserve all this for…" She drifted off there.

Crickets would have taken up chorus if the season were right. As it was, the engine purred louder.

"Only a psychopath would think you deserve that kind of treatment, and from what I understand, you're divorcing said psychopath, am I right?"

A tiny chuckle.

A stifled cry.

Sniffing. "Right."

"My family loves you, Abbie. We all do."

More sniffing. "Thanks."

If something could have torn and warmed his heart all at once, it was a moment like this. Of course, time with Abbie had often been that way. A forceful push and an urgent pull. Swells of satisfying bliss, thick with that longing, ever-present ache. She loved him—but that was forbidden. She was his—but she wouldn't be for long. She was there—but soon she'd be gone.

Still, there was a reason Abbie picked *him* to call in her time of need. And though Thatcher wanted to believe it was due to some undying romantic connection between the two of them, he knew it went far beyond that. It was the same reason that—when Thatcher's aunt and uncle died—his cousins, Wyatt and Nash, came to live with them instead of the other candidates. The Copeland family was synonymous with the term *open arms.* As imperfect and flawed as his family might be, they loved hard, forgave often, and accepted folks as they were.

Abbie Carrington had always known she was loved on the ranch, and he'd see to it that that didn't change. Thatcher made a mental note to text his family in their group chat once he pulled up to the house. He'd make sure they knew that Abbie had endured years of abuse from the man she married—while in her teens, no less. She needed love and kindness as well as protection, and he trusted they'd find it in their hearts to deliver. Even ornery old Wyatt.

"Hey," Abbie said in a curious tone. "Remember how your granddad had that old enlarger and all that processing equipment?"

Thatcher's brow furrowed for a blink. "Oh, you mean for the dark room? To do, like, pictures from film?"

"Yeah," she said. "He had an old camera too. Do you think they got rid of that? Or that it's still around someplace maybe?"

Abbie had always taken an interest in that old camera. Once, Gramps even helped her develop a few prints for her grandparents, that glossy finish in black and white.

Thatcher pictured the old ranch house and shrugged. "The ranch hands take up the rooms there, but it could still be in the attic, I guess."

"I'd love to take some classic photos of your family," she said. "As a thank you for letting me stay a while."

Thatcher didn't want Abbie to feel like she had to repay them somehow, but he understood why she'd want to just the same. He didn't bother saying that the family had had their fill of photo shoots at Wes's wedding earlier that week. Or the fact that she'd happened to call him at the tailend of that —just before the guests tossed snowflake confetti on the bride and groom as they dashed toward the decorated truck.

"Sure," he said. "I'll ask Grandma C. if she kept that stuff."

"Thank you," Abbie said for the second time.

"You bet." *I miss you.* Abbie had said those three words just moments ago, and Thatcher would be danged if it hadn't sent his mind to racing like a crazed bull. He missed her too. And spending time with her now, it almost made him miss her all the more.

As they neared the ranch, Thatcher inwardly pleaded with the heavens. He couldn't articulate the words or phrases—heck, he wasn't even sure what he wanted—just for Abbie to feel welcome, he guessed. For her to be safe from the man she'd fled and, selfishly, for the ability to guard his own heart from one who'd already broken it once before.

Mere weeks ago, while the family prepared for Wes and Taja's wedding, it seemed all was right with the world.

After a deadly close call during a trial Taja was set to testify for, the couple had returned home, albeit banged up and bruised, but safe all the same.

Tomorrow was Christmas Eve. And just who should roll into town to help make the season bright but Abbie—the very woman who got away—bearing bruises of her own, weighed down by a past Thatcher wished he could rewrite somehow.

He considered the sparks that still pulsed between them, the camaraderie that hadn't waned, and the sound of her laughter as they revived the old call-in radio pastime. She'd told Thatcher she'd initiated the paperwork for a divorce. Why had she made a point to tell him that?

To put his mind at rest, he decided. If he knew she was already planning to leave Quinten for good, Thatcher wouldn't pester her about possibly going back to him. Whatever the reason, it most definitely wasn't to encourage Thatcher or make him think he stood a chance. They both knew better than that.

Still, Thatcher would make sure Abbie was safe from harm during her time there, then let her go as he'd done year after year at the summer's end—with that all too familiar longing in his heart.

Abbie smoothed a hand over the soft, red sweater Thatcher had purchased for her at the department store. She'd sent him in with a list of her sizes for everything from underclothing to shoes, and he hadn't done half-bad. Granted, most of the tops he'd picked out were a shade of red—one crimson silk blouse, one cherry red tee shirt, a burgundy sweatshirt, and this sweater, which leaned toward a rusty orange when compared to the others—but perhaps the selection in a place like that was limited to seasonal items this time of year.

In addition to the street clothes, Thatcher had purchased a six-pack of white tee shirts and boxers from the men's department so she could *"be comfortable around the house. You'll thank me,"* he assured. She guessed it was better than him wandering through the lingerie department in search of women's nightwear.

Compared to what Abbie was used to wearing, the everyday clothing wasn't nearly as fashionable, but Abbie didn't mind. She didn't want to stand out for her high fashion and expensive taste. In fact, the further she could get from the stifling pressure to reflect some so-called *first-class lifestyle*, the better. Abbie would never be slave to that again.

When they'd arrived at the Copeland home, the sights and scents warmly familiar, his family had, as predicted, been gone. But as she'd sifted through the purchased clothing in the privacy of Thatcher's room, Abbie had heard them return. It was oddly comforting, the clanks and clatters in the kitchen, the exuberant greeting from the dogs, and the muffled sounds of joking and laughter.

Abbie and Quinten's home was the opposite—library quiet and museum still. Free of dust, clutter, life. It was bittersweet, being in Thatcher's room, surrounded by his clothes, his collectables, his smell—heavy on the leather with hints of spicy aftershave. Masculine, the scent of a rugged, hard working cowboy.

She and Thatcher would be staying here—Abbie in Thatcher's bed and Thatcher on the couch in the den until the day after Christmas. Once Belle and her husband flew home, Abbie and Thatcher would move into the ranch house with Rem, where they'd each have their own room.

Suddenly, a metallic clanking echoed into the room in a rhythmic pattern that had Abbie picturing the old triangular dinner bell out back.

"Dinner time," came Jacki in that sweet, southern tone.

A soft knock came to the door. "You ready for this?" Thatcher asked from the other side, voice low and thick with wry insinuation. He knew his family could be a lot, especially compared to hers, but Abbie had always welcomed the differences.

Today, however, was different. At the mere thought of stepping into their presence, Abbie wished she was back in Thatcher's truck, hidden from the rest of the world. Safe from judgment about her life—present and past.

She walked slowly to the door, grasped hold of the doorknob, and gave it a twist. "I'm not coming," she said in a whisper, the words coated in a nervous laugh.

Thatcher chuckled, low and deep. "C'mon," he crooned. "It'll be fine. They're not *all* here, so it'll be less intimidating. Belle and Scott are doing their own thing. So are Wes, Taja, and Rosie. And Rem's on duty. Tomorrow, being Christmas Eve and all—*that's* when you'll get the whole gang."

She pulled the door open, locked eyes with Thatcher, and felt a spark of warmth kindle in her chest. "Okay," she said.

Thatcher moved as if he were about to extend his hand or arm to her. Just as quickly, he stopped short and tucked both hands into his pockets. He proceeded down the hall before her, a welcome shield from the eyes of his family as she followed him into the glowing kitchen, fragrant with savory sweet scents of barbecue and fresh-baked rolls.

At once, Thatcher slowed his pace, shoulders high and still. He stepped aside slowly, reluctantly, angling himself toward her, and nodded toward the large group scattered throughout the kitchen. Jacki hustled about in a floral apron, an oven mitt over one hand as she swung a tray of hot rolls toward a rack on the counter. Lloyd pinched a chunk off one of the rolls and blew on it before tossing it into his mouth.

Nash went to do the same, but Jacki gave his hand a swat. "Set the napkins on the table, will you?"

Like Thatcher, Nash looked older than he had when she last saw him.

Wyatt and Wade were hovered over a crockpot.

"No," Wyatt was saying. "Let me see them."

Wade handed over a pair of what looked like claws. He slid his fingers through slots at the base of each tool and made fists to show the plastic, spikey knives. "You tear into the meat like this." He rotated his wrists so his palms faced outward and made a raking motion. "Tears it right up if it's tender enough."

"It's *always* tender enough," Jacki inserted.

"That's for sure and for certain," Lloyd said.

"Unlike Lilly's," mumbled Grandma C. "Her pot roasts are tough as rawhide." She'd scored one of the rolls and was spooning red jam onto it. She popped it into her mouth and moaned.

Abbie felt her limbs go lax. She'd missed this cozy atmosphere. A world that only one word could describe: home. The sort of home you saw on wholesome TV shows with a moral at the end of each episode. Johnny learned how to share. Jimmy discovered his joking manner could go too far. And gol-darn it, Ma needed help around the house once and a while or she'd lose her marbles.

On the after-school specials Abbie had seen as a kid, the main character never had homes like this. But their friends did. They'd go there one day and see what it would be like to have a home and family they'd only ever dreamed of.

Abbie always thought back on her summer getaways in the great state of Montana, where Buck and Dottie knew everyone in town. Where the Copeland family worked the ranch together, ate and prayed together, and played together too. They actually enjoyed one another's company, as rowdy as they might have been, all those boys cooped into one house.

"Well, howdy, Ms. Abbie," thundered Lloyd, drawing her attention back to that corner of the room. The burly cowboy climbed off the barstool with a grunt and headed her way.

Thatcher rested a hand on her lower back and gave her the slightest nudge. "Go ahead," he said under his breath.

"Let's have a hug," the man boomed, lifting one arm as Abbie headed in his direction.

"Oh, save one of those for me," Jacki said, rounding the bar and heading through the dining area.

In came the warmth. First with a slightly measured embrace from Lloyd, who smelled exactly like Grandpa Buck.

Once Lloyd released Abbie and stepped back, Jacki swooped in like a mother hen and wrapped both arms snugly around her. "Oh, precious Abbie, I was absolutely devastated when I heard."

"Don't smother the poor girl," Lloyd mumbled.

"Oh, I'm not." Jacki pulled back, cradled Abbie's elbows, and stared at her through watery blue eyes. "I'm so sorry, hon. Who could have predicted this?"

It was a gracious thing to say. It gave Abbie the much-needed benefit of the doubt, as if no one, not even those closest to Quinten, could have seen it coming.

But then Grandma C piped up. "*I* could have," she snapped.

Wyatt and Wade looked up from the crockpot.

A stack of napkins slipped from Nash's grip and toppled to the floor.

Thatcher's eyes narrowed while Jacki's doubled in size.

"Pardon me?" Abbie managed.

"I said *I* could have predicted this by that man's creepy, sneaky compositions. I hate every danged one of them. I figure the composer himself is as unstable and erratic as his music."

A bubble of laughter snuck up Abbie's throat as the humor of Grandma C's words tickled her mind.

"Grandma," Jacki scolded.

"*What?*" she shrieked innocently. "It's one thing to hear it with a movie when there are actions to go along with the chaos. But to listen to one of those albums while trying to paint or think or…breathe? *Kill* me!"

That earned a whole new round of laughter that rocked Abbie's shoulders and chest. How many times had Abbie felt exactly the same way? Trying to cook a meal while the frantic melody jumped and lulled without rhyme or reason. And here was someone half across the country, virtually speaking Abbie's very own thoughts aloud.

Fancy prancy Quinten who thought every person on the planet worshiped him. Not Grandma C. Grandma C *hated* him, and she wasn't afraid to say so. Abbie covered her mouth with one hand and doubled over as more laughter came. Uncontrollable, hysterical, wonderful.

"I'm sorry," she said through more laughter still. "It's just…I've never heard anyone talk about him like that. Quinten slaves over his compositions, certain every last note is perfect and beyond reproach." She wiped at her eyes, working to smooth the smile out of her cheeks as she turned to look at Grandma C. "And you *hate* it." She couldn't get the words out without laughing yet again, another hearty round that rumbled low in her chest.

"Ah," Abbie sniffed and wiped her eyes as the laughter subsided at last. "I needed that."

Grandma C flung her arms out to either side. "Hey, kid, that's what I'm here for."

Nash had retrieved the napkins and was placing them beside each plate on the table.

"Whoa, whoa. Didn't those fall on the floor?" Thatcher asked.

Nash shrugged, glancing at Abbie before looking back to Thatcher. "Twenty second rule. How you doing, Abbie?"

"Fine, thanks."

"She's not doing fine," Wyatt grumbled from the kitchen. "Find something else to ask her next time."

"It doesn't bother me, honestly," Abbie said. "I just… appreciate you guys for letting me come here. Intrude on your family at Christmastime, no less."

"Don't pay any mind to Wyatt," Thatcher said as he nodded toward the dining room table. "The poor guy still hasn't figured out that he's not perfect."

"Ooh," came Nash and Wade.

"Let's sit down to dinner, everyone," Jacki said as she rushed back to the counter.

The interaction reminded Abbie of the beef between the cousins-turned-brothers. While Thatcher was the youngest in his family with Wade just a bit older, Nash and Wyatt were the same ages respectively. The youngest brothers stuck together, the older two did as well, which meant they were often defending one another.

The rest of the group joined them at the table, and Wade said grace as everyone bowed their heads. Soon, serving plates and platters were being passed around the group. Tender pot roast with roasted carrots and potatoes, a garden salad with crispy croutons and bacon bits, and Jell-O salad with whipping cream on top.

"I made that with you in mind," Jacki said as Abbie scooped up a serving for herself.

"You did?"

Jacki nodded. "Strawberry Jell-O with mandarin oranges and banana slices." And there they were—the pale slices of fresh bananas, the small, juicy-looking orange wedges. Just seeing it made her feel like a kid again.

Abbie told herself this was not something to get emotional about, but that didn't stop the tears from welling in her eyes. "That was so sweet of you," she said. "Thank you. I can't wait to taste it."

"Me neither," Grandma C said. "Pass it this way next, will you?"

"You should have heard what Rosie said to the fake Santa today at the shelter," Lloyd said.

"Oh, man," Wade said with a laugh. "It was hilarious."

"That girl is something," Nash added.

Thatcher chuckled softly under his breath. "Yeah, she is. What did she say this time?"

Lloyd broke into the tale with a wide smile and a gleam in his eye, explaining how seven-year-old Rosie asked if she could look for bugs in Santa's beard, insisting that several must live there.

And while Abbie was charmed by the story itself, she was also warmed by the interest and amusement that lit each face. It was clear that this little girl had stolen their hearts. It was no surprise that the family would love and treat her like one of their own; they'd always done that with Abbie. And, she realized, emotions welling to the surface once more, they were doing it again now. Forget the fact that she'd left someone they loved heartbroken when she married shortly after her last trip there. They were welcoming just the same.

She took a spoonful of the Jell-O dessert and closed her eyes to taste each delectable flavor. Oh, how she loved the simplicity of good, country food. Better than any chocolate torte or crème brulee. Abbie cracked open her eyes to see Jacki watching in anticipation.

Abbie gave her a nod and grinned. "So good," she said.

"You've got a little something right here," Thatcher told her.

Abbie licked her top lip to discover a dab of cream there. "Thanks," she said with a laugh.

"Everyone lift a glass," Lloyd said, reaching for his own and lifting it high.

Abbie followed suit with the rest of the group.

"To our unexpected guest and longtime friend, we're glad you're here. May the Lord be with you through the steps ahead."

"Hear, hear," Thatcher and his brothers said in turn.

"Cheers," Jacki chimed.

Abbie bowed her head slightly. "Thank you." A deep burst of gratitude pushed through her. Perhaps she *had* come to the right place after all. In fact, no place could be better than this, she was sure of it.

But then Abbie recalled the source of her misgivings. It had less to do with his family and how they might treat her, though that had been a slight concern. The bigger one, however, was the fact that she could put them in danger. Was it fair to stay here, knowing that a madman was after her?

The simple answer was no, it wasn't fair.

Sure, Quinten wouldn't find her anytime soon, with as many more obvious options as there were to rule out, but eventually, he would come. And by that time, Abbie would need to be long gone.

CHAPTER 9

Thatcher was deep in sleep when a soft tap came to his shoulder.

"Don't be mad at me," came a whisper.

He forced his eyes open, blinking against the darkness, and forced himself to sit up. He was on the floor, he realized, in the den. And that was Abbie talking. Abbie Carrington was here, a fact he could still hardly believe.

"Why aren't you on the couch?" she asked.

Thatcher shook his head. "Why would I be mad at you?"

"Is the couch not comfortable?" Abbie persisted.

"Abbie," he said.

"Yeah?"

"You said not to be mad at you. What did you come in here to say?"

"Oh. Well…"

He could tell by the muffled sounds that she was moving to sit more comfortably on the floor. Something rough scraped against his arm as she did, which didn't make sense.

"I just got word that there's an opening in a women's shelter north of Boise. The train headed there has a stop here in less than five hours."

Thatcher didn't speak, only chewed on the unpalatable words, trying to force them down.

"I wouldn't have you drive me all the way back there, of course, and I hate to even have you take me anywhere at this hour, but if you could just help me get to the nearest bus stop, I can get myself to the train station on time."

Boy, was Thatcher glad he hadn't let himself sink any deeper into the feelings he had for Abbie. The words *close call* ran through his mind. Last night at dinner, he'd been tempted to entertain a possible future together. She got along so well with his family. They'd relived fond memories and a few embarrassing ones too, mainly at Thatcher's expense, but he didn't mind. It felt right.

Still, he'd kept up a firm guard—a warning, really. She was taken. Abbie could return to the man she was running from. Many women did. But even if she didn't, she wouldn't stay. She never had, and she never would.

Case in point—this painful moment in the dark of night in the stupid den of his childhood home. A home he hadn't moved out of yet. Sure, ranch life was ranch life. You work, eat, sleep, and wake up to do it all over again. Until he married, Thatcher wouldn't need to build a house of his own. Heck, he wouldn't even inherit the land until he did so.

But it wasn't enough for Ms. Abigail Benedict Carrington, was it? Nope. She was married to a millionaire who wrote creepy music and strangled his wife. Thatcher groaned in response to his own crude thoughts.

"Fine." He flung off the covers.

"Fine?" She sounded stunned.

"Yep, you want to leave on Christmas Eve so you can spend time with strangers in a shelter instead of staying here with me? Fantastic." He climbed to his feet quickly, wobbling back on his heels.

"Thatcher, that's not—"

"Don't explain it to me, please. I'm not going to hold you captive against your will, Abs. I'm a better man than that."

Something razor sharp sank deep into his gut as Thatcher realized what he'd said. It wasn't the low blow he'd made about holding her captive. That part got lost in the fact that he'd called her Abs, something he hadn't done in years.

The sharp ache went deeper, spread wider, seeped clear up his chest and into his throat where emotion threatened to well up and make his voice crack. Having Abbie here was dangerous, all right. Not because that scum-of-the-earth husband of hers might find them, but because Thatcher was already falling back into his old patterns with her.

"Let's go." He headed down the staircase, listening carefully to the soft creaks as she followed him down.

He shouldn't have been surprised to see the ratty backpack on her shoulder as they walked through the dimly lit kitchen, but he was. She couldn't get out of there fast enough. The fickle woman had already made up her mind before waking him. Knowing he was sucker enough to do whatever she wished.

Thatcher led her through the washroom where he stepped into his boots and snatched his keys off the hook. Quietly then, he creaked open the side door, stepped onto the shoveled wraparound porch, and guided Abbie down the wide set of steps and onto the slick, trampled snow.

"You okay?" he asked, tempted to give her a hand.

"Yes." Only halfway through that one, simple word, Abbie yelped as she slid.

Thatcher spun to catch her by the elbow and hoist her back onto her feet. "You can hold onto my belt loops if you want," he offered.

He felt the weight of her first on one side, fingers latching onto one of his belt loops.

She balanced it out by securing a loop on the other side next. "Thanks."

It reminded him of the way she'd sheltered herself against the storm at the train station. Which reminded him. "Are you going to put your wig and stuff back on?" he hollered over his shoulder.

"I already did," she said.

He was surprised he hadn't noticed. Of course, it'd been dark in the den. And once he had been able to see, the stuffed backpack had stolen his attention.

After walking to the passenger side of the truck and

helping her in, Thatcher stomped behind the truck, crushing his boots into the snow and cursing his crappy fate. What sort of Christmas Eve was this? Probably go down in history as the worst in his life.

He climbed into his truck behind the wheel, shoved the key in the ignition and roared the thing to life. A quick glance in her direction said she'd taken no more than the backpack. It was slightly fuller than it had been before, but it couldn't possibly hold all the clothes she'd had him grab for her.

"Where are the rest of your clothes?"

"I left the tags on them. The receipt is in the bag. I figure you can take them back, get the money, and it'll repay you for all this trouble."

"I don't want you to repay me, Abbie. Would you just take the dang clothes with you so you have more to your name than that punk outfit and that freaking pink wig?"

Abbie pinned her lips together hard. In the punk getup, she looked exactly like a rebellious teenager. "No."

"I'm not the one who paid for those—"

"Which is why I said it's my way of paying you back," she snapped. "Sort of."

"Sort of?"

"I know I can't repay you for this, Thatcher, geez."

Now it was Thatcher's turn to pin his lips closed. The last thing he wanted to do was raise his voice at her. So he focused on the road instead, watching the spot of light beneath an upcoming streetlamp, counting down the seconds until the light poured over the cab of his truck, then waned completely. He was angry, bitter, and hurt.

Disappointment was there too, leading his mind to ask the question *why.*

Exactly why did he want Abbie to stay?

Because he loved her, that was why. Because he wanted the chance to finally have her in his life. He couldn't help but shake his head at the truth of it. He had some nerve, didn't he? Thinking he could swoop in during her time of need, wait until her divorce was final, then move in to claim her as his? *Such foolish notions follow when our selfish nature reigns.* He'd seen that quote on the tin sign on the old barn more times than he could count, but never had it rang more true.

If he cared about Abbie, he'd want her to...to do what she wanted to do. And what she wanted to do was hop onto a bus in the middle of the night and board a train to Idaho so she could walk into a women's shelter on Christmas Eve and do who-knew-what from there? Would she keep on running? Just Abbie and her tattered backpack—a vagabond with no real home.

And who's to say someone else wouldn't harm her? Quinten Bromley wasn't the only dangerous man out there. How many train and bus stations would she visit before someone tried to take advantage? She wasn't safe on her own, which meant Thatcher's interest went beyond his own desire to have her near.

Copeland Brothers Ranch had served as a safe haven for Taja and Rosie. It could serve as one for Abbie too, he was certain of it. But how could he convince her of that?

"Can you tell me what your initial plan was?" he asked

calmly. "When you first decided to come to Montana, that is. How long did you intend to stay?"

"I didn't want to be presumptive, but if it wasn't too much of a burden, I planned to stay for a few weeks. Maybe a month."

He nodded, surprised she'd admitted that. "Okay. But we've established that your stay here *isn't* too much of a burden..." He glanced over expectantly, relieved when she nodded in agreement. "So what changed?"

"I got scared," she said. "If anything happened to your family because of me, I'd die. I'd never ever forgive myself. Never."

"Rem's a cop, Abbie. In two days, we're moving into the ranch house where it'll be just us and him. That's it. Between Rem and myself, I'm sure we could protect you if Quinten showed up at our door."

Silence. He hoped that meant Abbie was considering what he said. He only hoped she'd consider fast because they were almost at the bus station. Sure, he'd thought about skipping the nearest one and heading out to the next, but if memory served him, that stop was at some desolate corner off the interstate, and this one at least had a gas station across from it. He'd park there and see to it that she got on safe if that's what she chose to do.

"You must not think Quinten is likely to find you here, am I right? Otherwise, you'd have planned to go someplace else."

"Well, that's what I thought originally."

"Why?" he prodded.

"Because we own like a hundred properties along the

Eastern Coast and dozens more in countries like Italy and France."

"And he'll check those first?"

She nodded. "Probably."

"What would ever make him suspect you might be here?"

"He wouldn't suspect it. Not unless they ruled out all the other possibilities. And even then, it'd have to come from my mom. She's the only one who knows about—" It sounded like someone snipped off the rest of her sentence with a set of sheers.

"About you," she finished.

Thatcher pulled into the gas station and brought the truck to a stop. "So basically, you're leaving for no reason."

Abbie turned to look out the window. "Why prolong it?" she said softly, sniffing and wiping her nose.

Thatcher would give anything in that moment to wrap his arms around her, pull her in for a warm embrace like she gave his parents last night. Dang, did that make him jealous. The thing was, there *was* something between them. And if what Thatcher wanted for her was a better life than she'd ever known…he should *want* her to give him a chance. Because he'd be danged if he couldn't give her that exact thing and more. Thatcher was loyal, hardworking, and he knew how to treat a woman right.

"Abbie?" he dared himself to say.

She kept her gaze out the window. "Yeah?"

His heart thundered like an angry drum. He reminded himself that—if all went according to plan—Abbie would be single, free to date whomever she chose. At last he cleared his throat and forced out the words.

"Do you think there's still a chance for us?"

Her shoulders fell, her body slumped, and Abbie dropped her head in her hands. A stifled cry got caught in her throat, and then she was sobbing. Raw and untamed, crying into her hands as her body rocked forward, then back. Just as Thatcher tried working up the nerve to reach out, maybe run a hand over her back, Abbie pulled back the handle and pushed open the passenger door.

"I have to go."

"No," he argued. "You don't. Not if you still think there's a chance."

Abbie climbed out, and Thatcher did the same, hurrying to meet her around the front of the truck. Adrenaline pumping, heart threatening to explode, he stood before her, blocking the path to the street.

"Is your marriage over or not?" he challenged.

Abbie nodded adamantly. "Of course it is."

"Then once it's legal we can…see, can't we? Don't you want that?" He took in the tears glistening on her cheeks beneath the streetlamp. The agonized expression on her face. The dilemma behind her pretty blue eyes.

The sound of a distant engine hummed, and Abbie darted a glance down the street. "That's the bus. I've got to go. Bye, Thatcher." And with that, she pushed past him, ran across the street, and looped one hand around the bus stop sign. Her eyes found his as the bus neared, and Thatcher felt his heart ripping open once again.

"If you think there's still a chance for us," he hollered

across the street. "Then please…" His voice tore. His breath hitched. "Please don't get on that bus."

Bright headlights illuminated her slender figure a moment before the bus hissed to a stop, hiding her fully from his view. He heard the door lurch open, and he pictured her climbing inside with her combat boots and torn up tights.

With his head dropping, chest deflating, jaw clenching, Thatcher inwardly pleaded for the heavens to protect her. He lifted his head as the doors swung closed, watched the bus rock back, lull in place, and then pull back onto the road. His eyes fell to the spot beside the streetlight where Abbie had been standing—vacant. She was gone.

But then he spotted something, no—some*one*—standing on the opposite side of the sign, looking right at him.

His heart skipped two full beats. He blinked hard and opened his eyes again. Yep, she was there all right. "You stayed?" he yelled across the street.

Abbie nodded and tucked her hands into the pockets of her hoodie. "I stayed."

He'd be danged. "Well," he said with the wave of one arm. "Come on then. Let's get back to the ranch."

CHAPTER 10

Abbie had skied close to a dozen times—once in Switzerland, twice in Aspen, and a handful of times in Park City. What she hadn't ever done was go sledding down a steep hill while helplessly sitting atop a speeding tube or sled. She'd seen it in movies, of course, and heard enough horror stories to steer clear of the winter activity just as her mother advised.

But here she was, climbing a massive hill in borrowed snow clothes with Thatcher and his family so they could climb onto tubes, saucers, or sleds and go flying down the hill at dangerous speeds.

The day had started with Lloyd's famous sausage and egg biscuits, something they ate on the go while heading up to Snowy Peak. The hills here were so high visitors had to park halfway up and climb to the top by foot. Prior guests had stomped steps into the packed snow to make the climb easier. A rope dipped between wood posts alongside, offering a poor excuse for a railing.

The men in the group, Thatcher included, had taken a different route from the parking lot, driving ATVs up to the top while pulling a selection of tubes and sleds.

"It really is great to see you again," Belle said as she trudged up the next step.

Abbie grinned, remembering how much she always looked up to Thatcher's sister. She was beautiful, of course, but down to earth too. Never acting like she was better than Abbie just because she was older.

"Thanks, you too. How long have you and Scott been married now?"

"We got married shortly after you did," she said. "Of course, I was twenty-seven. You were practically still a kid." Belle glanced over to give Abbie a kind, knowing look. A you-could-never-have-known type of look. "I really am sorry," she said in a whisper. "About the abuse you've suffered."

Abbie nodded. "Thank you."

"And if you don't mind my saying," Belle added, facing forward and taking hold of the rope once again, "I'm glad you're old enough now to choose who you're *really* meant to be with."

It was a bold statement, but Abbie didn't mind it in the least. She only wished things were that easy.

"Hi, Abbie," came a little voice from behind.

Abbie slowed to glance over her shoulder, smiling when a grinning Rosie caught her eye. While the knit cap on her head did its best to contain the heap on top, curly blonde locks poked through and framed her bright, rosy cheeks.

"Hi, Rosie. Are you excited to go sledding?" Abbie asked.

"Yep." She smeared a gloved hand over her face and crinkled her nose. "This is the very first time I ever went."

Her mother, Taja, chuckled as she supported Rosie with a hand on her back. "It sure is."

"Do you want to know a secret?" Abbie asked. "This is *my* first time too."

"It *is*?" Rosie squeaked in surprise.

"Yep, and I'm scared. What's better to ride down on, do you think?" Abbie asked, glancing at Taja as well. "The tube or one of the sleds?"

"I prefer the tube," Taja said. "It's a smoother ride since it kind of absorbs the blow."

"Hey, guess what, Abbie?" Rosie said. "Arctic foxes have big, puffy tails that act like blankets. They also have super thick fur on the feet like built-in snow boots."

"That's so cool," Abbie said, imagining a playful fox dancing in the snow.

"Oh, and do you know what they call the female fox?"

"What?"

"A vixen!" Rosie giggled. "That's one of the reindeer's names."

"You're right," Abbie agreed with a laugh. "How silly."

"My mom has a sink cleaner called Comet too!"

Abbie grinned at Rosie and Taja in turn. "Another reindeer name—*wow*!"

"I like to notice stuff like that." Rosie nodded proudly,

then pointed ahead with widened eyes. "Look, we're almost at the top."

She was right, there were only a few steps left. Thatcher stood with the rest of his family, untangling the ropes from the tubes and sleds and divvying them out.

"You two made it!" Thatcher's brother, Wes, cheered as he hurried over. He hunched down, swooped Rosie into one arm and pulled Taja in with the other, planting a kiss firmly on her lips.

Abbie felt she should turn away, being witness to such a tender moment, but she couldn't get herself to do so just yet. What would it have felt like to have a family like that? Parents who loved and adored one another? It was obvious that these two females were Wes's world. She had to remind herself that Rosie wasn't Wes's daughter by birth. That fact made the moment all the more touching. And for a reason she couldn't explain, it gave Abbie a sense of hope. There were good men out there.

"It's pretty sickening, isn't it?"

The sound of Thatcher's whispered voice, the feel of him standing so near, startled Abbie enough that she flinched away from him and squealed. She pressed a hand to her heart and shook her head. "Oh, sorry, I didn't see you there." His question sank in, and Abbie felt her cheeks warm with embarrassment as she realized what he was referring to. He'd noticed her staring at the small trio.

"It's…" She sighed. "Beautiful," Abbie admitted.

"Yeah, yeah. Let's fly down some hills."

Already, Belle and Scott had gone down. Others were

hunkering onto the sleds and tubes, including Jacki and Lloyd, who were side by side.

"Want me to give you a push?" Nash asked, sounding far too mischievous.

Lloyd swatted behind him. "Heck, no. Rosie, hon?" the man called. "Come give your grandparents a push down the hill, will you?"

"Yep!" The toes of Rosie's boots caught clumps of snow as she trudged over, a wide grin on her face.

"Be sure to make Grandpa's push real good and hard," Jacki said playfully.

Lloyd chuckled. "Make Grandma's push even harder."

"No, no. I just need a gentle one."

Rosie reared up behind Lloyd.

"Careful, now," Taja warned. "You don't want to go down with him."

Rosie rubbed her lips together, eyes narrowed in on Lloyd like a bull seeing red. "One big push coming right up!" At once she hurried forward, then stopped as she got close enough to reach him with both hands. Her momentum all but lost, she grunted and dug her boots into the snow.

Lloyd's tube slid forward. One inch, then two, then it went far enough over the edge for gravity to take its grip. "Woo-hoo!" Lloyd hollered as he went speeding down the hill.

Rosie repeated the action with Jackie, and soon the grown woman was squealing like a schoolgirl. "Good job, Rosie!" she yelled from further down the hill.

Wyatt, Wade, and Nash lined up three sleds next. "Give

them time to get a little further so we don't knock them off their feet," Wyatt suggested.

"Good plan," Wade said before glancing over at Abbie and Thatcher. "You two going to race?"

Abbie shook her head.

"Maybe," Thatcher said.

"Don't let him get a head start," Nash warned with a grin.

"Yeah," Wyatt said. "He's a cheater."

"Sounds like someone's still salty about me kicking his trash on this hill last year," Thatcher razzed. "How about a push off?"

"Don't even think about it," Wyatt said. The three hunkered onto their sleds, counted down from three, then sped on down the hill with yelps and hollers. Wes, Rosie, and Taja went next. The sound of Rosie's squeal was followed by an ecstatic "ee-haw!" Her exuberant giggles came next, fading off the farther she went.

"And then there were two," Thatcher said. He was right. Rem had gotten called in to take a morning shift, though Thatcher suspected he'd volunteered to dodge the sledding activity without upsetting Jacki. It wasn't Rem's thing, he'd said. Abbie wondered if that excuse would fly for her too.

"You know what?" she started to say, but Thatcher was already shaking his head.

"Nope. You're not going to get out of this."

"It's not my thing," she blurted, though amusement coated her words. It was funny that he'd sensed she was backing out.

"Listen, the Abbie I knew wasn't scared of anything. She was the first one to do a cherry drop off the swing at the lake."

"That's true," she said with a nod.

"She tried jumping off the cellar roof with an umbrella in the wind."

Abbie cringed. "That one didn't exactly go according to plan."

"And she climbed the outside of the treehouse to get higher up the tree, then plopped onto our trampoline. I thought you were going to break your neck that day."

"I *probably* could have," she admitted with a nod.

"You just saw an elderly couple go down that hill. You just watched a seven-year-old follow them down. This can't be the thing that scares Abbie the Brave."

He'd never called her that before, but Abbie liked that that's how he viewed her. "I've never sledded before."

His gaze held hers as a flicker of surprise flashed in his eyes. He narrowed them, stepped closer, and performed that half-grin that sank one dimple into his cheek. Abbie's heart skipped a beat.

"That's because you never spent a winter with me. If you had, trust me, you would have dominated these hills."

There was no fighting back the grin that pulled at the corners of her mouth, but she tried just the same, biting her bottom lip.

"We'll hook our tubes together so you don't go flying into the woods someplace," he suggested.

"Or land in the pond with Biff's obsessed boss," Abbie added.

"Biff?" But then enlightenment washed over his face. "Ah, from the radio show. Right." He leaned in. "No matter how obsessed you were with me," he said, voice low and raspy, "I'd never do that to you."

Abbie cleared her throat as her heart hammered out of rhythm. "Good to know." And she liked the idea of having their tubes tied together. It sounded safer somehow. Unless, of course, they knocked heads or something.

Thatcher connected the tubes and set them in place at the top of the hill then hunkered onto his knees and steadied them. "Go ahead," he said with a nod. "Climb on while I'm holding it."

She did, and soon Thatcher did too. They were facing forward, legs sprawled out before them. The sight beyond the tops of her boots sent a new rush of adrenaline through her core. She blew out a shaky breath and gripped the handles on her tube.

Thatcher's shoulder grazed hers as he shimmied them closer to the edge. "There's one thing I didn't tell you about tying the tubes together like this…"

"Oh no. What?"

He scooted closer to the edge even still. "It makes you go…" He grunted, successfully hurling himself over the edge with Abbie right behind him. "Much faster!" he yelled. "Yah-hoo!"

Talk about thrilling. Speeding, rushing, whizzing over the smooth, snowy surface with bounces and bumps. She couldn't help but laugh and squeal and giggle like a child.

Brisk wind nipped at her nose and cheeks, the feel of it exhilarating against her skin. It'd been ages since Abbie had let herself do something reckless, wild, fun. Since marrying Quinten, she'd lost herself in the world of banquets, ceremonies, and public appearances. Beyond that, she'd become a metaphorical and literal punching bag to the man she'd devoted her young life to. Making herself smaller, quieter, softer. Shrinking, shriveling, fading.

Less of a person. Less of herself.

But this—*this* was who she was! Thatcher was right; Abbie had always been up for some good, thrill-seeking fun, and now she remembered why—this is what it felt like to be alive!

Adrenaline pumped through her, hot and fast, countering the cold breeze that whisked wildly against her face. She hadn't guessed that they'd spin, heading down backward one moment, sideways the next, and frontwards for a moment more before turning once again.

Thatcher's laughter was the cherry on top. That icing on the cake that made her crave more and more, long after that first delectable bite. At last, they whirled to a slow stop at the base, spinning so the world and trees whirled behind him as she locked her gaze on his.

Fresh laughter bubbled up her throat, rocking her chest as she gave into another round, the perfect harmony to Thatcher's deep chuckle. The thrill of the ride, the sheer surprise of how much fun it had been, and excitement of having unlocked the chains that bound her, created a cocktail of emotions. Emotions Abbie hadn't experienced for so long.

Thatcher cupped a hand behind one ear. "I'm waiting," he crooned, grin wide and chest puffed.

She knew exactly what he was waiting for. Knew because they were kids again. Or teens, perhaps. Back in their pattern of friendship, mischief, and fun. "You weren't wrong," she said. "That was incredible!"

"Right?" Boy, did he look pleased. "C'mon, I'll help you up."

Abbie, feeling constrained in the snow clothes, accepted Thatcher's help to get to her feet. Only then did she realize how beautiful their surroundings were. The hill had taken them right where they'd started, but Abbie hadn't seen if from this angle, as focused as she'd been on the intimidating slope. Yet as she spun slowly in place, she took in the endless frosted forest. Deep green, snow-flocked pines broke up clusters of gentle aspens and towering, twisty oaks. Bare branches, thick with shimmering snow, took on a magical quality.

Sunlight broke through a lofty bow, turning the untouched snow to a bed of glistening crystals, sparkling with every color of the rainbow. "Wow," she breathed. "This view is breathtaking."

"Yes," Thatcher agreed. "It is."

Abbie turned to see his eyes fixed on her. A moment passed where his words from last night thundered through her mind anew. *Do you think there's still a chance for us?*

If there was, she and Thatcher would have to go about things the right way.

Her divorce may have been all but final, but Abbie knew better than to behave as if she were single just yet. It seemed Thatcher understood that too. In their youth, the two had started out as friends. They'd enjoyed the chemistry between them, built off it over the years, and created something beautiful in the end. Perhaps they could follow that pattern once more. Take things a day at a time and see where it led them.

A knot of fear worked its way into her mind, reminding Abbie that her time there was limited. Sooner or later, Quinten would come looking for her. But there was always hope. Hope that he'd sign the papers and grant her the divorce. That he'd be willing to sign the slip that said this was mutual. He'd avoid scandal *and* come out looking like the good guy people thought he was. Something told Abbie not to rule that option out.

As Abbie climbed the snowy steps for another ride down the mountainside, pulling her tube on the hill beside them, she lifted a prayer to the heavens. It was Christmastime; perhaps Quinten would sign those papers after all, giving Abbie, as Leona suggested, a Christmas miracle she'd never forget.

CHAPTER 11

Thatcher could hardly believe the chain of events that had led to this moment. Sitting among his family in the warm, heavenly glow of twinkling Christmas lights was none other than Abbie Carrington. The deep rasp of Pops' distinct voice drifted over the room as he reclined in his favorite chair, reading from the Good Book.

Thatcher wasn't one to get sappy, but he'd be danged if his heart wasn't overflowing with gratitude. And hope too. Ma sat on one of the kitchen chairs they'd dragged in to accommodate the group. There she was, right beside Pops, with a dozing Rosie on her lap. The expression on Ma's face was one of utter peace. *"There's no place like together. When the family's all here, my heart is whole."* She'd always said it; tonight, more than ever, Thatcher understood why.

Beside Ma, Belle was curled into Scott's shoulder, the

pair tucked into the same couch as Grandma C and Nash, who gazed at the Christmas tree while Pops read on. Rem sat on one of the kitchen chairs in the corner with his feet propped on a second chair before him, that ever-present toothpick pinned between his lips. Wes and Taja took up the loveseat, snuggling and looking like the blissfully happy newlyweds they were. Wade and Wyatt sat on opposite corners of the piano bench, supporting their weight with elbows leaning heavily on their knees.

Sharing a beanbag with Thatcher, warm and fragrant, was Abbie. She'd bent her legs at the knees to partially sit on her feet. The length of her back leaned comfortably along his upper arm while her lower torso was plush against his hip. He keyed into the rhythm of her breathing, keenly aware that someone had tried to stifle that breath and failed. She was alive—a fact that took precedence over all other thoughts and desires. The severity of Abbie's situation didn't allow for casual feelings such as jealousy or lust.

What he felt for her went much deeper, past his own superficial longings, until it was all about her. Her safety, wellbeing, happiness—whether that would include him, that remained to be seen.

Perhaps he only felt that way because, in his heart, Thatcher truly believed he was meant to be part of that picture. Would he really be able to accept it if things didn't go his way?

He pushed past that thought, refocused on the familiar verses, and grinned at the mention of offered gifts. Grandma C had known just where Grandpa's old photo equipment had been stored—in a marked storage bin in the attic. She said Abbie was welcome to not only use but also keep the camera, the enlarger, and whatever developing paper and products were there too.

The chemicals, as old as they were, had crusted up around leaky lids from the heat. The undeveloped paper was likely damaged from the heat as well. Thatcher had hopped online and ordered new film, chemicals, paper, and a popup darkroom where she could develop the film and prints. Those wouldn't arrive until the day after Christmas, but he planned to tell her about them tomorrow while she unwrapped the camera.

He could not wait to present the camera and expected delivery slip to her in the morning. Thatcher hoped the gift would offer Abbie a distraction from the danger she ran from, an escape into her art and passion.

Just then, Thatcher had the impulse to wrap an arm around Abbie. He wanted her to curl into him while he dipped his nose into the silky strands of her hair and breathed her in. It caused his mind to drift further. Just when would it be appropriate to do such a thing?

Thatcher entertained different scenarios. Like what if she'd been there for an entire month with no cooperation from Quinten while—in Abbie's mind—the marriage was over. Was that enough?

Or if Quinten *did* suddenly sign the papers, leaving technicalities as the waning thread holding the atrocity of their marriage together, would Thatcher feel comfortable pulling Abbie into his arms for a warm embrace?

Other elements came into play, words like *too soon* and *on the rebound* kindling sparks of doubt and fear.

Just then, Abbie sighed deeply, causing more of her warm, heavenly weight to settle against him.

Thatcher closed his eyes and tuned into her breaths, feeling oddly in sync with her in that moment. Was it possible she was having similar thoughts? Was she, too, wondering about the potential between them?

It was too soon for romance, he figured that much, but a man's behavior should alter while interacting with a married woman. He wished there was some sort of gauge—a thermostat of sorts to indicate just when the climate was right.

But then it came to him: Abbie could set the tone. Thatcher wasn't the one running from an abusive spouse; she was. Why not let her set the pace—romantic or other?

If Abbie wanted to lean on him for comfort, his embrace would be hers. If the moment came when her lips sought his, he wouldn't deny her his kiss. What Abbie wanted from him, he'd give her, and let the consequences fall where they may.

Right or wrong, Thatcher felt more at peace than he had since she'd arrived.

CHAPTER 12

A sense of satisfaction swelled deep and wide in Abbie's chest as she lowered the camera and let it hang from the strap around her neck. The bright, red barn before her, rich and textured against the glowing blue sky, was the Mona Lisa of barns. The great structure might be boasting a fresh coat of paint, but beneath that layer, the weathered wood and rusty hinges told tales of old. Cutting through the white, snowy ground was a muddy trail to the barn door. Some might be tempted to digitally cover the path, viewing it as an interruption from the serene view. In Abbie's mind, however, that worn path was the glint in her smile.

Muddy as it may be, it spoke of the comings and goings of hardworking ranchers, from one generation after the next. She wished she could get pictures from this exact angle of each season. The lavender skies and lively blossoms in spring. The hustle and bustle of summertime

—chicks scurrying busily about, their tail feathers high as they pecked their beaks into the ground for food. Autumn would be a sight all its own. Rich, colorful sunsets casting a deep glow over the leaf-covered ground. She imagined framing the four photos to make a square on the wall—the four seasons of Copeland Brothers Ranch.

She hoped the tiny chicken tracks in the snow beyond the chicken coop would show. They added to the charm as well. Brave, feathered creatures venturing out each morning when the sun rose.

She sighed a contented sigh. Three days had passed since Christmas, and she had yet to hear from Leona. Still, the holiday had gone better than Abbie could have imagined. Thatcher hadn't forgotten her request to ask about the old camera. Not that it would have done her any good without film; he had her covered there too. In fact, Thatcher had ordered not only film, but he'd also purchased everything she'd need to develop it and make prints herself right there at the ranch.

Abbie could hardly believe how good it felt to have the familiar weight of that camera in her hands, especially in a place so rich with history, integrity, and interest.

After Belle and her husband Scott flew home, Thatcher and Abbie moved into the old ranch house where Grandma and Grandpa raised Lloyd and his siblings. Rem currently lived on the main level, where he kept track of the ranch hands when they came to stay for the season. Though since she'd arrived, Rem was scarcely home.

Abbie and Thatcher were staying upstairs, their rooms separated by a Jack and Jill bathroom at the end of a long hall. Her room was, in a word, charming. Wooden floors warmed by an old rag rug, a puffy pink comforter on the soft, creaky bed, and a bookshelf complete with worn books, well-loved toys, and charming relics. On the opposite end of that hallway were three other bedrooms with several beds, some of them bunks, to house half a dozen or more ranch hands.

Thatcher walked out of the barn then, carrying a large hay bale toward the stable. The horses followed his movement along the edge of the corral, the smallest of the three gaining his attention with snorts and neighs.

"Morning, Crew," he said in a jovial tone. "You must be hungry."

Abbie moved in closer, positioned the camera once more, and slowly followed him through the lens, keeping the muscular cowboy in the crosshairs as he walked.

At the gate, Thatcher tossed the haybale to the ground and dusted off his gloves.

"Thatcher," Abbie called.

He turned toward her, scanning the area before fixing his eyes on her. Abbie, whose finger hovered knowingly over the button, pressed quickly to capture the shot. She twisted the lens to zoom in, grinning slightly as she realized he was scowling at her. Another click.

"This is *not* what I had in mind when I got you the film," he said, lifting a gloved palm to block his face. The lens homed in on the worn leather instead.

"Come on," she urged, looking out from behind the camera. "Just be my subject for a few test shots. Please?"

"Fine, but don't expect me to pose for them." Thatcher

dropped his hand and secured the pitchfork resting against the fence. The three beautiful horses, still huddled on the other side of the corral, nudged noses and shuffled their weight in anticipation. Small, cloudy puffs drifted from their muzzles in the chilled air.

"Candid pics are great by me." Since Thatcher's back was to her now, Abbie circled around with the camera aimed on him, seeking a profile angle as he fed the horses in the winter scene. If the barn was the Mona Lisa, Thatcher was a cowboy version of David or Adonis.

A blast of warmth sprouted around her chest as she snapped a shot of him from that angle. Unlike the digital images she was used to taking, Abbie couldn't immediately see her work. This was old time film, which meant a limited number of images and a whole lot of guesswork. She toyed with the settings, mindfully tracking which changes she made, and readied the lens once again.

Thatcher in his element was something to behold. He clicked his tongue as he tossed forkfuls of hay over the fence. "There you go," he lulled. "There you go."

Abbie hoped the film would pick up the definition of his chiseled jaw, accented by the short facial hair he somehow kept trimmed at the exact same length. She liked the way it set him apart from Quinten and his obsession for a clean shave.

Thatcher was taller and broader than Quinten too. Even that corduroy coat with the wool collar couldn't hide the broadness of his shoulders and chest. He was clearly a man who'd worked hard on the field all his days. There was something about cowboys; they'd earned a reputation for being honest, loyal, and hardworking too. Their labor seemed to harden them to a degree, but in Abbie's interactions, she'd noticed gentle sides to them too.

Grandpa Buck would often say, *"There are three things a cowboy's loyal to in this life: His God, his woman, and his land."* The land, he'd told her, included the animals it kept. The comment had stuck with her, a sweet reminder of the man she admired most in her life and, sadly, a bitter contrast to the man she'd married.

Once Thatcher was done feeding the horses, he turned to Abbie theatrically, bent his arm with the pitchfork in his grip, and pulled a somber face. "You should come get in this with me. We'll be like the couple in that painting."

"This camera doesn't exactly work with a selfie stick," she joked. "But once I have a print, I could create a digital image and superimpose myself." She'd been halfway kidding, but the challenge of doing that very thing was incredibly appealing.

"Look solemn again," she directed, slightly twisting the ridged edges of the lens for a better focus. Her heart skipped another beat as she took in the features of his attractive face. The way the intensity behind his brown eyes pierced her even through the lens. She held very still as her pointer finger pressed the button. The shutter dragged, then clicked.

"Let me get one more," she said. "No smiling."

The comment caused a slight lift at the corner of his mouth. "I wasn't smiling until you said not to," he mumbled, bringing his lips over his teeth and going straight-faced once again.

"You smile with your eyes," she accused. "When you're looking at *me,* anyway."

Now he smiled wider and shook his head. "So full of yourself."

She giggled, quickly pressing the trigger to capture the wry, half grin on his face.

"Hey," he griped. "Okay, okay, that's enough. My turn to get yours."

Abbie couldn't wait to see how those photos would turn out, particularly the last one, where he wore one of her favorite expressions. If his hat had been off, she'd have also captured the lift of that one brow, and the small v between his eyes, which was likely hidden in the shadow of his hat.

While securing the camera with one hand, she lifted the strap up over her head. "Okay," she said as Thatcher approached her. "You'll have to take your hat off."

Thatcher removed his hat, tossed it over the fence post, and ran a hand through the wavy strands of his dark hair. She was used to it looking more blond in parts. It'd gotten darker over time. And of course, she mused, it was winter. He likely had natural highlights in the summer, even if he did wear a hat most of the time.

"Don't look at my hat hair," Thatcher said.

"I'm not," she lied. Thatcher had wonderful hair. Thick, textured, and far too wavy to show a dent from his hat this early in the day; it wasn't even lunchtime yet.

Abbie pressed up onto her toes to loop the strap over

his head, her wrist grazing the hair she admired. Gracious, he smelled good.

Thatcher bit the tip of one glove and yanked his hand free before spitting the glove from his mouth onto the snowy ground. He did the same with the other before taking hold of the camera.

Abbie leaned in, moving her cheek close to his so she could look at it with him. "You'll need to hold very still," she told him, "or you'll get a blurry image. With film, the shutter needs time to open and close. How much time depends on the lighting. Just get your subject in the crosshairs and adjust the dial until it's a nice, crisp image."

He gave her a nod. "Got it. Now," he said, making a triangle with his pointer finger and thumb and propping his chin with it. "Head over to the horses and face me. Think…smolder face."

"I'm not supposed to smolder," she said with a laugh. "I'm—"

"Hey," Thatcher interrupted, smoothing that same finger and thumb above his upper lip as if grooming a mustache. "I am the artiste, am I not?"

Abbie laughed some more. "A French one?"

"Oui, oui," he assured.

"Okay," she said, playing along. "You want a smolder, do you?" Abbie channeled her best fashion runway face. Gaze fixed on him, lips pouty, cheeks slightly sucked in, and eyes flaring with heat.

"Sweet *mercy*," Thatcher said under his breath.

She grinned. "What happened to your accent,

monsieur?" Was it just her or were his cheeks turning red behind that lens?

"Right now, I'm just trying not to lose my breath," he admitted with a laugh.

She liked hearing that. Liked it enough to assume the expression again, adding more heat behind her gaze as she pierced through the round lens he had focused on her.

The shutter let out a click. And then another. He turned the camera so it was horizontal, took two steps forward, and snapped one more.

"You better take this thing away from me before I click through the whole roll. I can't stop myself."

Abbie smiled, lifting a hand to stop him when the shutter sounded once again. "Okay," she said with a laugh. "That's good. Let me finish off the roll, then we can develop it. Are you going to join me for that?"

His face turned thoughtful. "Do you *want* me to join you for that part?" It seemed to be a new pattern of his since she arrived. Testing, treading cautiously, asking more than directing.

She envisioned the pop-up creation he'd gifted her, musing that, no matter how potent those chemicals were, she'd still catch hints of Thatcher's aftershave and the ever-present scent of leather.

At last, she nodded. Gulped. "Of course. It's a fun process. And I might need your help."

Thatcher lifted what looked like an insinuative brow while reaching to snatch his hat from the post. "Oh yeah?" He shuffled closer, giving her a second sample of the scent she'd just been thinking of.

Abbie took a step back, unsure why she wanted the distance. To clear her head maybe? "Yeah," she confirmed.

"Okay, I've got a few more things to take care of while you finish up. I'll meet you inside in a bit."

Abbie nodded, ducked her head, and hurried past him along the worn path through the snow.

She wasn't in the habit of carrying her phone with her, but Abbie was dying to check it when she got back inside. She resisted the urge to speed through her final three shots. With as many times as she checked that screen each day, it hadn't given her anything since Leona's text about Quinten being served.

Perhaps he'd signed the papers already and they hadn't yet been delivered. She guessed that was possible. Christmas was a busy time of year. There was no telling how long people might be out of the office. Possibly through New Year's.

Of course, there was always the alternative. Quinten could be more livid than ever. Rocked by a fit of rage, plotting his course to hunt her down and make her—as he'd said—"*slip quietly out of his life*" with his bare hands.

A deep shiver rocked through her body. Abbie pulled the scarf higher around her neck and spun in place, looking for something to catch her eye. Thatcher had gone back into the barn to care for the chickens. Rosie would come around noon to collect the eggs. And though she'd only been there for a few days, Abbie was already looking forward to Rosie's cheery daily visit.

She also enjoyed chatting with Rosie's mom, Taja. The friendly woman hadn't exactly shared the reason behind her recent move from Oregon to Montana, but she'd implied that she and Rosie had been in harm's way. Abbie had sensed there was more to the story that Taja was hesitant to share. Perhaps someday she'd hear the whole story.

At once, an old wagon wheel caught her eye. The rustic piece—fashioned of weathered wood and rusted metal—was mounted to a gate made of three horizontal posts. The contrast in color, along with the different textures, made for an interesting composition. The mound of snow on top caught sparkles of sunlight. Something she might not exactly be able to capture on film, but she'd do her best.

She had just two images left on the roll, so Abbie climbed the patio steps, trailed along the wraparound porch and into the front yard. This house was even older than Jacki and Lloyd's, but equally charming. And, according to Grandma C, the space was rich in romance, seeing that Wes and Taja had just fallen in love there.

Abbie couldn't help but envy Taja and Wes's relationship. Sure, it had come with its own issues, but at least Taja had been free to date when she'd arrived. Abbie's story felt so complicated in comparison. She had a crazy man, who was still legally her husband, that wanted her dead. And though Abbie wanted nothing more than to free herself of Quinten, he was the very thing still holding her back from Thatcher. It didn't seem fair that—even after she'd escaped him—he still had control over her life. Especially since she was there for only a limited time.

She couldn't help but wonder which would come first—word that Quinten had signed the papers at last or the dreaded, inward urgency that it was time for her to leave Montana. Abbie had felt certain that, once she'd signed the papers, she would feel okay about doing things that single people do. Like flirting and cuddling and…behaving like she had with Thatcher back in the day.

But she still didn't feel right about it. It was clear that Thatcher felt the same way. Maybe because her future was so uncertain. The last thing Abbie would want to do was hurt Thatcher again. It was possible that her hesitancy had more to do with that than a sense of loyalty to her marriage. If Quinten signed the papers, she wondered, would things change?

Yes, she decided, feeling as if that option was a million miles away. So out of reach the day might never come. Abbie entertained it just the same, allowing herself to waltz into a world of fantasy. She pictured picking up her phone and seeing a text from Leona that said Quinten had signed the papers—it had worked! She was free as a bird. Able to do whatever she desired, even stay at Copeland Brothers Ranch, perhaps.

Merely entertaining the idea caused a deep and sudden longing to carve through her center. It would never happen. She'd be running from Quinten the rest of her life. It came along with the territory—a fact that made staying with Quinten somehow easier. One woman who'd escaped years of violent abuse related it to a shark in the water with that ever-present fin announcing his every move. So long as she stayed with her abuser, she could see where he was. But once she left…there was no telling how and when he would strike. Only one thing was certain—that he *would* strike.

Abbie might have died the night Quinten choked her. What would he have done then? Who would he have blamed? Perhaps that thought came into play when she'd fought back to defend herself. He could have persisted, attacked once more, or snuffed the life out of her after she'd exhausted her energy, but he hadn't.

It occurred to Abbie that she'd been staring at the front of the ranch house, what Thatcher referred to as the bunk house, for some time. She walked from one side of the home to the next, assessing the structure, angles, and the light. Which perspective would create the most interest? Which would capture the humble, stalwart nature of such a home?

Just as she spun on one foot, stepped beneath the bare branches of a nearby tree, a bright beam of sun peered through a break in a high, puffy cloud, casting a stark glow over a corner of the pitched rooftop. Stunning. In black and white, it would offer the perfect contrast to the exposed shingles, the nearby barn, and the sheet of sky in the distance.

She lifted her camera, warm emotion and inspiration rushing through her veins, and snapped the picture. It was few and far between when a photo did justice to the real thing. She hoped that this one, on some level, would come close.

"Abbie!" The elated sound of Thatcher's voice caught her off guard. She glanced about the porch, trying to spot where it'd come from.

"Where are you?"

"Right here," he came, sounding even closer somehow.

Abbie traced over the home before spotting him, half hanging out the window. He was holding something in one hand and waving it about.

"What is it?" she asked.

"Your phone," he said. "You got a text from the attorney. At least, I think it's her."

Abbie hadn't bothered locking the new phone. In fact, she often had Thatcher check it when he went into the kitchen or headed up the stairs—depending on where she'd left it.

If a message came in and it wasn't from Thatcher, it *had* to be from Leona; no one else had the number. Abbie's heart broke into a frantic sprint, racing so hard it hurt. What if it was the news she'd been dying to hear? And why did she suddenly feel so much dread? Thick and heated, like a body of lava flowing into her gut, up her chest, weighing her down as she braced the camera and hurried toward the home.

"Does it say Leona?" she blurted. "What does it say?"

"Yeah, it's from Leona," he hollered. "It says he signed the papers!"

Elation sprang like a delicate sprout, tiny amidst the molten pool gushing through her. "You're lying," she said, though she knew Thatcher would never joke about something like that. But in this instance, the alternative didn't seem possible.

"Come see for yourself," Thatcher said, sounding as shocked as she was.

At once he disappeared from the window, and Abbie crossed the remainder of the yard through the wet, slushy snow. She hurried up the wide set of porch steps, stomping the snow from her boots as she went, and yanked her feet out once she made it to the rug. She'd barely grabbed the latch to the storm door when the paneled door on the other side creaked wide open.

Thatcher stood there, phone in hand, shocked elation on his flushed face. "Here." He thrust the phone into her grip, and Abbie fumbled awkwardly to take hold of it. The screen was black, so she pushed a button, swiped to the left, and tapped on her text app.

The attorney *had* texted her.

Leona Petrelli: *Good news! Quinten signed the papers. They were delivered to my office, certified mail. My assistant signed for them at exactly 1:04 p.m.*

Before reading the remainder of the text, Abbie glanced at the time on her screen. It was 11:14 there in Montana, meaning that Quinten's signed documents had arrived just ten minutes ago.

She finished reading the remainder of the test: *I'm glad we were in the office today. Happy New Year, to you, Abbie. You're one step closer to ringing in a whole new life.*

"Wow," Thatcher said over her shoulder, his warm breath grazing her temple.

Abbie tried to process the news. She was free. Only moments ago, she'd feared this was an impossible outcome. But here it was, evidence right before her eyes. Quinten was letting her out. Leona had said that New Hampshire had some of the quickest divorce options out there. She hadn't been kidding. Of course, it only worked if both parties cooperated.

"I can't believe it," she said, wondering how long it would take to sink in. She'd expected to feel different, more relieved.

Suddenly Thatcher stepped away, tugged the front brim of his hat until it covered more of his face, and cleared his throat. "I'm sorry," he rasped. "This is probably...difficult for you."

Abbie furrowed her brow. "Hmm?"

"No, I get it." He shook his head and started toward the kitchen. "You were married to him. I'm sure you probably still love the guy in a way—"

But Abbie was already hurrying after him. She grabbed him by the shoulder, the realization of what he said filtering in. "I don't love him, Thatcher. I'm sure it's that way for *some* women, but not me. I'm not sad, I'm just... not as relieved as I thought I'd be." She shrugged and looked down at her phone once more, somehow needing to make sure she'd read it correctly.

She had. It was all there, each word in its proper place. Quinten had signed it, agreed to her terms. It was all but finished.

"I never thought he'd let me walk away. Most domestic-abuse-related murders occur after the victim leaves, did I tell you that?" She didn't wait for an answer, just followed the trail of thoughts running through her mind. "I always worried he'd try to kill me if I left. He proved me right when I even mentioned divorce last week." She lifted her gaze.

Thatcher was studying her face. Jaw tight, nostrils flared, fury burning in his eyes. "He'll never touch you again." He said it like a promise. An uttered oath or vow.

Abbie nodded. "I think you're right. At least, that's what my head says. Why would he sign it if he was just going to come after me? This is him letting me go, but…"

Thatcher shuffled closer, the toes of his boots nudging her sock-covered feet. "But?"

"But the rest of me hasn't caught up. I don't *feel* like I'm free. I don't *feel* safe."

At once Thatcher was moving even closer and pulling her into a warm, heavenly scented embrace. "You might not feel it yet, but you *are* safe." He smoothed his hands over her back and mumbled into her hair. "You're safe, and if you want me to, I'll keep reminding you until it sinks in."

His warmth and smell were everywhere, seeping through her coat and her clothes and burrowing right into her heart where she needed it most. Soothing, comforting, filling her with new levels of assurance and peace. "Thanks," she said against his sleeve.

Thatcher pulled back to lock eyes with her. "You're here with me now," he rasped, "and I swear, I'll die before I let him lay another hand on you."

CHAPTER 13

Thatcher wasted no time telling his family the good news. In a matter of weeks, depending on the load at the courthouse, Abbie's petition for divorce would be granted by the state. More importantly, though, both parties had signed the dotted line. Technicalities, especially in a case like this, were of no consequence.

At least, that's what he'd told Nash as they'd hauled fresh food to the cattle in the east pasture. Thanks to a recent rise in temps, the snowfall had turned into rain the last few days, which meant a whole lot of gross and goopy mud.

"You want my *real* opinion?" Nash asked as he climbed off his horse, Copper.

Wyatt and Wade were yards behind Nash, hauling fresh hay bales from the supply barn into Thatcher's flatbed.

Thatcher eyed the two of them before setting his gaze

back on Nash. The flickering of a microburst sparked to life in his chest. "If you can tell me quietly, yes."

Nash tossed a look over his shoulder and nodded. "You're putting your whole life on hold. Canceling all your plans, probably burning bridges to Camille and Leah, at least. Deborah obviously doesn't mind since she's planning to let *me* take her out for the night." He popped his brows.

That was true enough. The busy investor hadn't seemed to mind when Thatcher canceled his plans and offered up Nash, whose date wound up with the flu, in his place. Not that Thatcher had been surprised. He assumed a woman like Deborah Springfield had men in every city she frequented, most of whom were probably willing to give her more of what she wanted; Thatcher had his limits.

Still, what Nash said about Leah and Camille was likely true. If weeks or even months went by, he'd be forced to give them a reason for not taking them out.

"Plus," Nash added as if knowing he was gaining ground, "you're going to turn me into a third wheel for the bronco brothers and I can't deal with that." Nash chuckled over the words, but Thatcher knew he meant what he said. Abbie had monopolized his time since she'd arrived, and Thatcher didn't see that changing any time soon.

He shook his head. "I feel you," he said, "but what can I do? The woman can't exactly have a social life since folks around here could recognize her. I'm all she's got."

Nash gave him a one-shouldered shrug. "Not exactly.

There's Taja. Abbie would probably love hanging out with her and Rosie. And Mom too. Heck, they could do a girl's night. Watch movies, eat bonbons, paint each other's nails."

Thatcher shook his head. "You've watched way too many chick flicks," he accused.

Nash gave him a wicked grin. "If it works, it works."

Thatcher laughed. "Yeah, yeah. Just don't forget where you got that advice."

"I won't," Nash assured. "I always give Rem the credit he deserves."

"Rem?" Thatcher tried to sound offended but failed. "Yeah, that's where I got it too."

"If she wants to watch a chick flick, say yes and take notes," the pair recited in unison.

Thatcher stifled a groan as he noticed Wyatt and Wade coming up behind Nash, the two glancing from one another before pinning their eyes on Thatcher.

"Is she all ready to go?" Thatcher asked with a nod toward his loaded truck.

Wade tipped his hat. "Yep."

Wyatt rested his work gloves on the fence post and folded his arms across his chest. "So, you're really going to spend New Year's Eve here with Abbie tonight?"

"Don't forget Ma, Pops, the newlyweds, and Rosie," Thatcher added, tucking one hand into his coat pocket to secure his keys. He looked down at the mud caking his boots, a pretty picture depicting the messy state of his life. Turned upside down by circumstances beyond his control, yet he'd take the heat for it all the same.

"And Grandma C," Nash added with a laugh. "She parties harder than any of us."

"Oh, I'm not forgetting about them," Wyatt said, blue eyes narrowing. "But don't you think it's a little risky to spend New Year's Eve with another man's wife?"

"Everyone knows you kiss the woman you're with when the clock strikes twelve," Wade added from his spot beside Nash.

And there it was, the type of remark Thatcher had been waiting for. Fire-like heat shot through his veins, forcing his pulse to spike in a blink. He fisted his keys and gave them a shake within his closed fist. "Why don't you mind your own business, *cousin.*"

Sure, it was a low blow, pointing out that Wyatt wasn't his real brother. Thatcher would never do that to Nash, but Wyatt didn't act like a loving or concerned brother the way Nash did. Still, as Thatcher surveyed the discomfort spreading within the group, he realized he'd stepped out of line.

Wade shifted his weight and ducked his head. Nash tugged the brim of his hat and looked at the ground as well. Wyatt, however, narrowed his eyes at Thatcher, his nostrils flaring and his jaw clenched.

"There's a reason you like Nash more than you like me or even your *own brother,* Wade. It's the same reason I get along with Wade better than the rest of you. Birds of a feather flock together. Wade and I are ambitious. We take responsibility for what we do, how we behave. Sure, we can get wild in competitions, when bull-riding to take the prize, but we keep it in the corral where it belongs. We *ride* wild bulls, we don't act like them."

"Thanks for the human psych course." Thatcher shook his head, not wanting the conversation to go any further. He was about to step around the group when he thought better of it. The quickest path to his truck was straight down the center—right between Wyatt and Wade. Thatcher squared his shoulders and took two long strides past Wade and Nash on his left. Yet just as he moved to pass Wyatt, the pushy guy stepped right into his path and rammed shoulders with him.

"No," Wyatt said. "I'm not going to let you off that easy."

"C'mon, Wyatt," Wade mumbled, but Wyatt pressed on.

"Guys like you and Nash do whatever you want. You act before you think, get yourself—*and* other people, I might add—into trouble, and pretend you didn't know any better. You make girls like Leah feel like they're not enough because you're too immature and conceited to commit."

"Ah." Thatcher tipped his head back. "I should have known this was about Leah. It's not my fault she prefers my company to yours. Good luck finding a woman who's looking for a stick in the mud."

Wyatt shoved Thatcher in the chest, forcing him two steps back. "Your *face* is going to be in the mud if you don't shut up."

Thatcher closed the gap and shoved him in return.

Nash and Wade flanked Wyatt at either side, ready to step in if things got out of hand.

"There's a reason your only brother doesn't like you," Thatcher said, glancing at Nash before pinning his gaze back on Wyatt. "You're always getting after him, putting him down, making him feel like crap all the time."

"I'm *trying* to help him become a man, is what I'm doing."

"So you think you're his father or something?"

Wyatt took a step back as those words, uttered louder than Thatcher meant to speak them, echoed off the walls of the nearby barn.

"No," Wyatt rasped with a head shake. "I'm well aware that *our* father is *dead*." With that, Wyatt tossed one last glance in Nash's direction before snatching his work gloves off the fence. And as he stomped off, leaving furious energy in his wake, Thatcher caught a disapproving look from Wade.

Nash evaded Thatcher's gaze altogether by glancing out over the land.

"We already told Ma and Pops," Wade said, gaining his attention once more. "But you may as well know that Wyatt and I enlisted in the Navy. We passed the aptitude test before our final comp in Arizona, and have since passed the physical exam as well. We signed up for delayed entry, so we head to Fort Worth shortly after the new year."

"Will you be close to Belle and Scott?"

He nodded. "We'll be on the same base. It's a naval air station, joint reserve. But Wyatt hates Scott, so I doubt we'll see them much."

That's because Wyatt hated everyone, Thatcher wanted to say, but didn't. Instead he turned his thoughts to what he'd just learned—Wyatt and Wade were leaving. He didn't know how to feel about that. Sure, the two had talked about becoming Navy SEALS since they were kids, but Thatcher was sure they'd set that goal aside for life on the ranch.

He glanced at Nash. "Did you already know?"

Nash nodded. "Wyatt told me when we all went out the other night."

"So that whole comment about becoming a third wheel was..."

"Was *honest*," Nash assured. "I *am* a third wheel right now. When Wade and Wyatt take off, I guess I'll be flying solo like Rem."

"Well," Wade said, wrangling Thatcher and Nash into a haphazard three-way hug. "I know you two are going to miss us whether you admit it or not."

"Yeah, yeah," Nash said.

"I won't miss you," Thatcher lied. "Just don't come back any stronger than I am, you hear? I like being the buffest brother in the bunch."

"Oh, ho ho! You're the most delusional one," Wade said, "that's for sure."

"You mean *second* buffest," Nash added while flexing the bicep hiding beneath his coat sleeve.

Thatcher untangled himself from the trio and headed toward his truck, Nash and Wade at his heels. "You guys have fun tonight," he said, shifting his gaze to Nash. "And you—watch out for Deborah. She's...aggressive."

Nash only laughed and rubbed his palms together. "I'm counting on it."

Wade rolled his eyes. "Poor kid. He's already in over his head and he doesn't know it."

"You've got that right," Thatcher said.

A series of clatters and clanks sounded from the garage, causing Thatcher to glance over his shoulder.

"It's just Wyatt," Wade said. "He's working on your bikes. Wants to get them done before we leave."

Guilt burrowed into Thatcher's center. Even after they'd argued, Wyatt planned to fix his motorcycle?

"You know...Wyatt has a lot of crap he's still sorting through," Wade said, adding another heap of guilt to the load. "I know he rubs you guys wrong, but he means well."

Thatcher gave him a curt nod and climbed into his truck. "Yeah. See you guys next year."

"Next year?" Nash squeaked. "Oh, you took that one from Ms. Davis? She liked saying that."

"*Every* teacher liked saying that," Wade said.

"Right, but Nash had a crush on Ms. Davis." Thatcher busted into laughter as he finished. "When *she* said it, he cried all the way home until I finally explained to him that next year was right after winter break."

Nash shook his head. "Didn't you say you were leaving?"

"I am. See you guys later." After Thatcher pulled onto the dirt road, he spotted Nash and Wade in the rearview, shoving one another playfully as they headed toward the garage. The fact was, Wade used to be a lot more like Wyatt. It seemed though that—over the years—Wade had decided Wyatt was doing enough big-brother-bullying for the both of them.

On the short drive back to the bunk house, Thatcher considered what Wade had said. Wyatt *had* gone through a lot. Not only had he lost both of his parents, the guy lost his first crush to cancer back in junior high. On top of that, he had a naturally crabby disposition, making him unpleasant to be around, especially for those with such opposite personalities like Thatcher and Nash.

All too soon, his thoughts were back on Abbie. He didn't exactly get what he'd been looking for during his discussion with Nash. Just a lesson on how much he was messing up the current state of his life. In some ways it was cushy, like Nash implied. He was casually dating three women, two of whom would drop their plans at the last minute to go out with him whenever the notion struck. But the sad fact was, his feelings for them were lukewarm compared to the flames he still torched for Abbie.

With that thought, his phone let out a buzz. Thatcher pulled alongside the barn and parked the truck before checking the screen.

Abbie: *sandwiches are ready.*

His pulse quickened. Warmth pooled around his heart. Since moving into the bunkhouse, he and Abbie had fallen into a lunchtime routine. While he was out taking care of the daily chores, she'd tidy up the home and prepare a nice lunch. If Jacki hadn't invited them to supper, Abbie would cook that too.

He allowed himself to soak in the sight of that text once more. If this wasn't a taste of married life, Thatcher didn't know what was. No wonder Wes went and fell in love with Taja while the single mom and her daughter stayed with him. Playing house, it seemed, could be risky. In more ways than one, he mused, recalling the danger Abbie was in.

Thatcher was suddenly grateful that Wes planned to spend New Year's at the house with the rest of them. After what he'd been through, the man was sure to have some advice. And perhaps Taja would open up about her side of things as well. It might do Abbie some good to hear that Copeland Brothers Ranch had been the safe haven Taja and her daughter had been searching for. Maybe, just maybe, that would encourage Abbie to stick around.

CHAPTER 14

Abbie rearranged the sandwich halves on the plate to add some height on one side. The thick slices of homemade bread—that Abbie had made herself courtesy of Grandma C's old bread maker—made her smile in satisfaction. Even better was the sight of that processed cheese layered between two slices of bologna. Talk about nostalgia. Abbie hadn't enjoyed a simple bologna sandwich since her memorable lunches with Grandma Dottie. A pitcher of iced tea, a plate of pickle spears, and a bowl of potato chips completed the scene.

Abbie sighed at the mere recollection. She'd wanted to replicate simple meals like that. For most, mastering a layered chocolate and cream torte might feel like an accomplishment to be proud of. But for Abbie, her efforts had only been to appease, impress, keep up. It's true that she took comfort in the solace of the kitchen when Quinten wasn't around, but even then, even when he was tucked into his music studio for hours, he'd often blast a selection of his songs throughout the house speakers, forcing his presence on her like a ghost—as haunting and erratic as the man himself. A presence she'd never escape.

But she *had* escaped him.

A burst of warm gratitude coated her skin like a hug. *Thank you, God. Thank you for helping me get away.*

At once, the back door creaked open. She envisioned Thatcher prying his muddy boots off at the door, stretching as he straightened back up, and stepping into his Lakers slides, a sporty contrast to the rest of his cowboy getup. Abbie had to admit, she was enjoying these daily glimpses of Thatcher doing life on the ranch.

Her heart fluttered as she heard him walking through the mudroom. She glanced up in time to see him enter the dining area. "Howdy." He shot her a grin and peeled off his corduroy coat, having to nearly pry his muscled arms from the sleeves. He flung it over the back of a nearby chair and reached for his hat. Yet before he pried that off too, he tipped his head and narrowed his gaze on Abbie. "Do I dare?"

He was worried about hat hair, of course. Abbie shrugged. "It's nothing I haven't seen before."

Thatcher thrust a fist over his chest. "Don't sound so unimpressed," he teased. "These locks are spun from real life gold." He removed his hat and raked fingers through the thick, wavy strands.

"I hate to be the one to break this to you," Abbie said with a grin, "but your hair is brown now."

Thatcher gasped. "It is *not.* My mama told me it was

spun from golden hay by a lovely maiden and I'll never stop believing it."

"Right, but you better not trim it, or the gold will be gone."

"Will not."

"It would too," Abbie insisted with a laugh. She tipped her head, trying to picture him with slightly shorter hair. It would look good, she mused. Of course, with looks like Thatcher's, he couldn't go wrong. "You hungry?"

Thatcher looked down at their plates. "I sure am. Let me wash up real quick." Thatcher hurried back into the mudroom and twisted the knob.

Scents of pine soap wafted into the kitchen as Abbie studied his worn cowboy hat and coat. Thatcher Copeland was a good, hardworking man, that much was true, and oh, how she admired that. Equally admirable though, was that fun, playful side of him. Thatcher had a way of igniting Abbie's zest for life, something that got stifled in the seasons spent away from him. Yet every summer, when she and Thatcher reunited, Abbie became a long-forgotten bulb on the cusp of spring. He was her sun, her rain, her encouragement to stop hiding beneath the mound of societal expectations and bloom to reveal her true colors.

Being here again, Abbie couldn't help but let herself imagine a life like this, the two of them on the ranch, enjoying rituals like lunch in the sunlit dining room on cold winter days. In the spring, perhaps they'd sit out on the patio instead, enjoying the crisp breeze while the birds chirped and the horses neighed.

After drying off with the hand towel hanging beside the wash bin, Thatcher joined her at the table, said grace over the food, and wrapped a hand around the glass of iced tea she'd poured him. He lifted it and eyed her glass to suggest she do the same. She did.

"Here's to closing out this year with a bang, Abbie. I'm glad you're here."

Abbie grinned and clinked her glass against his. "Thanks," she said. "Me too." And as she brought the drink to her lips, tipping it back to take a sip, she considered the evening ahead of them. "Can you believe he actually signed the papers?" she blurted as she considered it once again.

Thatcher shook his head and thrust a triumphant arm in the air like he was riding a bull. "Woo hoo!" he cheered. "I have to keep reminding myself that it actually happened," he said, picking up his sandwich and taking a bite.

"I know," she agreed, a hint of shocked laughter coating the words. "It's crazy. I'm actually free now."

Thatcher wiped his mouth with a napkin. "So is that how you see it?" he asked. "Even though it's not technically" —he used finger quotes— *"final?"*

Abbie didn't hesitate. "Definitely. I already considered it done once *I* signed the papers and left. I sort of *had* to, since I knew Quinten might try to drag things on for years. But ever since we got that text saying he'd signed them…" She shrugged. "I don't know, it sealed the deal, I guess. I'm finally free to do what I want to do."

Abbie shifted her gaze back to Thatcher. He did the

same, fixing those hazel eyes on her as those final words basked in the chemistry between them. Moments lapsed, the unspoken thoughts behind his gaze causing heat to spread up her cheeks.

"Knock, knock," called a cheerful Jacki while knocking on the back door. She hurried in with a pan and slid it across the counter before spinning to look at Thatcher and Abbie in turn. "Would you mind baking these rolls here before you head over tonight?" she asked.

"Of course," Abbie said, willing the blush to hurry and leave her cheeks. She felt caught somehow, as if the two were only kids again.

"Psst…" Thatcher whispered. "What did you mean when you said *'free to do whatever you wanted?'*" He popped his brow wickedly.

Abbie shushed him and turned back to Jacki.

"They'll be finished rising in about four hours," she was saying. "There's a sticky note on top with instructions."

Abbie made the mistake of glancing at Thatcher, half-expecting him to respond to his mother. Instead, he gave Abbie a wink.

She fought back a gasp and turned back to Jacki. "Sounds great. Is there anything else we can bring?"

Jacki scrutinized Thatcher for a blink, propped both hands on her hips, and bent low to inspect his face.

Abbie's heart pounded. Had she seen him flirting with her? Was she giving him a scolding look?

Suddenly, Jacki secured the napkin from the table and smeared it over his face. "Got a few crumbs there," she muttered, throwing the napkin back into place. She pointed a finger at him. "You behave."

Thatcher's eyes went wide and innocent. "I'm a full-grown man, Ma. What are you doing to me?" He spared a *help me* look in Abbie's direction, which planted a seed of humor in the moment.

Abbie couldn't help but giggle. "Yeah, Thatcher. *Behave.*"

Jacki straightened back up and pulled the lapels of her coat together in front. "See you tonight." And then she was gone.

Thatcher shook his head. "Tsk, tsk." He was baiting her, and Abbie knew it, but she couldn't help but bite.

"What?" she asked innocently.

"Always getting me into trouble, Ms. Abbie. I think she thinks you're a bad influence."

Abbie's jaw dropped. "*Me*?" She shook her head. "No way. You're the one she was pointing fingers at. She didn't tell *me* to behave."

Thatcher lifted a brow. Slowly, a Cheshire grin pulled at the corners of his mouth. "You're right," he said. "Mama knows darn well I won't listen, being the grown man that I am. And since she didn't give you that warning, I'd say we're *both* allowed to misbehave if we'd like."

That comment was a swarm of honeybees and her tummy was the hive. Zips, zooms, and tingles raced through her center. Abbie took hold of her sandwich and brought it to her lips, saying one last thing before taking a bite. "We'll see about that."

CHAPTER 15

Abbie's gaze drifted from one corner of the space to the next. Scents from dinner still hung in the air, sweetened by the tart tang of triple berry pie now cooling on the rack by the window.

Seated at the nearby card table, Lloyd pieced together a puzzle with Grandma C. Laughter often rose between them, not all of it reverent, Abbie mused. Lloyd's were innocent enough, playful accusations that his mother had numbered the puzzle pieces on back. Grandma C, however, kept making comments about the bare-chested men manning the sailboats in the puzzle, insisting her days of groping a man's muscled chest weren't over yet. If there was air in her lungs there was a chance for love in her life.

Jacki and Rosie were kneeled up to the coffee table, the two crafting a paper banner welcoming the new year like a guest of honor. Perhaps it was. Life was a gift, after all. Meant to be cherished, like Grandma Dottie always said.

Rosie's face beamed with excitement as she smeared glue over a paper flower, her tongue peeking slightly from her lips as she worked. "This is going to be the prettiest New Year's banner I ever saw," the little girl declared.

Abbie shifted her gaze to Taja, who sat across the table from her, the two of them waiting for Wes and Thatcher to round up some board games.

"They're like two peas in a pod," Taja said.

Abbie's grin grew; Taja must have followed her gaze. "That's wonderful," she said, recalling the many times she'd made Independence Day crafts with Grandma Dottie. "I used to spend every summer with my Grandma Dottie and Grandpa Buck, as long as he was living," she added. "They were some of the best people on this earth, I'm telling you. I really cherish those memories."

Taja's smile spread to the corners of her green eyes. "That's neat. I can't tell you how happy it makes me, raising Rosie in a place where she's surrounded by so much love."

"I can imagine," Abbie said with a nod.

"I'm an only child, myself."

Abbie's eyes widened. "Me too. That's why I always loved coming over here. Besides, of course, the fact that I had a massive crush on Thatcher."

"Of course," Taja said with a laugh. "Hey, Thatcher asked if Wes and I would mind sharing a bit about how we wound up here, if you're interested."

"I'd love that," Abbie said, resting her elbows on the

table as she leaned in. Even that action felt like freedom. Quinten was like a second father—scolding her for being improper, even in their own home. *"Must you rest your elbows on the table like a homeless child?'"*

"I've been a single mom since Rosie was born," Taja said, "seeing that her father bailed once he found out I was pregnant."

"I'm sorry," Abbie offered. "That must have been difficult."

Taja continued, telling of how she worked at a National State Park in Oregon, but Abbie couldn't help but dwell on one particular word, one that reminded Abbie she had a secret to share. One that Thatcher might not take well. She, too, had wound up pregnant. And instead of telling Thatcher like she should have done, Abbie said *I do* to another man—an abusive one, as it turned out—willing to let Quinten raise the baby instead.

"Rosie loved spending time at the giftshop," Taja was saying. "So, when she asked to have her birthday party there, I figured it was perfect."

"And she was turning seven?" Abbie thought she'd heard.

"Yes," Taja said with a nod. Her face fell flat then, and her gaze shot to where Rosie kneeled on the floor. "To make a long story short, a close friend of ours, a man who runs the shop, was shot. And though I didn't see the shooter in the act, I did come across him just seconds after, which made me the key witness in the crime."

A chill shook through Abbie. "How awful," she said. "And on your daughter's birthday?"

Taja went on to explain that she and Rosie had been sent to Copeland Brothers Ranch, which would serve as a safe house while they awaited the date of the trial.

"So you'd never met any of them before?" Abbie asked.

Taja shook her head and grinned. "Nope. Lloyd's a retired marshal and he's close to a family that has taken on a bunch of witnesses over the years."

"Psst," came a rather loud whisper from the bottom of the stairs. Thatcher peeked his head around the corner and made the sound again. "Psst, Rosie!"

Rosie shot a look over her shoulder, then popped to her feet, a grin filling her entire face. "Hi!"

Thatcher's heart-melting smile made Abbie sigh. "Get Grandma C and come upstairs with me and Wes," he instructed in that not-so-quiet whisper.

"Wonder what they're up to," Taja said with a head-shake. She set her gaze back on Abbie. "I can see why you took a liking to him. Thatcher is a lot of fun. And he's so cute with Rosie."

Abbie's heart melted a little more. Was it possible she could actually have the life she'd always wanted? Abbie rarely let herself entertain the idea, as frightened as she was about putting the Copelands in danger. But what if Quinten never came looking for her?

"So you stayed here, went back and testified," Abbie said, getting back to the events of Taja's story. "How did you wind up back here? Were you and Wes already serious by that point?"

Taja bit her lip. "We were, yes. I'll have to give you the details to that side of things another time." She lifted her brow. "And maybe you can catch *me* up on things between you and Thatcher..."

"Absolutely," Abbie said, enjoying the camaraderie brewing between them.

"Anyway," Taja said with a sigh. "I want to assure you, in case you have any doubts, that this is a safe place. And if you ever need someone to talk to, I'm here."

Abbie had always wanted a sister. She couldn't help but wonder if this warm feeling—the genuine kindness of this near stranger, was a small taste of sisterhood. Someone who would share their fears, and be a support in hard times.

"Thank you," she said through a sniff, moisture welling in her eyes. "That really means a lot."

"Why don't you come to breakfast next week? Rosie's going to start her at-home school again on Monday. While the guys are out doing their thing, we can swap a few more stories and pig out on pancakes."

"I'd love that," Abbie said. Already, she was looking forward to it. To making friends with someone so down to earth. With values similar to hers. A woman who knew and loved the Copelands as much as she did. And, from what Abbie could tell, appreciated the value of a good man.

But how long would it last? Did she dare build friendships she'd be forced to pull away from sooner or later?

Suddenly a celebratory song—like the kind they use to rile crowds at a sports game—blasted from the base of the stairs. Taja's eyes went wide, causing Abbie to glance over her shoulder.

There, boasting a curly, platinum wig, was Grandma C. She wore pink bell bottoms with white vinyl boots and a flowy white top that frilled widely around her wrists. She lifted a megaphone to her lips. "Let's get this party started!"

Grandma C stepped aside in time for Rosie to leap onto the scene in a neon leotard, layers of puffy socks, and a matching headband. If Grandma was representing the seventies, Rosie was rocking the eighties.

Out came Wes next, sporting a sixties vibe, looking like a young Sonny Bono with a thick mustache and a flashy, silk shirt snapped up only halfway. Rosie clapped and cheered as Wes, who was obviously outside his comfort zone, swayed this way and that to the tune. No one needed to tell Abbie that he was only doing this for Rosie, which made it all the more adorable. Taja, whose hands were clasped beneath her chin as she watched with a wide grin, seemed to agree.

At once, the music changed to a very familiar nineties tune from a grunge band Abbie knew quite well, thank you very much. Sure, it was only because she and Thatcher used to listen to it; he was a fan of alternative and grunge rock. It was Nirvana's "Smells Like Teen Spirit."

Soon came the lead singer of the band in ripped jeans and a flannel shirt. Thatcher had turned into a Curt Cobain lookalike, and she'd be danged if he didn't look good.

He motioned for everyone to stand up before resuming his air guitar and lip-syncing to the music. Rosie danced her way to a wooden chest at the base of the staircase and pried it open. "Come get an outfit everyone," she encouraged.

Thatcher walked right up to Abbie, eyes fixed on her as he mouthed the words with convincing passion. He took her by the hand, led her to the trunk, and pulled a familiar object from its depths—the backpack she'd been wearing when he picked her up at the train station.

She peeked inside to see the combat boots, torn tights, and the baggy sweatshirt inside. She spotted the pink wig and beanie there too.

"Go get dressed so you can be my Courtney," he encouraged. "Your song's up next."

Abbie was all for it. She hurried up the stairs, not wanting to miss out on the fun. Taja was right behind her, carrying a long, black wig and an evening gown. "Let me guess," Abbie said. "Cher?"

"You got it," Taja said. "Can't believe Wes is really doing this. I swear, the guy does not know how to tell Rosie no."

The two shared a laugh as they darted into opposite rooms to change. Soon they were back downstairs and taking in Jacki and Lloyd's matching duds.

As promised, Thatcher played a song by Hole, and Abbie went all out, musing the wardrobe was just right. After that, Rosie lip-synced to Cindy Lauper's "Girls Just Wanna Have Fun" while the group danced and cheered her on. And as the small rock party continued with "I Got You, Babe" and a memorable Abba song by Grandma C, Abbie had the distinct feeling that everything would be okay. Perhaps she wouldn't have to leave after all.

The countdown to midnight rolled in quickly. One minute Jacki was announcing they had two hours left, the next she was giving a twelve-minute warning.

"Everyone decide where you'd like to be," Jacki said. "Grandpa Lloyd and I are heading onto the porch," she announced.

"Rosie and I are going to watch the ball drop and blow the horns," Grandma C cheered. "Right, Rosie?"

Rosie nodded hugely. "Cuz Wes said he wants to kiss Mom into the new year." She clapped her hands. "Guess what, Abbie," she panted while dancing on her toes and twirling. "Bonobo apes kiss like humans do. Did you know that?"

"I *didn't* know that," Abbie said. "How cool!" Abbie found herself more and more charmed by Rosie as the days moved on. It hardly seemed like a dark day could go by without her presence lighting it up.

"Here's your horn, Rosie," Grandma said. Yet before Abbie averted her gaze, she caught Grandma motioning for Thatcher to go.

Go where? Was she suggesting he hurry and get lost? Or that he take Abbie with him?

"Abbie," Thatcher said, his low voice seeming to answer that question. "Let's go up to the den."

The den? A blast of heat stirred low in her tummy. The den was where Abbie and Thatcher shared their very first kiss in a game of truth or dare. In that same den, the two had done a whole lot of cuddling and smooching in the summers following.

She glanced at the hand he held out for her, wondering if she should leave the wig behind or keep it on. She opted to keep it in place and set her hand in his. Thatcher easily enveloped it in his warm, large grip, the scent of him—pine soap and leather—teasing her senses.

In the den, Abbie was met with more familiar scents. She glanced at the wall of dimly-lit books along one side, figuring that was the reason it had always smelled like a library—the bittersweet scent of yellowed pages and cracking spines. And though she'd only ever come in the summer, traces of wood-burning smoke seemed to be fused in the fabrics, telling tales of cozy winters before the wood burning stove below.

Thatcher stopped walking in the center of the room, turned to face her, and stepped in close enough to slide one boot between hers. With his face shadowed by the weak lamplight behind him, Thatcher smoothed a large hand up the small of her back.

He lifted their joined hands as if they were about to dance, turning his gaze to watch as he unlocked the grasp, then glided his calloused fingertips over her palm.

Mmm, so good.

"I must be the luckiest man alive," he crooned, eyes fixed on the way her hand responded to his touch. "I can't believe you're really here." His voice had gone raspy and weak. He lowered his head, and Abbie pressed up on her toes, lips parted, ready. Yet instead of meeting her lips with his, Thatcher planted a gentle, tantalizing kiss to her upper cheek. He moved over to her temple, his hot breath teasing along the way, and planted another sweet kiss to her sensitive skin. Gently then, he tugged at the strands of her wig. Abbie was quick to pull it off and let it drop to the floor. She smoothed a hand over her hair, but soon abandoned the action as Thatcher's parted mouth trailed over her hairline. Slowly.

Goosebumps surfaced over her skin and rippled in waves up her arms. Cherished. Thatcher made her feel oh, so cherished.

Abbie lifted a hand to his chiseled face, reveling in the feel of his stubbled jaw, somewhat guiding his lips to hers. She traced his full lips with one thumb, heart pounding with anticipation, when suddenly Thatcher's hand wrapped gently around hers. He stepped back, turning so the lamp shined in from one side. The look in his eyes said it all—their hazel depths wrought with conflict.

"I want to kiss you more than anything," he said, "but… I don't want to start off on the wrong foot. We're so close to things being official—"

Abbie's jaw clenched. She yanked her hand away and stepped back. "Why are you worried about *him?* Don't you think he's taken enough from me over the years? My dignity, my pride, my freedom and joy? Now—even though we've both signed papers to make it official—he's taking this from me too?"

"I'm just trying to do the right thing here, Abs."

"Because *I'm* doing the wrong thing, is that what you're saying? You're making it sound like *I'm* the bad guy here. Beaten, belittled, abused, yet *I* was the only one faithful to our vows. The man's been cheating on me for years. I barely escape with air in my lungs, manage to get him to sign papers and set me free once and for all, and *you're* worried about *bro code?"*

"I'm not thinking about him—"

"Then what are you worried about? Paperwork? You're worried that someone hasn't put some official stamp on the documents and filed them in their proper place?"

She spun to turn away from him, fueled with so much anger and hurt that she'd almost missed what he said.

"You're right."

She stared into the dark corner across the room. The part that led to the loft. Abbie wiped tears from her face and sniffed. "What?"

Thatcher spun her around, gripped her by both hips, and pulled her firmly against his chest. Abbie braced herself with her hands on his chest.

"You're right," he nearly growled, and crushed his fevered lips to hers.

Thatcher reveled in the feel of Abbie's body, soft and warm in his arms, as he savored the blessed taste of her kiss. Abbie, the vibrant woman who stole his heart at first sight. Abbie, the woman who escaped the clutches of an abusive man and ran straight into his arms. She'd endured enough heartache and shame at the hands of her ex, and he'd be danged if he was going to add to it. Hadn't he decided he'd let her set the tone?

Sure, doubts might have crept in once Thatcher was about to give in to his passion for her, but hearing Abbie's side of things put those doubts to rest like nails in the coffin of her past. Those doubts were six feet under solid ground. Meanwhile, he and Abbie were in the clouds.

The intensity of their kiss had taken them both by storm, as impulsive and driven as it was, but as the urgency waned, their pace got lost in this lulling, euphoric haze.

Thatcher tuned in to the hypnotic sensations as the kiss melded and slowed. He pulled back and, with his lower lip, traced the prominent shape of her mouth, the cupid's bow up top, then the luscious curve of her bottom lip. He lingered in the space between, allowing her heated breath to further entice him as he came in for another series of slow, lingering kisses. Savoring the slick heat of her mouth with each blessed push and pull.

Yes. Yes. Yes.

In the distance, the countdown was on. First ten, then nine.

More kisses. More of her.

Seven, six.

The feel of her fingers on his scalp.

Three, two.

A soft, whining whimper catching in Abbie's throat.

And in came the new year with Abbie in his arms, her breath on his lips, and the infectious vines of her love entangling his heart. He was in it, buried beneath a heap too deep to climb out of now. Whatever he'd gotten himself into, there was no going back.

CHAPTER 16

Laughter drifted over the charming dining area, accented by the incredible view out back. Abbie's morning with Taja and Rosie had flown by so fast it felt like she'd barely blinked.

Abbie had been to the Copeland's lake house a handful of times in her youth. She'd always loved dual dining areas —one outdoors, one in, the two connected by a patio door and a wall of windows.

In the summertime, the kids would eat on the outdoor patio since they didn't mind the heat or the bugs. The grownups ate within the air conditioned portion of the home while still enjoying the view. Glass panels created something that might look like a greenhouse on one side, giving a fair view of the sky as well.

She'd thought nothing could compare to the sight of that lake in the summer. The surrounding plush, green trees growing tall around it were reflected in the water with the blue sky and glistening sun. But today's view was breathtaking in an entirely new way. Frost-covered branches surrounded the frozen blue lake, its edges a rim of quartz-like crystal.

"Makes me wish I'd brought my camera," Abbie said as they took in the view.

Taja nodded and sighed. "There's always next time."

Abbie grinned, liking the sound of that.

A bowl of Sour Patch Kids sat in the center of the table. Taja reached in, plucked out the yellow ones. "These are Wes's new vice," she announced before tossing one into her mouth.

"Oh yeah?" Abbie asked.

Taja nodded. "It's usually licorice ropes, but he had a few of these from Rosie's leftover Halloween candy and he was hooked."

"That's cute."

"He likes all but the yellows, which happen to be my favorite." Taja leaned onto the table and squared a look at Abbie. "So, how are things with Thatcher?"

Abbie felt her cheeks fill with heat.

"C'mon, I told you mine." And that she had. Taja had told Abbie all about her and Wes's love story, and Abbie had lapped it up like a dream.

"You two seem closer since New Year's," Taja prompted.

Abbie sighed, recalling the spectacular kiss they'd shared in the den. Even in memory, it nearly took her breath away. "We are," she admitted. "Things are good. I mean, we get along as well as we always did. There's such an ease in spending time with him, you know?"

Taja nodded. "That's good, but am I sensing a *but?*"

Abbie hadn't meant to let her concern slip through, but Taja had picked up on it all the same. She thought back on that unforgettable day, the sight of the pregnancy wand, and the chaos tearing through her mind. "As great as things are," Abbie said, "there's something I need to tell him. It's probably going to be hard for him to hear, and it might make him furious with me."

Taja gave that some thought as she chewed on the candy. "Well," she said before swallowing it down at last. "Is it something that will affect your future? Like—you're secretly still tied to your ex or you plan to leave here soon?"

Abbie shook her head. "It's something from our past. Before I married Quinten, actually. I thought about bringing it up the day after New Year's, but then he had to say goodbye to his brothers, so I didn't want to take away from that."

"Right," Taja said. "It's already kind of complicated for Thatcher, I think, where Wyatt's concerned."

Abbie nodded. Just two days ago, on the day after New Year's, the Copelands had said goodbye to Wyatt and Wade, wishing them well as they left for the Navy. It had been a tearful farewell, especially for Jacki, who repeatedly dabbed her watery blue eyes with a wadded tissue. Lloyd expressed their shared support and pride, saying he felt honored to be sending two fine men off to serve our country.

A sudden urge prodded at Abbie's mind, the desire to confide in Taja about her secret. Perhaps if she got it off her chest, she'd be able to wait to tell Thatcher at a more appropriate time.

"I kind of want to tell you what it is," Abbie blurted.

Taja's eyes went wide. A smile pulled at her lips. "You do?"

Abbie nodded. "Just don't let Wes tell Thatcher. I'll tell Thatcher eventually. I just have to wait for the right time, like you say."

"Okay," Taja urged in a whisper. Not that anyone else was there. An hour or so ago, Jacki had picked up Rosie and taken her to the library for some new books.

Abbie considered the best way to phrase it. "Thatcher and I were in love, right? But I always knew I wouldn't be able to marry who I wanted, especially some cowboy from Montana."

Taja nodded encouragingly.

"But every summer when I came to stay with my great-grandparents—well, eventually it was just Grandma Dottie after Grandpa Buck passed—but Thatcher and I would just pick up where we left off each time. The summers were magic.

"But when it came to my last summer here, after I'd graduated, things got more complicated. We both knew we couldn't be together. I'd told him, in fact, that my parents wanted me to marry Quinten Bromley, so it was like...a sad, last exploration into this world we'd never get to visit again. We spent a lot of time just lying on the ground, holding hands, and looking up at the sky. Or balled-up and cradling one another, as if we could hold on tight enough to change our fate.

"On my final night here, when it was time to say goodbye, I begged Thatcher not to really leave. I asked him to meet me out back where Grandma said I could stay in the tent. He did. And, umm..." Her face went hot as she dropped her gaze. "I wound up pregnant."

Taja gasped. Her eyes doubled in size. "You *did*? With Thatcher's—"

"Yes," Abbie assured. "I didn't find out until I went home. You have to understand that my older cousin wound up in a world of scandal. I knew from the time I was young that I would *not* cast that sort of shame on my family. Quinten showed up to officially propose while I was locked up in the bathroom panicking over the test."

"I can't even imagine," Taja said breathlessly. "You poor thing."

"My mom confided in Quinten, probably saying someone had taken advantage of me, and he said he still wanted to marry me. We'd just have to move up the date. Which we did. I felt terrible sending Thatcher the wedding announcement, but I felt it was only fair that he knew. I had to give up hope for our future together, and if he was ever going to move on, he had to do the same." The pain from that time in her life was tangible even then, as deep as it had gone.

"Two days after the wedding, while we were still on our honeymoon, I miscarried. I cried for days, knowing my one connection to Thatcher was lost forever." She wiped at the tears trickling down her cheeks.

"So you're saying," Taja said, lowering her chin and looking at Abbie through her lashes, "that Thatcher doesn't know you were ever pregnant."

Abbie held her gaze, searching her face for signs of disgust or judgment. Neither was there. In the warm green eyes before her, Abbie sensed kindness and understanding.

At last, Abbie shook her head. "He doesn't know. I feel like I need to tell him, but I'm just not sure when or how. Especially now that things just got so good. I don't want to mess it up."

Taja nodded. "I think he'll understand," she said. "And I'm sure when the time is right, you'll sense it. You'll know."

Abbie turned her gaze to take in the view once more, sucking in a deep breath. "Thanks." She resisted the urge to bring up another concern, but it was there all the same. Despite the fact that Quinten had granted her the divorce she wanted, Abbie still feared he might try to find her.

What if he'd only signed to get her to feel more comfortable or safe? Safe enough to let her guard down. At what point would Abbie feel she could go out in public? Be seen in a small town? Or perhaps the time would never come. Perhaps Abbie was kidding herself, refusing to accept a truth too dark to accept: what if the only way to assure her safety and, more importantly, the safety of everyone on Copeland Brothers Ranch, was to leave?

CHAPTER 17

The familiar scent of chemicals filled the confined space in the popup darkroom Thatcher had purchased for Abbie over Christmas, and boy, was he glad he had. He was learning a lot from Abbie.

Three bins stood on the table before them, each filled with the appropriate solution. The developer first, the fixer second, followed by the stop bath.

They were nearing the middle of January now, with still no public word from Quinten on the divorce, and nothing from the attorney saying things were final. Abbie had spent the last few weeks toying with a particular image on Thatcher's laptop. Now was time for the big reveal; he couldn't wait.

"You're producing a headshot for my career in modeling, right?" Thatcher teased.

Abbie giggled and gave him a nudge with her elbow. "You're about to find out." Dangling from the first set of tongs was the paper Abbie had just burned the image onto. "Before you see the final product, I want you to appreciate the steps I took to make this happen." She turned to face him in the dim, red light.

Thatcher leaned in and stole a kiss. "I appreciate them."

Abbie smiled against his lips. "You have to hear them first," she said. "I took two separate prints, made them into digital images with my phone, pulled those images onto your laptop, downloaded Photoshop so I could merge and manipulate the images to my satisfaction, then photographed that image to get it back on film, which I processed yesterday, all to get this masterpiece of a print."

Thatcher scooted behind her in the small space and curved his hands around her hips. With his mouth very close to her ear, he said, "I love it when you talk nerdy to me."

She giggled. "It's not nerdy. It's cool."

He squeezed her waist and grinned as he buried his nose into the silky strands of her hair until he grazed her delicate neck. "Keep telling yourself that."

She laughed again, and he loved how she could take his teasing. "Okay, I'll stop distracting you now so I can appreciate your masterpiece." He moved into place alongside her once more and rubbed his hands together.

"I tested this already, so I know just how long I have to process it to get the perfect contrast." Abbie lowered the paper in the first bin and pressed a button on the timer. "Here it goes."

Thatcher leaned in, watching as the image gradually, and rather magically, appeared. Like an eraser in reverse.

Dark shapes growing darker. White shapes turning gray. He spotted the outline of Abbie's face with ease, and though his own face was not far off, he couldn't pull his eyes off Abbie. She wore a rather perturbed expression, which meant it was the final image he'd snuck after she'd told him to stop. Fire burned low in his belly at the sight of that fiery expression. He'd seen it so many times over the years. A millisecond before she splashed him good and hard because he'd splashed her. Or a moment before she dished out a verbal lashing that put Thatcher to shame after a playful joke aimed in her direction. He loved how Abbie knew how to put him in his place.

The timer beeped, and Abbie dunked the tongs back into the tank and secured the print. She was quick to drop it into the next bin and set the timer. "This one makes the image permanent," Abbie said under her breath.

Thatcher took a moment to look at the overall image. She'd done a mockup of the American Gothic, alright. Him and her standing side by side.

The timer beeped, and Abbie moved the print into the final bin. "Want to get that little wash sink ready?" she asked, setting the timer once it was soaking in the final bath.

It took him a moment to snap out of his daze, but he forced his eyes off the print, moved over to the small sink, and twisted the knob.

The timer beeped.

"Thanks." Abbie pinned the print with the final set of tongs and shimmied into the space between Thatcher and the sink. She glided her shoulder blades against his chest and giggled. "Hi there, stranger."

"Howdy," he crooned in a deep voice.

Abbie let the water run over the print, thoroughly rinsing it before twisting the faucet. She tipped her gaze up to where the rope stretched from one end of the space to the next. "Where did those clips go?"

Thatcher reached up to secure them at either side of her. "Right here," he rasped against her temple. Chills erupted over her arms as she lifted the print to the clips, and Thatcher grinned in satisfaction.

He pressed each clip in turn, enjoying the way she seamlessly slid the print into place on each side. "This," he assured, appreciating the new details catching his gaze, "really *is* a masterpiece. You're incredible, Abbie. I mean it."

He shook his head, appreciating more and more the woman she was. Intelligent, strong, resilient, hilarious, playful and fun.

Abbie shifted in the cramped space, grabbing Thatcher's forearm to steady her, until she was facing him. She rested her cheek against his chest. "I didn't hear what you said."

Thatcher laughed. "Yes, you did."

She giggled and shook her head. "The vent is too loud. Say it again."

"You want to turn me into one big sap, I know it."

She kept her face pinned against his chest, but nodded this time. "Umm hmm."

"That's you admitting that you do? Want to turn me into a sap?"

"Yeah," she said in a pouty voice, giggling some more.

He couldn't help but like the way she was asking for what she wanted, even if it was for a simple compliment on her work. How often had she been denied those very things in her life? Falling short of her parents' expectations only to spend years married to a psychopath who belittled and abused her.

Thatcher had felt a strong urge to shield Abbie from the moment she'd asked if she could come to Montana. As each day passed, that urge bulged and swelled and took up more space in his head, his heart, his soul. Thatcher had said he would die before he let Quinten hurt her again, and he meant that with every fiber and speck he was made from.

He rubbed his hands up the length of her back, slowly, sweetly, pressing the tips of his fingers into the tight muscles. "I love how creative you are," he said, gently massaging her back as he spoke. "And talented, too. The pictures of the barn brought Pops and Grandma C to tears, which is no easy feat," he pointed out, recalling the day she'd developed the first set of black and whites.

"You're smart too. You got into one of the best schools in the country and earned a degree. And though it's probably been a while since you used any of this stuff," he said, glancing about the space, "you still know how to turn blank paper into frameable art. Granted, with this one, you have *very* attractive subjects."

Abbie giggled and sniffed.

Thatcher kept rubbing, moving up to the round of her shoulders, pressing, softly pinching. "I was just thinking about the things I love about you," he admitted, "while you were working your magic."

"Because it's sexy when I work with chemicals?" she prodded, her breath warm against his chest.

He laughed. "Very." Thatcher didn't want to elaborate. It was uncomfortable for him to voice such intimate thoughts. "Let's just say that I think you're the package deal. Intelligent, funny, kind, and fun to be around."

Abbie sniffed. "Thank you." She moved her hands from their balled-up place beneath her chin, wrapped her arms around his lower waist, and squeezed. "Ditto."

Thatcher chuckled, moving his hands to her neck now. "Ditto? No, you're not getting off that easily," he said, pinching the skin up the back of her neck.

Abbie rolled her head from one side to the next and groaned. "You're a very talented masseuse," she said in a dreamy voice.

"Which is another way of saying I'm good with my hands," he said proudly.

She giggled. "Keep telling yourself that."

"I will."

"I always knew you'd be the type of man I wanted. Family minded, down to earth, loyal and strong. You know the value of...of the things that really matter, unlike my parents. Unlike the crowd I was taught to impress. If it weren't for Buck and Dottie, I might not have known what mattered either."

She squeezed him again before letting her limbs go

weak around him. "I absolutely *love* your playful side," she said. "I can't tell you how attractive your sense of humor is to me, the way you can take it as much as you dish it. You're never too prideful to be the butt of your own joke, and that shows an impressive amount of confidence in who you are."

A rush of warm gratitude seeped into his soul. Thatcher couldn't count how many times he'd been accused of being immature, of not growing up, of not honoring the social code for when not to joke around. But Thatcher had a sensitive side. He'd never purposefully hurt someone with his words. He only sought to lighten the mood.

He and Abbie seemed to have that in common. At least when she was here, they did. When she was being herself. Emotion threatened to rise in his throat, so he cleared it with a small cough and summoned his Irish accent. "Maybe I secretly believe I'm just a wee speck of a man who deserves to be the butt of a joke."

"No," she said through a laugh. "You don't."

"You're right," he allowed. "I don't."

Abbie lifted her chin to gaze at him in the red-tinted light, pink against her skin, lighting her up like a goddess. He smoothed his fingertips over her skin, cradling her neck with such delicacy, Abbie let out a whimper.

At last, he lowered his head and pressed his lips to hers in a slow, passionate kiss. The space around them came alive with more than chemistry this time. Now, floating thick in the air were their words of appreciation, adoration, and love. That's what it all narrowed down to—a deep and unyielding love that would consume him until the day he died. And hopefully beyond. They may not have exchanged the words, but he could tell by her kiss that she felt the same.

Suddenly, he was transported to a space in the heavenly realm, he was sure of it. He crushed his lips to hers once more, reveling in the fact that Abbie Carrington was truly there in his arms, in his life. They were together at last. Beyond that, what else mattered?

And as Abbie matched his passion in the ebb and flow of each drawn out kiss, Thatcher inwardly admitted that he was fully lost to her. What would happen from here, he couldn't be sure, but he desperately hoped that this time he wouldn't have to say goodbye.

CHAPTER 18

Nerves shot through Abbie's body as the big screen TV blasted a commercial. Something about durable kitchen garbage bags. She stared at the bulging bag of trash as it split and spilled onto the staged white carpet below.

Talk about triggering. Quinten was more anal than anyone she'd met, yet he insisted on sticking with a white theme in the entry room. Plush white carpet with matching vases and chairs, all to complement the glossy finish of his ebony grand piano at the far end of the room, propped on a small stage, as he'd have it.

When he insisted on having company linger in that room, Abbie felt the weight of that piano on her shoulders, knowing it was up to her to keep the marble, fabrics, and furniture impeccably white.

"If this guy tries to spin things on you," Grandma C

said over a mouthful of popcorn, "he's going to have *me* to deal with."

The great room was filled with several members of Thatcher's family. Lloyd was seated in his lounge chair, only he wasn't reclining in it the way he normally did. In fact, the way he sat on the edge of the seat reminded Abbie of the way he'd shift to sit during an intense moment in a ball game. Jacki held a similar position on the edge of the loveseat nearby, wringing a dish towel in her hands while staring intently at the screen.

Thatcher shifted on the sofa beside her. She sensed he wanted to acknowledge Grandma C's comment, the way she hoped to, but he must be as distraught inside as she was. Three days ago, as January came to an end, the divorce was made final. Thank heavens New Hampshire didn't have a waiting period. But on that same day they got word from Leona, the Copelands caught wind of an upcoming interview with none other than America's beloved, award-winning composer, Quinten Bromley.

Trailers for the interview showed spoilers that made Abbie's stomach churn. They'd edited the footage for the most dramatic effect, no doubt, but tonight, those glimpses would give way to Quinten's full and elaborate tale.

Rem sauntered into the room with a bottle of beer in one hand, a toothpick playing at his lips. Thatcher's oldest brother hadn't been around a whole lot recently, having taken on extra shifts at the station, but Abbie was glad he was there tonight, showing his support.

Rem patted Thatcher's shoulder, then Abbie's as he

walked by. "It's going to be all right," he assured them before sinking into the couch beside Grandma C.

"Thanks," Thatcher and Abbie said in unison.

"I'll say it is," Grandma snapped, her eyes sharpening on the screen.

Abbie leaned her head onto Thatcher's shoulder and let out a deep sigh. "You know what I wish we were doing right now?"

Thatcher glanced over. "I know what *I* wish we were doing right now," he answered playfully.

She gave him a nudge. "I wish we were lying on a blanket under a blue sky, watching the clouds and playing our radio show game."

Thatcher wrapped an arm around her back and pressed a kiss to her head. "That's what I was going to say." He continued to rub her back as the familiar theme song for the weekly show started to play.

"It's on!" Grandma C shouted.

Lloyd's shoulders stiffened. Jacki wrung the towel so hard her hands went red. Rem reached up and twisted the toothpick between his lips.

"It's going to be okay. Whatever it is, whatever he says, it can't tear us apart. What else matters?"

It might have been a simple thing to say, but it struck Abbie as profound in that moment. He was right. What mattered to her most was Thatcher and the family she hoped to spend her future with. So what if her now-legally ex-husband smeared her name on public television? Her parents would be stuck picking up the pieces of a mess they helped make. Abbie, on the other hand, could live her life far, far away from them.

Mental illness? *That* was this guy's angle?

Fury forced its way through Thatcher's blood like liquid fire. It had taken everything in him not to shoot to his feet and pace the floor like a madman. At one point, he'd bit into his knuckle so hard the teeth marks still hadn't faded.

Of course, he'd kept his cool more than *someone* else had.

After multiple outbursts by none other than Grandma C, Ma had suggested she go upstairs and finish watching it in the den so the others could hear past her heckling. She had, but she'd taken her popcorn with her.

Now that the show was through, the remainder of Thatcher's family having kept their peace until the show was done, Grandma was making her way down the stairs to join them. "If there's anyone I can't stand on God's green earth…" she was mumbling.

"Well," Jacki said, "I think we should start by getting Abbie's response to the interview before the rest of us speak up. Is that okay with you?"

Abbie scooted to the front edge of the couch and nodded.

The phone beside Pops' chair rang. "This must be Wes and the gang," he said, pressing the button to put it on speaker. "How are the sick-Os doing over there?" he boomed. If there was anything that could lighten Pops' mood, it was a call from the lake house, where his only grandchild was staying until Wes and Taja's house was built.

"I heard that, Grampa Lloyd," little Rosie hollered through the line.

Pops let out a hearty chuckle. "Are you feeling any better today, Rosie?"

"A little," she rasped.

Wes cleared his throat and sniffed through obvious congestion. "She and Taja are feeling a little better," he said. "I feel worse."

"Join the club," Grandma C blurted.

All eyes turned on Grandma.

"You're not getting sick, are you, Mama?" Pops asked her.

"No, but I almost threw up listening to that jerk's grandiose speech about the years he faithfully attended to his wife."

"Me too," Taja agreed, voice distant on the line.

"We know we missed out on being there," Wes continued, "but we wanted to join in on the discussion if it's not too late."

"Nope. We're just about to give Abbie the floor so she can give her two cents first."

"Perfect," Wes said.

"We're here for you, Abbie," Taja added.

Rosie piped up next. "I'm here too! But now I'm going to go take a bubble bath, so see you later."

Ma beamed with an affectionate grin. "Don't forget to wash behind your ears."

Thatcher resisted the urge to apologize for the goo-goo eyed grandparents in the room and rubbed a comforting hand over Abbie's back.

The rest of the group said goodbye to Rosie before Ma cleared her throat and turned back to Abbie. "I think we're all ready to hear your thoughts, dear."

"Thanks," Abbie said. "I'm still processing it all, to be honest. But so far, I mainly have this…overwhelming sense of relief."

"Relief?" Grandma C screeched. "That pompous pig face didn't take a scrap of responsibility for—"

"Grandma," Jacki warned, silencing the irate woman in a blink.

Grandma C curled her lips over her teeth and folded her thin arms over her chest with a *humph*.

Abbie grinned at Thatcher before turning that smile on his grandma. "I love your passion," she said. "And I appreciate all you guys' support in this. I can't tell you how much it means. And you're right," she said with a wave in Grandma C's direction, "Quinten didn't take any responsibility in the interview, but I never thought he would. I firmly believe that the only reason he signed the papers was because I agreed, in writing, that I wouldn't disclose the nature of his violence and abuse. But for him to tell the world that I'm mentally ill and spending time in a facility to get better…I don't mind that at all."

Thatcher shifted to better see her face as she continued. "Who in this world is mentally well *all* the time? No one. All of us need to give time, attention, medical care, even, to our mental wellness. There's no shame in it. In fact, I hope it encourages people to seek help if they need it. Especially those trapped in the society I grew up in, where discussing mental issues is taboo."

Thatcher had tried pinning up his anger—like hot air in a balloon as he sat beside Abbie, waiting to hear her speak. Yet as her words infiltrated the space, offering a new perspective, the heat seemed to seep right out of him. She had a point. Sure, Quinten got off scot free, but so long as Abbie could move on with her life, they could live with it.

"That's a gracious approach, Abbie," Ma said.

Pops nodded. "I suppose that if a man's going to be spreading lies about you, at least it's no skin off your back."

"You're a better person than me," Rem said while shaking his head. "But I still think he'll get his before this lifetime is through."

"I hope so," Grandma C said with a sneer. "If I ever had the chance, I'd knock his noggin like the Whack-a-Mole champion I am!" She bopped her fists down on her knees to prove it.

"I guess it explains your absence too," Thatcher pointed out.

"That's true," Taja said from the speaker of Pops' phone.

"If that interview is the only way he plans to lash out," Abbie said, "I consider it a win."

"Hear, hear," Pops thundered.

"Well said," Ma agreed. Other forms of approval filtered in, and though Thatcher nodded along, he couldn't peel his eyes off the fresh, pink splotches blooming up Abbie's neck. Or the sudden shift in her demeanor. What was it, he wondered, that had her feeling so unsettled suddenly? She'd seemed calm enough as she shared her opinion and others shared theirs.

Whatever it was, Thatcher felt it was best to get Abbie alone so she wouldn't have to hold back in front of the group. So she could open up to him, perhaps, though he wasn't so sure she would.

"Well," he said, coming to his feet and stretching his arms over his head. "Abbie and I are going to head back now."

"Aren't you going to stay for dessert?" Ma asked, hurrying to her feet as well. Already she was racing toward the kitchen. "Let me get you some to go. Rem? Grab me one of those tin containers with a lid, will you?"

Rem shot a questioning look at Thatcher. It was easy enough to interpret. *Why doesn't she have you do it?* Rem wanted to ask, but the look on Thatcher's face must have stopped him. Or perhaps he'd caught onto the shift in Abbie's demeanor, because he simply grunted to a stand and headed toward the kitchen. "Sure."

Abbie hurried to her feet and began hugging everyone goodbye.

"Hey, Ma!" Wes shouted through the line. "Tell Rem to bring some dessert out to us at the lake house, will you?"

"Come get it yourself," mumbled Rem.

"Oh, hush," Ma scolded. "Rem would be happy to bring you guys some dessert since you're sick and all."

Rem shook his head, rolling his eyes in surrender. "Umm hmm."

Thatcher couldn't get Abbie to himself soon enough. He figured that once they got into the truck, he'd feel safe to ask about the thoughts in her head.

Sadly, he found himself tongue-tied instead. He flipped on the music, turned up the heat, and snuck glimpses of a deep-in-thought Abbie on the passenger seat. Not the middle seat next to him. Perhaps that's what had him afraid to ask. Something had come to her mind tonight, between the time that she'd spoken to the group about her take on the interview, and the moment she'd tensed up before they left.

He hoped she'd speak up about it on her own, but if she didn't, Thatcher could come out and ask her himself. Whether he wanted to hear it or not. Something told him he wasn't going to like it.

CHAPTER 19

Abbie scrubbed her face in the too-bright glow of the bathroom. She avoided meeting eyes with the face in the mirror as she splashed cleanser off her cheeks, reached blindly for a hand towel, and dabbed her skin dry.

If watching that interview had lifted a great weight off Abbie's shoulders, coming back to reality had crushed her like a ten-ton train. *Relief,* she'd said, so foolishly, so naïvely. As if she hadn't spent the first five years of her young adult life learning Quinten's cunning ways.

It seemed some days, he'd wait for Abbie to peak. He'd alter the atmosphere so she'd start to feel comfortable, almost safe, hopeful that he'd changed his ways. Then, he'd deliver a shocking blow that would knock those notions soundly out of her head. That would incinerate any sprout of hope in her heart.

Quinten's interview, that entire display, was the man's

attempt to alter the atmosphere, put Abbie's mind at ease. To make her believe she could come out of hiding, be seen in public places like grocery stores, libraries, or on small town streets. Hadn't she known all along that it was only a matter of time before Quinten ruled out the properties she and her family owned? Any day now, her mother would recall the torment in Abbie's pained plea to let her go live with Grandma Dottie and raise the unborn child there.

Who would come to Montana first? Her mother or Quinten? Or would they send a private investigator to feel out the situation? Perhaps they'd already done that. If so, Abbie might have been spotted on the back patio on one of the properties. Or in the cozy dining nook overlooking the lake.

A shiver rocked through her. If somebody spotted her there, it could put little Rosie and their small family at risk.

Of course, Abbie didn't think her mother knew the Copelands by name. In fact, she was certain she didn't. And since Mom had never taken an interest in Buck and Dottie's life on the ranch, she wouldn't know any of the neighbors either. She'd have no one to ask or inquire. Heavens knew her father didn't have much to do with them either.

That settled her heart the slightest bit. Gave her a degree of peace as she planned out her exit.

Abbie scrubbed her teeth vigorously, not even recalling the moment she'd grabbed the brush and smeared toothpaste over it. She continued to brush all the same, gearing her thoughts toward her initial escape plan—a one-way flight to Australia, a place no one would suspect her to be. She'd buy a plot of land for homesteading, hire some local help to get the job done, and live a life of solitude. She'd be safe, the Copelands would be safe, and that was all that mattered.

A series of taps came to the bathroom door from Thatcher's side. "You did it!" he said with fake cheer.

Abbie glared toward the door.

"You broke the record for brushing your teeth longer than any other human in history."

Abbie spit into the sink and ran the water. Thatcher and all his joking around. She ignored him, tapping off her toothbrush and slipping it back into the slot.

"Mind if we talk?" he asked next.

Yes, she minded. Because if they talked, she'd have to tell him she was leaving, and if she did that… A flood of emotion rushed in, and Abbie did her best to suppress it. Chin quivering, eyes welling, throat tightening. She flipped off the faucet, ripped the hand towel off the rack, and shoved her face into it. A deep sob rocked through her, making her entire body tremble.

"Please, Abbie," Thatcher came again. "There's no need for you to go through this alone."

Abbie lowered the towel and glared at the reflection she'd been avoiding. She was putting him at risk. She was putting his whole family at risk. He didn't get it, did he? She *could* do something about that.

At once, she unlocked the door and flung it open.

"*Alone* is *exactly* how I need to go through this, Thatcher. Okay?"

"You're wrong," Thatcher said as he barged into the bathroom. He reached for her, securing firm hands on both of her forearms and fixing his eyes on hers.

Abbie looked down at each hand in turn, pointedly, before lifting an accusatory glare back on him.

Thatcher's hazel eyes went wide—awareness mingled with shock. He released her arms like they were hot coals in his hands. She watched as hurt and shame warred behind his gaze as he took in her face.

"I'm not going to hurt you, Abbie," he assured, tone gentle, but defensive too.

Abbie knew it was wrong of her to make him feel this way, but for some reason, she allowed him to think he'd frightened her. She folded her arms, took a step back, and then another until her heels met with the tub. She reached her arms down, bending at the knees, until she was sitting on the edge.

Thatcher went to sit down beside her, but she lifted a hand to stay him. "Just..." She sighed. "I need some space."

Thatcher groaned and dropped his head back. Even with her gaze set on the hand towel she'd tossed on the counter, she could make out his posture with ease. Shoulders rigid, chest puffed, jaw clenched tight. She felt bad for doing this to him, but it was inevitable, and the sooner they both accepted that, the better.

The devastating truth of it crashed over her so hard that the sobs came back with a vengeance. She dropped her face in her hands and gave in to the emotion that ripped through her like a jagged-edged sword. Tears gushing, chest convulsing, temples throbbing with pent-up sorrow and rage. She resented Quinten for taking this from her too. Her chance at true love with a man *worth* giving her heart to. Her shot at a future with a family that would give her all the love she'd longed for over the years. Love that didn't hinge on a list of dos and don'ts.

Thatcher had joined her on the side of the bathtub after all and was smoothing a hand over her back as he so often did. A silent gesture to show his support. So constant. Unwavering. Undeserved. This honest cowboy cared about her the way her stiff parents and abusive husband never had. To have someone care for her in such a way…it was a gift so rare and beautiful, she could hardly complain if she lost it altogether. Perhaps she was fortunate to get even a taste.

Especially if it meant keeping the man she loved and cared for in return safe.

"He's not going to stop, Thatcher," she managed through sniffs.

Thatcher didn't argue, just continued to gently rub her back. She'd miss this. Miss him. Miss the home and the family and old familiar smells. She'd miss the comfort and the unique feeling of belonging; it was more than she ever had in the uptight society she'd been born into.

"I can't keep putting you and your family at risk. One day they'll find me. My parents will assume I was being dramatic about him wanting me dead. Quinten will convince them that he's wracked with worry and grief.

They'll come looking for me. And when you have pockets as deep as theirs, you find what you're looking for."

It was the most honest she'd been with herself in weeks. And somehow, that helped steel her resolve. "I know where I'm going. I believe I'll be safe. And so long as I get far, far away from here, you guys will be safe too."

"I'll come with you," Thatcher blurted, his tone rich with enthusiasm. "That's it! If I come with you, my family will be safe, and you won't be alone."

"You can't live away from your family, Thatcher."

"I can't live away from *you*," he argued.

Her shoulders drooped, and Thatcher bent at the knees to squat low before her. Balancing on the balls of his feet, prodding at her with the heat of his gaze, he waited for her chin to lift, and her eyes to meet his.

If a person could ooze passion with their expression alone, Thatcher could. It was that youthful quality of his that allowed for such transparency. In that moment, Thatcher's expression, the light tremor rocking his limbs, nearly bled his vulnerability. His desperation to be heard.

He gulped, lowered his chin, and locked his eyes on hers. "I love my family, Abbie. But I'm *in love* with you. And if you plan to pack up your bags and take a one-way trip to Timbuktu, I'm begging you…"

Abbie shook her head as tears pooled down her cheeks. "I'm in love with you too," she admitted, knowing how deeply true that was. "Which is why—"

"Please," he rasped, "please let me come with you." He threw his arms around her then, squeezing as if he could never let her go. And the fact was, Abbie wasn't sure she could let him go either. Not after his declaration of love for her.

As if her mind had been working double time, a wayward thought popped into her brain. There was still one thing he didn't know. Taja had said she'd know when the timing was right. Perhaps this would test Thatcher's devotion to her. It was only fair that he knew just what she'd done, what she'd been keeping from him all these years.

"Thatcher," she breathed, pulling back enough to look at his face once more. "There's something I need to tell you."

CHAPTER 20

Abbie had been pregnant with his baby. Thatcher didn't know how to process that. He hadn't hidden his shock, though he wasn't sure how Abbie would interpret it. All he could think was that eighteen-year-old him and eighteen-year-old her had nearly become parents.

Pregnancy in and of itself was a gain, adding another person into a couple's world. And though Thatcher had a taste of that initial excitement from the news, the emotion quickly gave way to sorrow. Because she'd never given birth to that child. She'd lost it before it was ever born.

To complicate matters, Abbie revealed that she'd married Quinten before she miscarried, meaning, had the child survived, he or she would have been raised in that abusive environment. Heck, they might have become the brunt of physical violence as well.

It was too much to take in all at once. If Abbie had been trying to push him away by sharing that part of her past, it had come close to working. He went from not believing it, to being furious about it, and then becoming terribly sad, all in a matter of minutes. Even now, hours later, the cycle continued. Doubt, fury, misery, hope.

Yes, somehow, hope was in there too. She loved him, and he loved her. They may not be able to spend the life together that he'd imagined, but they *could* spend their lives together. And perhaps in time, they'd feel safe to move back to the good state of Montana where they could build a home on Thatcher's inherited land and be close to his family once again.

Thatcher let that idea offer a new round of comfort as he pulled the sheet up and over his head. He hadn't climbed into his bed after wrapping things up with Abbie last night. He hadn't dared. To keep the sneaky woman from trying to do something rash without his knowledge, Thatcher had set up camp right there in the hallway. If she wanted to come out of her room, Abbie would have to step over him to do it.

With that tidbit offering a layer of comfort, Thatcher closed his eyes and gave into the great pull of sleep at last. He wasn't exactly sure what the days ahead would hold, but one thing was certain, it was bound to be one heck of a ride.

"Thatcher, wake up!"

The sound of Rem's voice put Thatcher on high alert. He went from horizontal to vertical and forced his eyes open. "Huh?"

"Why are you sleeping in the hall?"

Thatcher only glared at him. "What do you want?"

"Ma and Pops just called. They tried to reach you first and failed. Abbie's folks were in a bad car accident last night. Nearly killed them. It's all over the news."

Thatcher shot a look at Abbie's closed door, squinting to see in the low, pale light. "They're alive though?"

"Yeah."

A wave of relief rushed in. "What time is it?"

"Seven. You slept in."

Thatcher nodded, not sure what to make of the accident. Would Abbie want to go back home now to see them? That wouldn't be safe. For a moment he was tempted to keep it from her, but he couldn't do that. At the very least she'd want to call the hospital, get an update on her parents' conditions.

He groaned and pushed the single sheet off his legs. As he came to a stand on the creaky floor, a memory flashed to his mind. *I was almost a dad.*

That detail hit him like it was new all over again, stirring up the round of reactions he'd been through before falling to sleep. Thatcher tried to imagine a petrified Abbie, hovered over the pregnancy test. The fear, the uncertainty, the slight thrill, perhaps. It gave him a thrill just thinking about it, Abbie pregnant with his baby.

With so many hazardous roadblocks ahead of them, the country house with the picket fence, barking dogs and playful kids, seemed like no more than a pipedream. Still, he prayed to the heavens for a chance to make it so. Then, with a heavy heart, he knocked on Abbie's door.

CHAPTER 21

Through a social media website, Abbie messaged her aunt for details on the condition of her parents. Critical, yet stable. Only then did she get word of what Mr. and Mrs. Carrington had told family and friends about their only daughter. Sure enough, it was the same story Quinten shared during his interview. Abbie went along with it, grateful that her aunt hadn't pressed for any specifics.

As for the accident, a mysterious diesel had rammed into the rear corner of their Bentley and sent them careening into an off-road tree. The driver had not been located.

Though her parents would never suspect it, Abbie had the distinct impression that the hit-and-run hadn't been an accident at all. What if that driver had been hired by Quinten?

If one or both of her parents had died, Abbie would surely go home for the funeral, which was right where Quinten wanted her to be—within arm's reach. She could just picture standing over an ornate casket propped over a freshly dug grave. Quinten sneaking quietly behind her as the crowd stood nearby. He'd slither a snake-like arm along her shoulders, coil his too-strong fingers around her arm, and hiss into her ear, *"You should never have left me. You're the one who caused this. I hope you're happy."*

A shiver rocked through her. Some might call it a hunch or suspicion, but it was more than that. Abbie had been Quinten's captive for years. Years that boiled down to minutes, hours, and endless days, witnessing his manipulative tactics and twisted ways. If her parents had missorted priorities, Quinten outdid them by having only one priority—himself.

He justified his selfish tendencies by saying *he'd* never been the priority in his own home. No one looked out for him. With an abusive father and what he described as a weak mother, Quinten was forced to sink into a world of his own creation. Mind spinning, weaving, crafting music to suit the madness.

He'd form images too: cinematic scenes to better suit the dramatic inclines and sudden drops—a world far, far away. It was a sad tale, she'd give him that, but he didn't rise above it as the hero everyone saw when he took a bow on stage. For a reason she'd never understand, Quinten Bromley became the villain instead.

When Abbie told Thatcher she thought Quinten had arranged the accident, he'd contacted Lloyd and arranged for a meeting of sorts to discuss their best move. And though Abbie would have rather disappeared than stick around for even one more day, she knew two heads were better than one. Besides, she wasn't thinking clearly anymore. How could she, with so much running through her mind? A combination of guilt for her parents' accident and rage toward the man she almost knew had caused it.

"I hope you don't mind," Lloyd said as he motioned toward a gray-haired man likely older than Grandma C. "I asked Earl Emerson, a fellow retired marshal, to join us for this. He and his family have taken on several witnesses over the years. They've dealt with many dangerous people hellbent on hurting the persons in their care."

The man extended a hand to her. "Sorry about all your troubles, hon," he said, his kind, gray eyes creased with age. "I'm here to help in any way I can."

"Thanks," Abbie said.

Also seated at the table were Wes, Taja, Nash, Rem, and Thatcher. Grandma C and Jacki had taken Rosie to the store to get supplies for the Valentine's craft they intended to make.

Abbie felt a nudge along the side of her foot. She peeked down to see Bonnie beneath the table, guarding a stuffed toy under her knotted paws and lowered chin, daring a sleepy, tail-wagging Clyde to make a move for it.

"Why don't you start by telling us all why you think Quinten is responsible for this so-called accident involving your folks," Lloyd said. "Then we can all brainstorm and figure out the best move to make from here."

Abbie nodded. "Okay, but I want you guys to be open

to ideas that…" She glanced at everyone except for Thatcher. "That allow me to set him up. Even if it's dangerous." The fact was, Abbie already had a few ideas of her own.

"During the interview," Abbie reminded, "Quinten mentioned a charity banquet he was sponsoring to raise funds for mental illness awareness."

Heads nodded.

"If Quinten's so worried about awareness, why doesn't he seek help for himself?" Nash grumbled.

"He's too busy claiming his *ex-wife* is the sick one," Thatcher added.

"I probably *do* need mental help after all I've been through," Abbie said. "I'm not ashamed of that."

Thatcher and Nash pinned their lips closed.

"Anyway," Abbie said, "my parents were on the way home from that event when a diesel smacked the driver's side bumper, which forced them off the road and headfirst into a nearby tree. The driver took off and the cops don't have any real leads yet."

"That *is* pretty fishy," Lloyd's buddy, Earl, allowed.

Abbie lifted a finger to count out the ways. "Quinten knew exactly where they were, when they left, and where they were headed. Plus, the accident happened to be in a spot where there's a massive off-road tree and *no* yard or house cameras within miles. He could have had someone stake out the whole thing."

"Everyone has yard cameras these days," Nash said. "Except us."

Rem lifted a finger. "I installed one at the front door of the bunk house."

"And I put one at the lake house," Wes added.

"My son-in-law put one in for us," Earl said.

"Sheesh." Lloyd looked around the table. "No one tells me these things."

"I'll install one here," Nash volunteered.

Lloyd only waved him off. "So, let's say it *was* Quinten who did that. How would you go about proving it? And is *that* what you hope to do?"

"Mostly she doesn't want him to try again," Thatcher said for her.

Abbie nodded as the truth of his words scraped over her skin. "Exactly. If this is his way of trying to lure me out of hiding, who says he'll stop there? That could have killed both of my parents, which is probably what he was hoping for. I don't think he'll stop.

"Even if it *had* killed them both," she added with a shiver, "who's to say he wouldn't have gone after my cousin or my aunt?" She could just see this rash of misfortune following the Benedict family like a dark cloud. All the while, Quinten was the very evil looming behind the scenes, orchestrating the madness like he did his music.

"We need him to reveal his hand," Thatcher said.

"Let's say you went to the hospital while you were wired," Rem said. "If this is a lure as you suggest, he'll be watching the place, right?"

Abbie nodded. "A funeral would have been simpler for him since he'd know exactly when I was coming. Since that didn't happen, I assume you're right. He's probably having the hospital, more specifically their rooms, watched."

"Would he blatantly admit to arranging the accident?" Thatcher asked. "Like, in conversation?"

"If we were alone—maybe. But even if he couldn't get me alone, he'd try to take credit without coming out and saying it. He's used to being sneaky. Saying things that only I'll catch onto while others are present. Like some sick inside joke." She recalled an evening in particular when the two were on camera as they entered an award ceremony. Quinten had lashed out hours prior and severely bruised her ribs because she'd "*taken a tone*" with him.

Then, on the drive there, Abbie expressed that the seatbelt was tender against her wounded center, adding that it hurt to even breathe. "*Good,*" he'd said smugly. "*Perhaps next time you'll watch your tone.*'"

As they walked the red carpet, a live interviewer asked if he was excited for the event.

"My heart is pounding so hard my ribs are aching," he'd said while pinching the back of Abbie's arm.

The host, a well-known beauty in the industry, giggled.

"At this rate," he'd continued, encouraged, *"I'll be afraid to fasten my seatbelt on the drive home, I'll be so bruised."* He gave Abbie's arm a second squeeze.

Abbie had hated him in that moment. His smug smile, slightly red knuckles, and his Mr. Nice Guy facade.

Thatcher cleared his throat, pulling Abbie from her

musings. "Has your aunt gotten back to you with the visiting hours and room numbers?" he asked.

Abbie opened her phone and pulled up the social media messaging app. Her heart gave out a thud as she spotted a new message with Quinten's name in it. Not from him, of course, since she'd blocked his profile from all sites to keep him from reaching out to her. It was her aunt who'd mentioned him.

"She just wrote me," Abbie announced. "It says, *Quinten asked if you'd be willing to meet him for lunch when you come to visit. He says you left some things behind that he'd like you to have. He also wants to give you his condolences about your parents' injuries. He feels responsible; the charity was his idea, after all.*"

"Wow!" Thatcher's chair screeched against the floor as he pushed himself from the table and shot to a stand. "That's rich. *Feels responsible?* That's because he *is* responsible and he's practically admitting it with that cryptic message."

Thatcher was right. He wanted Abbie to get that message loud and clear so she'd accept his offer.

"Well, this is good, right?" Earl said, turning to Abbie.

She nodded, though her head was swimming.

"I agree," Rem said. "If he really did orchestrate the accident with your folks, and you can get him to admit it, he'll go away for a long time."

"Two counts of attempted murder," Lloyd added.

"She's *not* going to meet up with that psycho!" Thatcher growled. "*I* am. And I'm going to pound his freaking face in the dirt."

Earl lifted a hand. "We'd make sure she was safe, Thatcher."

"You're darn right," Lloyd agreed.

Abbie was testing the idea for herself, flares of anticipation like hot pokers in her gut. This was similar to the plan she'd been plotting all morning; it might be easier to make it happen than she imagined.

"We'll make it a public setting," she said. "But I'll need enough privacy that we can talk without others hearing."

"And we'll have you bugged," Rem added. "I can arrange for that."

Thatcher groaned as he paced. It reminded Abbie of their first night in the cheap motel when he'd paced back and forth in the small room with the blizzard raging outside.

"I can't believe you guys are actually entertaining this," Thatcher said. "Even if she gets away with some scrap of evidence, who's to say that scumbag won't get his hands on her before she leaves town? Look what he did to her parents!"

That final comment quieted whatever objection Nash had on his lips.

Earl dropped his hand and began to nod.

"What's his weakness?" Lloyd asked. "He knows yours is your family, even if you *are* estranged. What's *his*?"

Abbie didn't hesitate. "Ego. How the public perceives him."

It went quiet.

The sound of the clock ticking picked up volume in the extended pause.

But then Nash sucked in a breath. "I know what might work. Let's not record things to show authorities *later.* Let's make sure the public sees what's happening…*while* it's happening," Nash gave Thatcher a knowing look.

"Oh," Thatcher said. "That's not a bad idea."

Rem sighed loudly. "Would you two stop speaking code and spit it out?"

"Remember when Nash and I did those live videos to raise funds at the auction?"

A light sparked bright in Abbie's mind. "That's a good idea. It's one thing to have documented evidence that may or may not see the light of day. That route takes things like hearings, trials, and a whole lot of time to pursue. Quinten could do a lot of damage in that time. But if I had our interaction secretly broadcasting—worldwide, even—he wouldn't be able to hide the evidence or distort the narrative. He'd be caught."

Rem pulled the toothpick from his lips. "So, you agree to meet him for lunch and start up one of those live videos from your phone?" Rem asked.

Clyde yawned loudly beneath the table, gaining Abbie's attention once more. She glanced down to see the daring dog inch closer to Bonnie and the toy she was guarding. Bonnie responded by giving Clyde's nose two solid licks before chewing into the toy with a relish.

"You think you can get him to admit anything?" Thatcher asked.

"Possibly," Abbie said, tearing her gaze off the dogs. "One time during a live interview, Quinten purposely made a comment about bruised ribs, having just bruised mine so bad it hurt to buckle up."

Thatcher groaned as if someone had crushed his own ribs. He was biting his knuckle, she noticed before continuing.

"It was almost as if Quinten was *daring* me to speak up, yet he *knew* that I wouldn't. It was the perfect place for me to say, *'Like the way you bruised mine with your fists?'* I totally could have said that. I even considered it then. It was live, you know?

"I can't tell you how many times I wished I had. What would he have done besides deny it? Even still, the seed would have been planted in his fans' minds…he would have freaked. And," she realized with a nod, "I would have paid for it later."

Thatcher stopped pacing. "He's the one who's going to pay now."

"Let's say we do this," Nash said. "Your goal is to get him to fess up to whatever you can get out of him. The thing with your parents, his violence throughout your marriage…"

Abbie nodded, confident he'd reveal enough to expose the side of him he'd managed to bury beneath his perfectly-polished façade.

The plan settled over the room like a tarp covering a puddle of mud—the mess wasn't gone, but at least it was covered up for now.

Abbie glanced over her shoulder to lock eyes with Thatcher. "What do you say? You on board?"

"We'll go with her, of course," Rem said. "She won't be alone."

Thatcher's jaw clenched as he eyed those seated at the table, his gaze ping-ponging between Rem, Nash, Lloyd, and his Uncle Earl. "You guys are sure we can keep her safe?"

"If we go about it the right way," Lloyd said. "I don't see how we could go wrong."

CHAPTER 22

Thatcher's chest was tight, his throat hot, and his skin agitated to the point his running shorts felt like sandpaper against his upper legs as he paced. Nash and Rem occupied the motel room two doors down while Abbie lay asleep on the hotel bed at his side; heaven only knew how she'd managed. Thatcher's brain was much too busy for shuteye. Busy creating one scenario after the next—possible encounters during Abbie's visit with her ex.

With Abbie's aunt as the go-between, Quinten had set the time and place which, in typical Quintin fashion, revolved around a special appearance. He'd been invited to participate in a celebrity ice sawing challenge at a winter festival near Alton. Prior to the contest, the two would have lunch at the festival in a dining globe he'd reserved for them. They'd seen the setup online—some octagonal structure made of glass and brass.

According to Abbie, Quinten would have plenty of fans present; many locals made a point of being at his public events. Some of his diehards would even travel for it with hopes to get a signature or a photo. All things that would keep him on his best behavior.

"Are you going to pace all night?"

The sound of Abbie's voice made him jump.

"I'm not going to *try anything* if you cuddle me," she added.

He shook his head. "You still manage to make jokes, half asleep with a dangerous mission ahead of you?"

"I'm not half asleep. I'm fully asleep. Dreaming."

He sighed, dragged himself to the edge of the bed, and plunked onto a corner at the foot. "What are you dreaming about?"

"You. Me. Our future."

Her words were a blanket—warmth, softness, comfort. Thatcher climbed further onto the mattress, made his way over to where she lay, and curled himself around her from behind. Thighs lining the backs of hers, knees tucked into the nook hers made, chest flush against her back. He wrapped an arm around her waist and buried his face into the feathery strands of her fragrant hair. "Help me dream about our future too."

Abbie smoothed a hand over the arm he'd wrapped around her, dragging the tips of her fingers up and down the length. Thatcher sensed some of the tightness drain from his body.

"We're free," she started. "All of this is behind us, so we get married and build a house on your land. It has sanitizer mounted at the front door with a sign that says, '*A germaphobe lives here. Kindly wash the nastiness off your hands before entering.*'"

"Man, I really *am* dreaming."

"It also has a dark room, of course, and a place for your workout equipment so you don't have to punch that bag in the garage."

He yawned. "Nice. What about Crew?"

"We have an awesome stable for Crew and Drew."

"Who's Drew?"

"The horse you bought me as a wedding gift. She's bold, blonde, and beautiful."

"Like you," he crooned.

"Naturally."

"Wait," he said, drifting back over her words. "Did you just propose to me?"

She laughed, then swatted his hand. "Shh, I was getting there. Each night when we fall asleep, we relive the wild way you proposed to me."

"How's that?" he asked, a grin already forming at his lips.

"Your motorcycle, of course. You carved each letter into the snow with the skillful navigation of your Harley. When I arrived, you dropped dramatically to one knee, hurting yourself in the process on a piece of ice, so we had to go to the emergency room."

"Wait, but I proposed to you first, right?"

She shushed him again. "I had no choice but to drive you to the ER while you clung onto me with one hand and pressed at your bleeding knee with the other."

"Did you rip your shirt and make a tourniquet to slow the bleeding first?" he asked.

"Of course. And you could hardly wait. As the female doctor stitched you up, calling you a stud for refusing anesthetic, you held onto my hand, gazed into my eyes, and asked me to marry you."

"And you said yes," Thatcher said.

"I said no because you weren't on one knee."

"My knee was bleeding."

"Yes, but I'm still a lady and I deserve a proper proposal."

He kissed the back of her head and grinned. "Noted."

"Good."

"You didn't get to the part where we honeymooned in Ireland."

"Oh, we did. Marrying me has its perks, you know. You were the king of the castle. It was hot."

He laughed. "If you were my queen, it was."

"Exactly." She breathed deeply, slowly, and he sensed that she was done telling her tale.

"Thanks, Abs," he rasped. "Goodnight."

She shifted slightly, cozying into him and sighing deeply. "Sweet dreams, Thatcher. Everything's going to be okay."

He hoped so. And as he dozed off at last, Abbie's dream painting pictures into his mind, Thatcher prayed those things might indeed come to pass.

CHAPTER 23

Abbie clicked the *Go Live* prompt on her screen—a profile she'd created specifically for this purpose—and then tucked her phone into the front pouch of the small shoulder bag they'd picked up. Similar to the size and shape of a fanny pack, the bag looped over her head to run diagonally along her chest with a clip in back.

She glanced up to see Thatcher and Nash watching from their phones.

"Yep," Nash said first, "I see us." The sound of his voice echoed from each of their phones in turn.

Thatcher scrutinized her phone where it sat tucked in the bag. "Hmm. It looks natural enough." When his statement echoed the way Nash's had, both men turned down the volume on their phones.

"We're the only followers on this profile for now," Nash said, "which is perfect. We don't want word getting to Quinten before you're through with him. But if things go awry, we can share it, blast it, and even send it directly to him, if needed."

Abbie nodded, recalling an earlier discussion they'd had on the trip there the day before. She'd given both Thatcher and Nash Quinten's phone number. If she felt she was in danger, Abbie could always warn Quinten that their interaction was being broadcast live over the internet. If he didn't believe her, they'd send him the link as proof. What could he do then? Attempt to strangle her while people were watching online?

Rem twisted the toothpick in his lips and nodded toward Thatcher and Nash. "Well, you two have a bus to catch. Arrange yourselves close to the dining domes, but make sure you look like spectators, happy to be there. You can each have in your earbuds, but if she's within eyeshot, you won't need to be staring at the screen the whole time. We won't be far behind you." With that, Rem opened the motel door and stepped aside.

Nash walked into the cold air first.

"We'll be right there," Thatcher said, stepping closer to Abbie while waving Rem off. Rem stepped out and closed the door behind him. "You can stop the video now," he said. "Can't have Nash eavesdropping as we say goodbye."

"Boo," Nash said from the other side of the door.

Abbie tugged the phone from the bag, stopped the live feed, then pushed it back into the pouch. Thatcher nudged in closer with small steps until he rested his forehead on Abbie's shoulder and groaned.

"I hate this."

"It's going to be okay," she said, feeling the truth of it in her heart. "We couldn't have arranged a better setting ourselves, and *he's* the one who set it all up. I'm sure those domes are fairly soundproof, meaning Quinten will feel free to speak candidly, and we'll be right within eyeshot of nearly everyone there. It's perfect."

He found Abbie's hands, slid his long fingers through hers, then pulled back to press a kiss to her head. "You're not scared?"

She shook her head. "No. Are you?"

"Heck no," Thatcher said. "Badgers don't get scared."

She grinned. "You better hurry. You don't want to miss the shuttle."

There was a reason they'd arranged for Nash and Thatcher to go ahead and for Rem to stay back and drop Abbie off at the event—Rem had a permit to carry a weapon. He was a police officer, after all. Besides, the coming and going would be the most dangerous part.

Thatcher leaned in, pressed a warm kiss to her lips, then pulled back to meet her gaze. Abbie looked into his hazel eyes and felt the first streak of fear for the day. Until then, she'd been calm. At peace. Confident that all would go well. Sure, she'd been nervous, but not scared. Not until she looked at the man she hoped to have a future with. The future they'd talked about just last night while he'd curled up behind her on the bed.

She didn't like that he was going to be there too, in the same place as Quinten. Thank heavens Quinten wouldn't know who he was. The two probably wouldn't so much as cross one another's paths. That was as it should be. Abbie could hardly believe she was about to come face-to-face with Quinten again. She was certain she'd done that for the last time.

"This is my chance to be free from him," Abbie said to herself as much as him. "We have to take it. Make the most of it. At least try."

Thatcher nodded and kissed her again. "I know." He squeezed her hands.

"We're going to miss the bus," Nash warned on the other side of the door.

"See you soon," Thatcher said against her lips before kissing her once more. "I love you."

"Love you too."

Abbie took one more look at the latest direct message from her aunt as they neared the Winter Festival. It was cloudy out, but bright due to the snow. Rem wore his sunglasses as he drove, a toothpick pinned between his lips.

She read over the message her aunt sent. Abbie's parents were still in stable condition and continuing to improve each day. Next came the part about today's meet up.

Quinten has a lunch reservation arranged for 3:30 sharp. He invites you to stay afterward for the celebrity ice sawing competition, which will air live on the local 5:00 news.

Her aunt went on to thank Abbie for being willing to

meet him for lunch, the poor guy. He looked wretched when she spoke with him at the hospital, and he was beside himself over losing her. She even went on to say she hoped the two could reconcile, which led Abbie to think that's what Quinten was hoping for too. Not because he loved her, of course, but because he didn't want anyone else to have what he felt was rightfully his.

"One thing that gives me comfort," Abbie said, turning to Rem, "is that he's got this live competition less than two hours after we meet. He can't be planning anything crazy, right?"

Rem shot her a look. "You tell me."

She shrugged. "He *is* nuts," she allowed, "but…" She considered her aunt's words once more. "What I really think, and I didn't want to say this to Thatcher and upset him even more, but Quinten actually might think he can get me back. I only say that because it's all he's known of me. I cower. Stay. Put up with whatever he dishes out."

"True," Rem said, his voice somehow even deeper than Thatcher's. "But you left. He's got to know it won't be so easy this time around."

She nodded. "Right. If I'm not around to terrorize, he'll terrorize my family until I agree to be his eternal captive."

Rem cursed under his breath. "He won't get away with that. We'll make sure of it." After a bout of silence, Rem spoke up again. "Thatcher seems to be at his best lately." He shook his head and chuckled low in his throat. "I wasn't sure when he'd grow up and stop breaking hearts. Leading women on only to kiss them goodbye. I sometimes wonder if he didn't know you'd come back to him.

Like...you two were just written in the stars or something."

Abbie liked hearing that.

"I'll tell you one thing. You're the only woman who could ever match his energy. That one's always been a wild child, and so were you." He glanced over and tipped his head. "In a good way."

She grinned. "Thanks. I have the feeling you secretly like that about him."

Rem scowled, then lifted a hand off the wheel. "Guilty as charged. Just don't tell *him* that. I'm kinda glad he found a woman who lets him be himself. As obnoxious as he can be at times, we'd miss Thatcher if he wasn't *him* anymore. We have enough grouchy men in the family, myself included."

That made her recall the blowup Thatcher had with Wyatt. "Do you think he and Wyatt will patch things up?" she asked.

Rem pursed his lips as he considered that. "I don't think they'll ever be best pals or anything, but yeah. Eventually, I think they'll at least learn how to see eye-to-eye. Even if they never *do* have the exact same perspective."

Abbie nodded. "I hope so."

Rem chuckled again and shook his head. "Man, you really *are* in love, aren't you? Thinking about Thatcher's family affairs at a time like this."

A grin spread warmly across her lips. A spot of joy that slipped its way deep into her heart. She mimicked the way Rem had lifted his hand. "Guilty as charged."

She set her mind back on the mission ahead of her.

There was a lot at stake. Her entire future—the life she and Thatcher hoped to have. If she succeeded, Quinten would spend most of his life in prison while Abbie finally lived free.

But if she failed, Quinten would be the free one. Free to haunt Abbie like a living ghost for the rest of her days.

CHAPTER 24

Talk about torture. Normally, this was a place he and Nash could seriously get into. The winter festival was packed with people young and old while music blasted over the speakers. Scents of fresh barbecue, funnel cakes, and burgers on the grill wafted from the food trucks while a team of ice boats raced around the track at impressive speeds.

And though Thatcher knew it was something he'd normally enjoy, he was fiercely agitated by the boisterous crowds, blasting announcements, and the fact that Quinten *freaking* Bromley was anxiously awaiting his date with Abbie. He glared at the dumb dining domes just off from the entrance. The glass cases looked even fancier than they had online. Fabrics and feathers, plush red roses accented by candles, candles, and more candles.

He checked the time. Abbie wouldn't get there for fifteen more minutes. Rem, who was acting as her Uber driver, would drive out of the lot, take a long circle to come back around, and park nearby where he could watch live from the rental car and call any authorities necessary. Pops and Earl were okay with the plan, Rem was good with it, and Abbie too. Things should be fine. Things should be just fine.

"Hey," Nash said, gaining his attention. "Is it just me, or are the Pigtail Twins coming our way."

Thatcher glanced up. "They *are* coming this way. And they're filming live." He hurried to spin around, but Nash stopped him.

"Of *course* they're filming live. That's what they're famous for."

"And right here we have two handsome cowboys who've braved the cold to join the fabulous winter fun," one said. "Aren't you ladies at home sad that you're missing out?"

"Hey, wait a minute," one said. "You cowboys are familiar. Didn't we repost one of your videos once?"

"Sure did," Nash said proudly while tipping his hat. "Was our Boot-Scootin' Fundraiser at the county fair."

"I remember," the other twin said. They were identical, but one accented her mole darker than the other to help set them apart.

"Who could forget faces like these?" crooned the one with the beauty mark. "Tell us what got you out here today," the other said. "The races? The food? The *women?*"

"Definitely," Nash said. "I wanted to see you lovely ladies take a crack at the ice today."

They squealed in unison. "How cute," one said, pinching his cheek.

"And you?" they said, turning their sights on Thatcher.

"I'd love to see one of you gals take the win as well." Boy, did he mean that.

"Especially over that wussy composer," Nash added.

The twins laughed. "He's not so bad," one said.

But the other gal leaned in. "I heard he made someone make a special trip to the nearest supermarket to get the mints he likes because they had a different brand in his trailer."

"Hey," chimed the other. "Do you already follow us? If so, shoot us anything you want us to post while we're here."

Thatcher's ears perked up.

"Will do," Nash said, tipping his hat. "Catch a drink later?" he added as they walked away.

The one with the beauty mark glanced over her shoulder as they headed off. "Definitely."

Thatcher checked the time again. "Seven more minutes." He looked toward the entrance. Rem planned to time it close to the minute so Thatcher and Nash wouldn't be caught off guard or have an untimely distraction like the Pigtail Twins. At least that was out of the way. Now it was time to watch the woman he loved have a romantic lunch with her violent ex-husband who either wanted her back or wanted her dead—he wasn't sure which. Heaven help them.

CHAPTER 25

"Thanks," Abbie hollered as she climbed out of the back seat and pulled out her phone. She feigned hitting pay for the Uber and pulled up the *Go live* screen instead. She gave the prompt a tap, recognized the circle that appeared in the center, and felt her heart leap when it showed the words *You're live* along the top.

"Paid," Abbie said cheerfully.

Rem gave her a nod from the front seat. "Have a nice day," he mumbled around the toothpick.

"You too." She closed the back door, tucked the phone into the pouch with shaky hands, and shivered from the chill that ran through her. She could practically feel Quinten's presence in the air. His menacing gaze and ill intent. She made her way to the back of the line, tugged the bills from her back pocket, and tried seeing past the crowded entrance.

It was no use. She'd have to wait until she got closer to

the front. Still, Abbie reminded herself that Thatcher was there, mingling among the attendees, possibly within eyeshot of her dangerous ex.

A rash of panic crawled through her at the thought. Suddenly the music overhead changed. She might not have even noticed, as preoccupied as she was, but the song that started up demanded her attention. They were playing one of Quinten's pieces, warming up the fans who'd come just for him. Abbie wasn't a fan by any means, but the egotistical man *was* the reason she was there. The reason Thatcher and Nash were on the other side of the crowded entrance, vulnerable.

An eerily beautiful string quartet drifted, nearly danced and twirled in the air. A ballerina came to mind, light on her toes as she moved this way and that, exploring the world around her, unaware of the danger lurking ahead.

Chills erupted over Abbie's skin, the feel of them nervy and sharp against the sleeves of her sweater. His compositions were so erratic, it was only a matter of time before the song would dart and stray into territory that—without words—sounded nearly vulgar.

It came on cue, the frantic clamor of a clashing chord from an ill-tuned piano. Abbie hated that it made her jump even then; Quinten loved it when his music did that to her. An accompanying trumpet belched loud and low, then piped into a steady, quiet gallop. Sneaking, creeping, advancing, seeming to say, *I'm coming for you; ready or not, I'm coming.*

The heat in her chest mounded and ached. Her throat tightened.

She tried again to see Thatcher or Nash, but the jammed up entrance still wouldn't allow it. How could she let Thatcher get anywhere near Quinten?

A flood of ideas poured in, made worse by the haunting composition playing overhead. Hadn't Abbie entertained a very frightening possibility already? Had she forgotten that Quinten might have hired a private investigator, discovered her whereabouts, and secured photos of Thatcher? It was possible Quinten had staged this whole thing with hopes to spot Thatcher in the crowd.

Heat sprung like a geyser in her chest. Bubbling, bloating, forcing red splotches to climb up her neck. She wanted to tell someone to shut off the song already. It was torture listening to it.

The line inched forward. Abbie's eyes landed on a toddler gripping a plush polar bear, reminding her of sweet little Rosie and her fascination with animals. Rosie adored her Uncle Thatcher, and he adored her. Nothing could happen to him. Abbie wouldn't allow it.

She tried once more to see past the crowd, wishing she could pull out her phone and text him. Warn him. *Be alert; he could be coming for you.*

The line inched forward once more, the temporary break in the crowd giving sight to where the ice boats were lined up side by side. *He's fine,* she told herself. What could Quinten do to him in such a large crowd? Besides, he had Nash with him. And the truth was, Abbie realized after the song came to its violent end at last, if Quinten had discovered where they were, he would have used that to his advantage with a sneak attack. He wouldn't have been so desperate as to cause the accident with her parents.

Abbie allowed those thoughts to settle over her as she closed her eyes and slowed her breath.

"He *is* handsome, isn't he?" she heard a woman whisper from behind.

"It doesn't hurt that he's good with his hands," another said.

"He can conduct my symphony any time." The two broke into laughter.

Abbie's eyes shot open. *If only they knew.* She glanced slightly over one shoulder to see the banner hanging along the fence. It featured the Celebrity Ice Sawing event with a photo of each special guest.

Quinten's image was one Abbie had taken in a downtown studio. She'd used a black velvet backdrop to contrast his blond hair and accent the angles of his jaw. He wore a charcoal turtleneck with an open sport coat and matching, pleated slacks. He looked smart and sophisticated.

Some women, like the ones in line behind her, might find that slight lift of his face on one side charming. But to Abbie, the quirk in his brow, that minor flare of one nostril, revealed his villainous side. She could just hear his inner thoughts in that moment as he peered at her through the lens. *She better get this one just right.*

She tore her eyes off the sight and walked ahead with the rest in line. Yet, as she approached the collection booth, a new dose of determination gripped hold of her; if she revealed Quinten for the man he really was, Abbie might save other women from falling into his trap. She liked that. In fact, running as she had, agreeing to sign the NDA, had left Abbie with only one regret: she was keeping Quinten's secret too. Not that she could have let that stop her from breaking free.

But now she could right that wrong, tell the world what he was really like. Warn the women who, like the ballerina, might inadvertently tiptoe right into his trap.

Abbie nodded, welcoming the adrenaline that raced through her at that thought. She was a fan of justice, and today, in the hours ahead, Abbie was determined to see that Quinten Bromley finally got what was coming to him.

At that thought, the group standing before her dispersed, and a pair of cowboy hats caught her eye from the distant crowd. Thatcher's gaze met hers for the briefest of seconds, proving he'd been watching for her, before he looked away. She could tell, even from there, that he was filling his lungs with air, his chest puffing.

Not wanting to give anything away—Quinten could be watching, after all—Abbie forced herself to scan over the goings on.

"Do you have a ticket?" the attendant asked.

Abbie turned back to the booth to see the child with the polar bear hurry inside with his mother. "No, I need to buy one, please," Abbie said. She handed over the bills, got a stamp across her hand, and thanked the gal at the stand.

"Have fun," the girl said.

Abbie tried to keep the wry reaction off her face as the word *justice* rang loud and clear in her mind. "I will."

It didn't take long to spot the domes Quinten must have been referring to. Five—no, six—of them were lined up like small glass houses. Since they were on land, facing the lake, pine trees weaved around them, creating a more private feel. Three of the domes were occupied, each with couples enjoying a romantic-looking date.

The sight made Abbie's stomach churn. Thatcher was probably losing it. She resisted the urge to look in his direction once more and made her way toward the domes instead. Quinten would surely be waiting for her nearby. Yet as Abbie neared the closest available structure, weaving through clusters of excited visitors, she spotted a young man wearing a smock with the festival's logo. A lanyard hung around his neck, that same logo on the card. He watched Abbie as she neared. Either Quinten had sent the kid and he was waiting for her, or he was waiting for whoever had rented this thing out.

"Are you Abigail?" the kid spoke up as she approached him.

Chills broke out over her skin. No one had called her that since she'd escaped. "Yes," she said, moving to open the glass door at the employee's back.

He put a hand out to stay her. "Wait," he said. "Yours is this way. Follow me." He proceeded to walk back toward the entrance.

"Okay..." Abbie muttered, eyes shifting to find the cowboy hats in the crowd, something made easier by the fact that Thatcher was now standing. Nash rested a hand on his shoulder, seeming to encourage him to take a seat on the bleachers once more. *Crap.*

It wasn't such a big deal that she was going someplace else, Abbie decided. The potential problem was the fact that Thatcher could lose his cool and blow their cover, making it impossible to get what she needed. Again she wished she could text Thatcher. She'd tell him to stay calm. Things were fine. He'd have audio along with somewhat of a view of whatever took place.

The kid led her past the booths and to the entrance of a small building of sorts. It must be the gift shop, she decided. The photos on the location's website showed a charming gift shop and learning center built right into the mountain like a hobbit's home.

After allowing Abbie to step inside first, the guy weaved through a crowd lined up at the register, far back into a quiet corner where he opened a door and motioned for her to precede him once more. "Take the stairs all the way down. Where it comes to a T, go left and follow the path around the bend until it leads to the crawlspace."

Abbie's heart clanked out of beat. "Crawlspace?"

"It's not as scary as it sounds," he assured. "It's over five feet high. Plumbers, electricians, wi-fi guys, all of them use it to access what they need."

Solid, earthy-looking walls cased either side of the dark, narrow stairwell. She gulped, trying to picture what on earth Quinten was doing down there. Waiting with a knife in his grip, blade sharp and ready to slice through her heart?

"But I'm not…any of those guys," she said with a laugh. "I thought I was coming for lunch? In one of the domes?"

The kid's face went red. "Yeah," he allowed, raking a hand through his hair and grinning as if he'd only now looked at her face. "This area is typically restricted, but he arranged to have the date down here. Whoever this guy is—your date—he knows how to get his way."

Abbie leaned in a bit. "Have you seen what it looks like down there? Is there really a table? With lunch?"

Suddenly a man in a white shirt and vest came bouncing up the stairs, a round tray tucked beneath one arm.

"Dude," the kid asked as the waiter approached. "Did you just take food down there?"

"I did," the gentleman said with a nod. He glanced at Abbie. "He's waiting for you, miss."

The kid grinned, looking relieved suddenly. "You heard the man."

The waiter disappeared into the crowd.

Abbie nodded, blew out a pursed breath, and moved to lower one foot onto the first step. She reached to rest a hand on the kid's forearm as she sensed he was about to close the door behind her. It was so dim that the light from the gift shop was a big help.

"Do you mind leaving this open until I get to the bottom?"

The kid nodded knowingly. "Sure thing."

"And…" she added, wanting to ask him to escort her until she got there. And then throughout the entire date too. Abbie did not want to be alone with Quinten in some dark, underground space. But how else was she going to get what she needed?

The hot, red splotches were climbing up her neck once again. She could feel the heat of them rising all the way to her cheeks.

"Are you okay?" the kid asked. "What else were you going to ask me?"

Abbie shook her head. "Nothing, I'm fine, thanks. Just…keep that open if you don't mind." She steadied herself by placing a hand against the cold, chalky walls at either side. The steps were like the ones she'd seen outside ski lodges. Slotted metal with small spikes to take the snow off your boots while wide, airy gaps between each step gave view of the ground below.

She moved down another, and then the next, her pulse rising with each descent. At last, Abbie made it to the bottom where it teed off like he said. She turned over her shoulder to see the young guy giving her an enthusiastic wave. "Nicely done! Just pull out your phone if you need more light."

She considered the live feed; she couldn't disrupt the video or even the perfect placement of her phone. Just how dark would it be?

"Have a fun date."

There was that word again—*fun.* She gulped, willing the tightness there to ease. "Thanks."

The door swung closed with an ominous boom, snuffing the light out with it.

Abbie blinked and stared into the grainy darkness, willing her eyes to adjust. It reminded her of a photo she'd developed in her first photography class in middle school. She'd tried to capture a nice shot of the moon, but as she hovered over the ever-darkening print soaking in the first bin, all she could see were tiny grainy dots in the darkness. The moon hadn't even come through among the stars. Puzzling, since she was positive it had been in the frame.

She later realized that the moon, which had been in the corner of the shot, had been hidden beneath the template during processing. Abbie had learned so much since then, something she should be proud of. She was working on that.

For now, she had to finish conquering the physical demon holding her back. Threatening to force her back into a life of misery. It was time to put Quinten Bromley in his place.

Abbie lifted her hands out before her and took her first few steps, not fully lifting her boots off the ground as she shuffled one foot in front of the other There had to be at least some light down here. The waiter had just delivered their food, he'd said. Had he used his phone light for the occasion? Or was he so familiar with the area that he hadn't needed to?

She'd probably missed a light switch. She was tempted to walk backward and check, but decided against it. The kid said she had to follow the path around a bend. Once she got past the bend, there was bound to be light. So she walked on, one hand in front of her, the other hand sliding lightly along the wall at her side, chalky like the one in the stairwell. Any minute, a massive spider could crawl onto her hand. There could already be one crawling up her sleeve.

The thought made Abbie yank that hand away from the wall. She placed it before her face, palm out like the other, to keep her from running into anything. A few steps more, and suddenly the ground dropped slightly beneath the sole of her boot, letting her know she'd stepped off the path. She righted it, or at least she hoped she had, with the next step, only this time she landed on a small pebble that caused her boot to skid and slip.

Her heart skipped its next beat as she reached out to steady herself.

Each step took her further away from the watchful eyes meant to keep Abbie safe. Further from Thatcher, Nash, and Rem. This is not what she'd prepared herself for.

Still, this was being broadcast, she reminded herself. They were still with her. And if Quinten tried anything, she'd make sure he knew he had an audience.

At last she spotted a fray of yellowed light outlining the bend in the wall like a crescent moon in the night. She moved quickly toward it, fixing her posture as she went. This was intentional, Abbie realized. One of Quinten's tactics to put Abbie ill at ease from the very start. Here, even in darkness, he had the home court advantage.

That might be true. He may have the advantage of being more familiar with the surroundings, but Abbie had an ace up her sleeve. At last she rounded the bend, welcoming the glow that met her path. She squinted toward the source of it.

There beyond the darkness, tucked into an even further recessed alcove, stood a mockup of the dining domes outside—minus the dome, of course. But there was the quaint table draped with swatches of fabric. Brass chairs, flowers in vases, and enough candles to melt the frozen earth around them.

Across the way, Quinten scooted his chair back and came to a hunched stand. "Abigail," he breathed, then cleared his throat. "Thank you for coming." His shining blue eyes locked on her, and a chill slithered up her back.

Abbie gave him a nod and continued to walk toward him. She'd learned over the years that there was a tone he liked her to use most. Agreeable, soft, coaxing. An approach that validated the power and authority of the beast he'd proven to be. And while the last thing Abbie wanted to do was to validate him or play the role of his victim, she'd need to use whatever tactic would work.

It was obvious he'd hoped to intimidate her with the setting. Any fool knew it was far from romantic to eat dinner under a structure where the sewage pipes ran and mice gathered in hiding. So which card would he play? The manipulative, I-desperately-miss-you-and-need-you-back tactic, or the I-plan-to-keep-threatening-the-lives-of-your-loved-ones-if-you-don't-come-back-to-me approach?

Abbie had been through enough with him that she could guess the answer. He'd start off by saying he missed her, see if she missed him too, and if he didn't get the response he hoped for, he'd work his way into the veiled threats.

Abbie was about to step off the path to join him when she noticed a netting of sorts draped around the parameter. She took a step back and eyed it.

"Oh," Quinten said. "In case there are critters down here. There's a magnetic strip down the center where you can step through."

The seam he spoke of came into view. Abbie gently pressed at it, causing either side to split apart so she could walk through. She hunched slightly so as not to scrape her head. "Interesting place for a lunch."

"Indeed. I'm nothing if not interesting." He reached for her hand, but Abbie dropped her gaze to the vacant chair.

"Let me get that for you." Playing the perfect gentleman he wasn't, Quinten hunched his shoulders, pulled back her chair, and motioned for her to sit. She did, scooting up to the neatly set table, and rested her hand beside an empty champagne glass.

Quinten covered it with his own. "Abigail," he crooned. "To think of what happened to your parents." He shook his head, reached for the ice bucket, and pulled out a frosty bottle of champagne. She watched as he pried off the foil and popped off the lid. Abbie checked her glass for any trace of a pill or drug before he tipped the bottle over the rim.

"To think that they could have died," he said as he poured.

"I know," Abbie said. "I was shocked to hear the news."

She felt his posture change at her remark. He had to be dying to know where she'd been when she heard the news. Who she'd been with.

"I hope you don't mind that I already ordered our food. Wasn't much of a selection, but we both like salmon. It's fresh, local, and wild, not farmed." He removed the cover from her plate, and then his own, before lifting his glass expectantly.

Abbie took hers by the stem and lifted it toward his.

"To..." he began to say, but paused as his eyes dropped to where her purse was strapped over her chest. His brow furrowed.

Abbie's pulse spiked.

"Why don't you take off your...shoulder bag? Make yourself comfortable?"

Did he suspect something? Her heart was pounding so hard she worried he might hear it. "Yeah, good idea." She set her glass down, gently tugged the strap over her head, and turned to hang it on the back of her chair. She didn't want Quinten to reach for it, but if she didn't have the phone close enough, it might not pick up his end of the conversation.

"Better," he said, nodding toward her glass once more. "Here's to unfortunate events that, in a strange twist of fate, reunite old lovers and friends."

Abbie grimaced and held her glass in place. Quinten made up the difference by tipping his glass enough to clink against hers. As he lifted his glass to his lips and took a sip, Abbie lowered hers and set it back on the table. She wasn't about to drink to a toast like that. He'd essentially said he was celebrating her parents' accident.

Quinten lowered his glass and pinned a look at where she'd set hers back on the table. He looked at her, alarm sparking in his eyes. "Why aren't you drinking? You're not pregnant, are you? With our—"

"No," she blurted. "I'll have some. I just don't want to drink it on an empty stomach." No need to start an argument just yet, she decided. She still needed to see what angle Quinten would take.

He pressed up his bottom lip, something he did when he was impressed. "Well, don't you sound sensible. I'm usually the one saying things like that. Perhaps I've rubbed off on you over the years?" He'd said it like a question.

"Perhaps."

He reached into his coat pocket and produced a small, velvet satchel. "You left this behind." Quinten dangled the bag from a silk ribbon that cinched it closed.

Abbie cupped a palm beneath it, and Quinten let it drop. She closed her fingers around the velvet bag, feeling exactly what she figured she would beneath the thin material.

"Aren't you going to look?"

She sighed. "I assume it's my old wedding ring."

He flinched. His nostrils flared. "Old? The word is antique, and it's worth millions. A simple thank you would suffice."

She set the satchel beside her plate. She'd donate the thing to charity. "Thank you."

He tilted his head and took another sip from his glass, amusement playing over his face. "I can tell what you're thinking."

Abbie resisted an eye roll. "You think so?"

"I know you so well. You're thinking, why in heaven's name would Quinten arrange for lunch in a dungeon?"

"Actually," she said, lifting her glass at last, "I was thinking, this is *so* like Quinten. Predictably dark, dramatic, and bizarre." She took a sip of her drink, letting him stew in her words.

He chuckled wryly. "Well, well, well. Aren't you feisty today. I always liked it when you got feisty." He picked up his fork, then secured the knife in his other hand. "Until it stopped being cute, that is." He went straight for the capers, reminding Abbie of the final meal she'd made for him. It had been smoked salmon, of course, over eggs benedict, but there he was, piling capers onto one flat edge of his knife and transferring them onto a forkful of food, just like he'd done that morning.

"Tell me," he said after lifting the fork to his lips, "why did you agree to come?"

Her heart gave out an extra thud, warning her that the answer should be just right. Now that she was here in his presence, getting a sense for his mood, Abbie felt it'd be best to appeal to his ego.

"I was coming anyway to see my parents." She watched for his reaction, knowing that she very well may not visit them at all. It'd be too risky, and fortunately, they were both now in stable condition. "But," Abbie added as she secured her fork and speared one of the glazed Brussels sprouts. "I also felt bad about the way I left."

He studied her for a blink, seeming to gauge her sincerity. "*Do* you?"

No. "Of course."

He gulped, then reached across the table to secure his phone. "A bit of ambiance," he said as he toyed with the screen. He tapped at it, and suddenly a classical piece of music blared from his small speaker. He set it down. "The incompetent staff here couldn't even spare a decent speaker. I hope you can hear it well enough." He moved it to the center of the table, and the noise grew—a round of violins chanting, bouncing, light and carefree.

She reminded herself that Grandma C hated Quinten's compositions as much as she did. The thought fueled her with a new level of confidence. Enough to ask something that might shift the tone of their conversation. Take it from cordial to clashing in a blink.

"You told my aunt that you felt responsible for the accident." Abbie watched his face carefully as he assumed a perplexed expression, so exaggerated it looked more theatrical than real.

"Did I now?" He folded his arms, lifted one hand and stroked his baby smooth jaw. "I suppose I feel *slightly* responsible. I assume *you* do as well."

There it was. His trusty tactic—planting seeds of doubt, blame, and outright lies.

Abbie gulped. *Play it carefully,* her inner voice warned. She didn't want to mess this up. Didn't want to leave New Hampshire only to hear of his next attempt on her parents' lives. Maybe he'd aim for Dorothy, her wayward cousin, next. Claim she died of an overdose. *"Poor thing,"* she could hear him saying. *"Seems like the people in your life keep stumbling into harm's way. I wonder what you might do to stop that..."*

"Why would *I* feel responsible, Quinten?" she asked, working to hide the disdain in her voice.

"Because you left them. Left without even saying goodbye. How selfish. How terrible."

Her mind shot to what he'd said in the interview. "How is caring for my mental health selfish?"

Quinten furrowed his brow and glanced about. And then his lips curled into a serpentine grin. He fixed his eyes on her. "You watched my interview. I knew you'd miss me."

"I didn't miss you."

"You're obsessed with me."

"Is *that* why I left?"

His face changed. The music did too. Soft thumps from a bass drum, like the beat of a heart. And then a piano chimed in, offering a soft, cheery sounding melody as the steady beat of the bass played on. *Ba-bump. Ba-bump.*

"You made me cover up your tracks. Do you think I was going to let you make me look like a fool? I am arguably the world's most desired artist in the civilized music industry—"

"Arguably is right."

"People are supposed to believe that my wife—who was quite fortunate to score me in the first place, *knocked up* as you were—just up and left me one day out of the blue?"

Abbie gritted her teeth. "I could have told a different story," she warned.

His nostrils flared as he glared at her.

Heat jumped from her gut to her chest. Now they were getting into it.

Quinten glanced away, a distant look in his eyes as the music took a drastic dive—chords clashing as the pace began to build.

"Here is the climax of the song," he said, eyes flashing with excitement. "Inspired by our final night together."

Quinten made a show of conducting an invisible orchestra as if he were live on stage. Bent arms stiff, poised wrists bouncing like pebbles down a dirt hill.

"Picture it," he said in a whisper. "Our last night together. My hands teasing the delicate curve of your throat. You, so enraptured by my touch that you're left gasping for air." He closed his eyes as a string quartet reached a fevered pitch, sharp enough to cut through the surrounding stone. The drumbeat came slower, weaker.

Ba-bump.

Ba-bump.

Ba... And then it was gone. Silence filled the space with chilling finality. Quinten gazed at her with a dreamy, blissful look on his face.

"Perfection, unlike the evening itself. With this piece, I imagined finishing what I started."

Abbie was speechless. Inspired by their final night together? His hands on her throat? Her gasping for air? Add to it the waning heartbeat and it was all very clear.

"What you started?" she said. "You tried choking me to death that night."

He stared at her, his wild eyes saying what his words did not. Was it possible he suspected she was recording him? They were alone, after all. Why not openly admit to what he'd done?

"Abigail," he said at last. "I chose not to finish the job, it's true. But I assumed we'd come to an understanding."

Abbie leaned forward in anticipation. "What understanding was that?"

Quinten used both hands to inch his plate away from the table edge. He rested a forearm there and leaned far over. "I'm bigger. Stronger. Superior. You said you wanted a divorce and I *showed* you what I thought of that idea. I wasn't unclear about it."

"Yet I *did* get away and I *did* get a divorce. I wasn't unclear about *that* either."

Quinten's hand darted like a snake's tongue in her direction. Suddenly her throat was in his coiling grip. "And look what happened," he hissed, shoving her back so hard her chair went tipping back.

Abbie scrambled to catch herself as she tipped back with it, barely grasping the under edge of the iron table enough to get her feet beneath her. The chair tumbled to the cold, dirt ground. She looked down to see her purse pinned between the dirt and the chair. "What in heaven's name are you referring to, Quinten?"

Come on, spell it out. Please, just spell it out.

Her face broke into a sweat. Her palms did too.

"I know how to make things happen, if you haven't learned that by now."

Abbie gulped, feeling as if her heart might stop beating in favor of better hearing his next words. "What kinds of things?"

"The kinds of things that make unsuspecting couples careen into tall trees on the roadside after a charity event."

Abbie once battled a fierce fever as a child. When it finally broke, a cold sweat surfaced over her entire body. That was the closest she could come to describing the odd sensation rippling from her scalp to her feet. Her body's response to what her mind was still trying to process.

He'd done it. Quinten had really done it. He'd revealed his hand. It almost felt too easy. She glanced down at the tipped chair, shock rippling through her as she considered her next steps.

"Why are you so worried about that bag?"

Abbie's eyes widened as she lifted her gaze back to him. "What?"

Quinten pushed his chair back, a knowing, nearly triumphant look on his face. His gaze dropped to the bag once more. "You heard me. What are you hiding in there?"

CHAPTER 26

"Thatcher, wait!" Nash was hollering from behind, but Thatcher didn't wait, didn't slow, only continued to cut through the crowd in the gift shop and hurry toward the stairs he'd seen in Abbie's live video. He pried open the door, spotted a row of employee lanyards and grabbed one for himself. He took off his hat, tossing it in Nash's direction before yanking the lanyard over his head.

"Start sharing the video," he said over his shoulder. Thatcher used the flashlight on his phone to guide his way as he barreled down the steps, rushed along the path, his mind racing for what he could say to end Quinten's little rendezvous.

"Evacuation," he hollered before reaching the bend. "Attention, Mr. Bromley," he called again, anxiously rounding the bend at last. "We have to evacuate the crawl-space immediately, let's go."

Abbie hunched down and snatched her bag out from under the chair.

"I was given special permission to be down here," Quinten said indignantly.

"Yeah, well the higher-ups say we have a gas leak that needs fixing. The crew's on their way now and you and the lady have to leave. Miss," he urged with a nod. "Let's go."

Abbie moved to duck beneath the bug net, but Quinten moved to stop her by grabbing her arm.

"Hey," Thatcher blurted. "Why are you grabbing her like that?"

"None of your business, *boy*," Quinten snapped. "Go on upstairs, tell your boss you did your job, and we'll be up shortly."

"Ma'am?" Thatcher waved his arm. "Please allow me to escort you outside."

Abbie tore her arm out of his grip and hurried through the break in the net. It took everything in his power to not pick her up in his arms and carry her out.

"It's not going to end here," Quinten warned from behind.

Abbie moved past Thatcher, but paused to look over her shoulder. "What's not?"

Thatcher extended an arm in Quinten's direction, dissuading him if he thought to advance.

"The misfortune," Quinten said, snatching something off the table. "And you'll have no one to blame but yourself."

"Let's go," Thatcher urged Abbie again. She met his

eyes for the briefest moment, and he gave her an encouraging nod. They had enough. He'd seen the live footage himself. Quinten was toast.

With one hand on her lower back, Thatcher urged Abbie the way they'd come.

"Wait a minute," Quinten hollered.

Thatcher leaned forward. "Run," he rasped under his breath.

To his surprise, Abbie did as he said. Thatcher guarded her as he kept pace from behind, shining a light from his phone on their path. If they could both get up the stairs, Quinten would have to stop his pursuit. They'd be in public, after all.

At the stairwell, Abbie tripped, and the purse fell into the darkness. He'd barely helped her to her feet when a hand gripped Thatcher's shoulder from behind.

He jerked free, rammed his elbow into the guy's face, and snatched the bag off the ground.

The door at the top of the stairs swung open. "Come on!" It was Nash.

"Go," Thatcher urged. He moved to race up the stairs behind her, knowing if he stuck behind to confront Quinten, she would too.

"Abigail!" Quinten demanded from the bottom of the stairs.

They'd made it to the top, where they spun back to look at him.

His face, red with fury. Blood dripped down his nose and over his lips. "There's a vial in the hospital with your dear mother's name on it," he continued. "Your father will be next."

Thatcher only urged her ahead.

"I swear to you that if you leave town, I'll make you sorry."

They hurried aside to close the door behind them, but Thatcher peeked through to say one last thing. "You'll be the one who's sorry soon enough." And with that, he let the door close.

CHAPTER 27

"Thank you for being at the Thirteenth Annual Winter Festival," an enthusiastic host boomed from the stage. Abbie watched the goings on from a small watch tower above the gift shop. A panel of tinted windows showed a broad view of the event outside, while the surveillance screens above the desk gave more specific views depending on the angle. The laptop on the desk, however, operated by the city's police chief, displayed the televised version of the online event.

Nash rubbed his hands together. "This is gonna be good."

Thatcher smoothed a hand over Abbie's back. "I hope so."

"You sure you have enough men down there to detain him?" Rem asked.

"Half a dozen should do it," the chief said.

"Let's get to know our celebrity guests, shall we?" the

host continued. He introduced the weatherman first, listing the guy's credentials before moving on to the town's mayor. "And now, for a man whose masterful compositions have haunted households for over a decade. A man who, my wife claims, is her celebrity crush, which means I'm not exactly rooting for him to win…"

The crowd laughed.

Thatcher growled. "He'll lose, alright."

"And last but not least, we have the lovely Pigtail Twins, Tyla & Tieka. This dynamic duo has made waves on the wide web with their…"

Abbie's stomach did flips as she listened to their introduction. The twins, after all, would play an intricate part in what Nash had named *the big reveal.* Abbie reflected on the pigtails she'd sported as part of her breakaway costume. She'd liked that side of her, the spunky girl with ripped tights and combat boots. A girl that would fit right in with the gals who would—as fate would have it—help the private meeting between Abbie and Quinten go viral.

"And in true Pigtail Twins fashion, Tyla & Tieka have been mingling with the crowd and getting loud. Let's take a look." The host nodded to the massive screen as the audience on the ice cheered.

"Get ready, guys and gals," the police chief said into a mouthpiece hooked to his ear. "He may try to make a run for it."

Abbie's heart clanked out of beat.

Suddenly, Abbie's video footage flicked onto the screen. The angle was slightly tilted to one side, which caused audience members to tilt their heads in unison.

There was Quinten, seated at the table, the candlelight bright against the darkness. Abbie had often assumed that her ex-husband's justice would come, but not until the next life.

Yet as she took in the moment, saw what was happening before her eyes, she realized the moment was now.

"Here is the climax of the song," he was saying, waving his arms all about.

A hush fell over the crowd as the song, which sounded like background music at first, approached its crescendo.

"Picture it. Our last night together. My hands teasing the delicate curve of your throat. You, so enraptured by my touch that you're left gasping for air."

Oohs and *ahs* filled the space. "Lucky girl," someone yelled from the crowd.

"I imagined finishing what I started."

Abbie's voice came next. *"What you started? You tried choking me to death that night."*

A collective gasp sounded over the crowd.

Abbie spared another glance in Quinten's direction. He took a backward step as his reply echoed over the icy ground.

"I chose not to finish the job," he was saying. *"But I assumed we'd come to an understanding."*

"What understanding was that?" came Abbie's voice next.

"I'm bigger. Stronger. Superior."

More gasps sounded.

"I don't think he's joking around," one lady said.

"What is this?" asked another.

"'You said you wanted a divorce and I showed you what I thought of that idea. I wasn't unclear about it."

"I did *get that divorce and I wasn't unclear about* that *either."*

Abbie flinched as Quinten's angry hand reached out, earning more gasps even still. *"And look what happened."*

"What in heaven's name are you referring to, Quinten?" Her voice came out tight, pinched, but not wavering.

From the tower, Abbie darted a look out the windows once more.

Quinten looked over one shoulder, and then the next, seeming to notice the three men and two women in uniform closing in on him.

"The kinds of things that make unsuspecting couples careen into tall trees on the roadside after a charity event."

"Mr. Quinten Bromley," one of the officers said, his voice magnified by the nearby mic as he moved in and secured Quinten's wrists. "You're under arrest for the attempted murder of Spencer and Eloise Carrington. Anything you say can and will…"

Abbie felt herself exhale as she watched them cuff a nostril-flaring Quinten in front of some of his biggest fans. "I was only joking," he declared. "I didn't mean any of that." He continued to ramble, but the microphone no longer picked up his voice as they guided him through the crowd.

The footage played on, and one of the officials in the tower addressed Quinten's threat about the vial with her *"dear mother's name on it,"* saying they already had agents guarding each of their rooms. They were safe, and so was she.

"Wow," Abbie breathed. "Thank you."

Thatcher pulled her into a warm embrace. "Didn't I say he'd be sorry?"

She managed a slight nod, hardly able to believe the moment was real. They'd really pulled it off, and now Quinten would have to answer for everything he'd done. Hopefully he'd go away for a very long time.

"You did," she said, enjoying the great feel of being in his arms. "You sure did."

CHAPTER 28

Thatcher watched as Abbie drummed her fingers on the table for the hundredth time.

"Let's go for a horse ride," he suggested. Sure, it was cold out, but the air would do them some good.

"No." She drummed some more.

"We could get something to eat."

She shook her head. "Can't."

"Drink? If we drive far enough, I'll find you a Starbucks. What kind of coffees do they have in the spring? Leprechaun lattes?"

She kept her posture the same, but her gaze darted his way.

"Blarney Brew with Irish Stew?"

Her brow furrowed.

"Come on," he finally said, throwing his head back in an exaggerated fashion. "You can't just sit here and wait all day. It's torture."

Abbie sighed and turned to him at last. "A jury is deliberating Quinten's fate. Which feels like it's also our fate. There's no distracting me from this one."

"Then maybe we should talk about it."

Abbie shook her head again. "It's better if we don't."

Up to this point, they'd talked of their future in terms of *when* he was found guilty, not *if,* meaning they hadn't broached the topic of what they'd do if Quinten went free. There seemed to be an unspoken pretense that it'd be bad luck to speak of the unthinkable outcome. Inwardly, however, Thatcher had been quietly formulating a plan B.

The fact was, Quinten had gotten away with a lot over the years. If he got off this time—if that jury actually found him to be innocent—Thatcher and Abbie's world would tip upside down. Quinten would be angrier than ever, set on reaping his revenge.

Thatcher's Plan B involved leaving Montana for a time, moving to a place away from here, and starting anew. His heart ached at the thought of leaving his family behind, of raising his kids someplace that was not Copeland Brothers Ranch. They'd be away from his family, miss out on Sunday dinners and birthday celebrations, and live under a constant cloud of fear. They'd worry about the safety of Abbie's family too.

It wouldn't be easy, but if Abbie was by his side, it would be worth it. At least they'd have each other, and he'd do everything in his power to give her the best life he could, no matter what.

Still, the waiting period was a torture of its own. They'd been hoping for a short deliberation time.

Assuming the evidence had been enough to snuff out any doubt. The driver had come forward, admitting to his part in the crime, and revealing a whole new aspect to the case —Quinten had been threatening the man's family, saying he'd kill them all if he ever came forward. Quinten had also accused the man of failing the mission on purpose, saying he'd chickened out and only tapped their bumper.

What more could the jury need? And why in heaven's name did they need—he glanced at the time—three and a half hours to agree that this creep was guilty with a capital G. At this rate, it could go on for days.

Abbie was drumming her fingers once more. The tips would be bruised if she kept that up. Thatcher worked to pull himself from the funk. If he was good at one thing, it was lightening the mood. Bringing the humor. Distracting from whatever event had caused upset or pain. He wanted more than ever to do that for Abbie, a woman who'd done the same for him during the summers throughout their youth. Like she had while Thatcher paced in the motel room before the set up with Quinten.

An idea came to him then, a recollection of the morning after he'd picked her up at the station. While the two ate breakfast burritos in his truck, Abbie revived their old radio show pastime. She'd been the DJ, he'd been the caller. That meant it was his turn to start things off.

"This is *TC Spill the Tea*, here on this brisk spring day to take your cares away."

He feigned tapping a button and leaning into a mic. "Hello, caller, who do we have on the line?"

Abbie stared at him with a blank expression.

"Shy, are we?" Thatcher urged. "Come on, friend. There must be a reason you dialed this number. What's on your mind?"

She lifted a finger and looped it in the air.

His shoulders drooped defeatedly.

"Turn around," Abbie said, making the same motion with her finger.

Thatcher perked up. "Oh yeah." He spun to face away from her, a triumphant grin pulling at his lips. Anticipation sprouted through him as he waited for her to speak.

"I'm calling about BBW," she said. "Do you know who that is?"

"I do not. Unless we're talking about barbecue basted wings, which happen to be good friends of mine."

"The big bad wolf," Abbie filled in.

"Ah, okay."

"He's done a lot of bad stuff to me and my family, and I'm not sure if he's going to get in trouble for it or not."

Okay, so they *were* going to talk about it.

"Well...I'm sorry, who am I speaking to?"

"Little Pig."

"Well, Little Pig, let's take a look at both scenarios. If he does get the punishment he has coming to him, how would you live your life?"

"I'd get to romp and skip and dance and play my flute by the fire at night."

"That sounds mighty fine," he said. "And if BBW goes free, how would you live your life?"

"I'd probably just sit home and oink all day."

"Oink?"

She made snorting sounds to prove it, and he could almost hear a smile coming on.

"No dancing? Skipping? Playing the flute in the firelight?"

She sighed. "I don't know."

He hadn't wanted things to take such a serious turn, but at least now maybe he could assure Abbie that he had a backup plan.

"You know what?" he said, clearing his throat.

"What?"

"I bet there's a special pig in your life who's willing to help you find happiness and safety no matter how things go."

"You think? How?"

"I bet this pig—or maybe he's a big, strong badger—will take you wherever you want to go. He'll find the best puddles of mud for you to bathe in."

"Mmm," she said with a laugh. "Would he get in the mud too?

Thatcher shivered. "Nope. He…doesn't like mud. But he'll dance an Irish jig in a wig to make you laugh. And he might even cut open his knee to kneel and propose to you."

"Do badgers have knees?" Abbie asked.

Thatcher spun back around to face her as he considered that. "We'll ask Rosie about that one." He took her hand and looked into her eyes. Thatcher had meant what he'd said. Quinten still had no idea where Abbie was living, but if he did run free, it was possible the man would find out somehow. It was unlikely he'd ever try and hurt her parents again, or anyone from her family, for that matter, after the video that had gone viral. For the most part, the video's population had done a whole lot of good. It had, however, made selecting a jury harder, according to prosecutors.

"You could still press charges for what he did to you," Thatcher said. "If he gets off for the attempted murder charges. You have your attorney, the woman from the library—"

Suddenly Abbie's phone began to buzz.

Thatcher's chest went tight as she swiped the screen and tapped the speaker prompt where it rested on the table.

"Yes?"

"We have a verdict," the prosecutor said.

"Okay."

Thatcher's heart pounded so hard it hurt. He worried it would keep him from hearing the verdict.

At last, a single word came through the line in the man's deep voice. "Guilty."

Thatcher threw a celebratory fist in the air. "Woo hoo!"

"Oh, my gosh," Abbie breathed, "I can't believe it." She scooted her chair away from the table as if she were about to stand, but she didn't. Like a puppet whose strings were abruptly snipped, Abbie crumbled in on herself, covering her face as a heart-wrenching sob got caught in her throat.

Thatcher was on his knees and by her side in a blink. He smoothed a hand over her back as that deep cry broke free in a round of raw, aching sobs. Her emotions pierced their way deep into his heart, testifying to the years of torment she'd endured. Thatcher closed his eyes against the sudden sting of welling tears.

"Finally," she said, the single word broken with her cries.

If Quinten had kept Abbie locked in a case for his keeping, the glass had shattered. Every intimidating glare, abusive phrase, and act of violence trickled off her like weightless shards.

"Let it out," Thatcher encouraged, allowing this to be a time of his own release. In his desperation to protect her, Thatcher had revisited the scene in the crawlspace, where he'd elbowed Quinten before following Abbie up the stairs. In his dreams, he produced a knife and slit the man's throat. Or brought a barrel to his head and pulled the trigger with ease. He'd woken up in a sweat, worried that perhaps they should've taken things into their own hands while they had the chance.

But justice had been served, and now they were free. His limbs went warm and lax, the extreme weight of that burden disintegrating like vapor in the sun. At last, he wiped the moisture from his eyes, lifted his chin to the heavens, and offered a wordless thanks he didn't know how to voice.

Abbie straightened up enough to throw her arms around Thatcher. She squeezed him tight as jagged breaths rocked through her, quickening at first, but slowing ever so gradually.

"It's done," Thatcher assured. "It's really over."

"Congratulations, you two," came the prosecutor through the line, letting them know he was still there.

"Thank you," Abbie said with a sniff. She patted Thatcher's back before releasing him. "Thank you so much." Her body trembled as she lifted the phone between them, but the smile on her face said it was all good. She would heal from this, especially now that she was finally free.

The prosecutor relayed the details next. Quinten had been sentenced for fifty years to life, twenty-five for each count, with no chance at parole. As public as the crime was, and related to domestic violence, the judge hoped to make an example out of him. Additionally, Quinten would face charges for threatening the driver's family, which, prosecutors said, could add another twelve years onto his sentence. Of course, the driver would be on trial for his part in the crime soon, too.

Once Abbie was off the phone, she threw her arms around Thatcher again and squealed. "It's going to take a while for this to really sink in."

Thatcher nodded. "Definitely. But you know what makes it more real?"

"What?"

He grinned. "Telling people about it."

"You're right! Let's call your parents and Grandma C first. Then let's call Taja and Wes. No, Nash—you'll want to tell Nash first maybe. Then Rem, Wyatt and Wade..."

"If you'd like," Thatcher said, "we can tell the ones living here in person."

Abbie nodded, seeming to test the idea. "Yes, I'd love

that. Especially Grandma C. She's going to be stoked!" She lifted her chin and sucked in a breath. "Wow," she said, puffing her chest with air. "We're actually free. Looks like we might get the future we've been hoping for after all."

Thatcher pulled her in for a hug, allowing their joy to fuse and swell, in, around, and through them. They really were free to pursue life together here at the ranch, just like Abbie had said. He kissed the top of her head. "You can count on it."

Abbie felt freer, happier, and lighter than she'd felt in years, if not her whole life. For as long as she could remember, Abbie had known there was a life she longed to have, while knowing that life could never be hers.

What Great-Grandma Dottie and Grandpa Buck had was a life of simplicity and fulfillment on the ranch. Sure, it was filled with hard work, physical labor, and the demands of farm and ranch life. But they were happy, humble, and down to earth in a way that grounded Abbie despite her uppity upbringing.

Now here she was, on the back of a Harley motorcycle, arms wrapped solidly around her real-life cowboy. They were headed to the lakeside for a day of fishing and a picnic lunch. It was the perfect way to start a new day.

Upon hearing the verdict, and telling Thatcher's family the good news, Grandma C and Jacki threw a celebration dinner the following night. Grandma said she'd let Abbie burn his albums if she had any; she didn't, of course. What she *did* have, however, was the daily newspaper with Quinten's photo and verdict plastered on the front page.

Grandma had torn off the section, crumpled it into a ball, and passed it to Abbie. From there, Abbie gripped the black and white wad of trash—a symbol of the years he'd hurt her—and tossed it right into the bonfire. Belle, Scott, Wyatt, and Wade were on FaceTime, meaning the whole family was there to cheer as the hot, hungry flames consumed the article representing her past in a fiery breath, turning it to ash in a blink.

Thatcher had said that, if Abbie would only step over the ashes in a pair of high heels and throw herself into his arms, it would reverse a horrible dream he'd had when Abbie first arrived.

"Maybe tomorrow," she'd said with a grin. "I haven't mastered that walking-on-fire thing quite yet." She'd thrown herself into his arms just the same, and whispered words of gratitude, relief, and love.

Abbie's parents weren't mentally in a place to celebrate the verdict. Their physical wounds had healed for the most part, but the pair admitted that they hadn't yet reconciled the loss of what they viewed as the son they'd always wanted. Abbie wasn't surprised that they hadn't greeted her with anything warm or fuzzy when she'd reached out after Quinten's arrest; she knew well enough how they were. Good thing she'd gained a bonus family in the Copelands.

Abbie considered that as Thatcher slowed the bike while he wound through a quiet trail not far from the lake house. It led to a clearing where they used to play as kids.

An old swing once dangled from one of the massive trees where they'd dare one another to do tricks.

He pulled up to an arbor with a set of picnic benches and helped Abbie off the bike.

"Okay," she heard a woman say from somewhere beyond the trees. "Run it on over."

Abbie glanced in that direction in time to see little Rosie dart out of the surrounding woods with a picnic basket in her hands. She grinned big at Abbie, tiptoeing as she went and set it on a table that had been covered with a checkered tablecloth.

"That's my girl," Thatcher said, voice filled with pride as he hunched down and held out a palm.

Rosie ran over to them and gave Thatcher a high five, followed by a hug. The sweet girl tossed her arms around Abbie too, her soft, warm cheek flush against Abbie's while the little one's hair tickled the side of Abbie's face.

"You're such a sweetheart," Abbie told her.

"So are you!" Rosie said, then gave them both a wave. "Have a romantic date!" she cheered, then skipped back toward the trees.

"Wait," Thatcher called after her. "Where's our animal fun fact?"

"Give her one from your new spring book," Taja suggested from her spot near the woods.

"Oh, I have one!" Rosie clapped and jumped in place. "Baby chicks can remember up to a hundred faces! It helps them tell their mama apart from all the siblings and aunts and stuff."

"Wow," Thatcher said. "I can only remember *ten* faces!"

Rosie flicked up her fingers and started to count. "Na-ah," she said doubtfully.

"Seriously." Thatcher turned to Abbie. "Who are *you?*"

Abbie swatted his arm. "He's teasing."

"I know that," Rosie said, then reached for Taja's hand.

"Nicely done," she heard Wes say as he stepped beyond the wooded area and wrapped an arm around Taja's waist. "Remember," he called, "date night with the Emersons this weekend."

"Sounds good," Thatcher assured.

Abbie had been surprised to hear some interesting facts about the family of Earl Emerson, the kind, older gentleman who'd met with them to construct a plan for Abbie's trip to New Hampshire. Earl had mentioned that he and his family had taken on a dozen or so witnesses over the years, the way the Copelands had harbored Taja and Rosie while they awaited the trial. What she hadn't known was that three of the women they hosted had married Earl's three nephews. This weekend, Abbie would get to meet the couples. She could hardly wait.

"Thanks, guys!" Thatcher hollered.

"Bye," Abbie called.

And as the small family said goodbye and headed back toward the lake house—visible in the distance—Abbie couldn't help but picture her and Thatcher having a little one of their own one day. Perhaps a girl who wouldn't mind getting messy or worrying about germs. Or a little boy who, like his father, had a mild fear of catching germs from the people and objects around him. Or perhaps their little guy would start off with blond hair like his dad and not realize that the years had turned most of it brown. Speaking of which…

Abbie moved in to run her fingers through Thatcher's newly cut hair.

He grinned. "This is you gloating again, isn't it?"

She shook her head. "This is me admiring you again. It looks nice. And," she added with a laugh, "I still can't believe this is what it took for you to realize you're not blond anymore."

"I will be," he promised. "Come summer. You just wait and see."

"I'm looking forward to it."

Thatcher took her by the hand and motioned toward the lake. "Before we eat, I have something for you over here."

Abbie walked toward the lake with him, noting where the grass gave way to a wide span of mud. In the summer, the area would dry out, allowing them to lay out towels and set up coolers and chairs.

"Man, this is a lot of mud…" That final word fell off her lips as something caught her eye—a strange pattern carved into the mud like wet sand on a beach. She squinted, making out a Y, an M, and an E.

Abbie leaned back slightly to get a broader view. There was something before that Y: two Rs, an A and another M. She gasped, and her heart skipped at least two beats. *"Marry me,"* she breathed. It was then she noticed the words further out—*Will you.*

Thatcher turned to face her and reached for her other hand. "The snow was gone, but I still wanted to give you the proposal you dreamed about, minus the cut knee and stitches." He glanced over at the mud and added, "Hopefully," before shivering.

Abbie loved the way the mere look of that mud made him squirm.

"But to prove how much you mean to me," Thatcher continued, urging her to step onto the muddy part of ground. He looked at her expectantly.

"You're not—"

"I am," he assured, and plopped a denim-covered knee right into the mud.

He lifted his chin, pulled a ring box from his pocket, and flicked it open to expose a beautiful ring. A simple engagement ring—an elegant gold band with one simple, embedded diamond—like the ones she'd shown him online.

"Abbie Abs Carrington," he said, making her laugh a little. She loved that he hadn't used her full name. That he'd thrown in his nickname for her instead.

"You were my very first crush. In fact, I didn't know what a crush was until you came along. Now, today, I'm asking if you'll also be—not just my last crush, but my lasting crush, the one I love and put before all others until the end of time."

The view of him there on one knee in the mud, his hazel eyes so welcoming and warm, became blurred by the tears welling in her eyes. She sniffed, smiled, and basked in the wonder of the moment. Thatcher Copeland was on one knee proposing to her. And she was free to say yes!

"Will you make me the happiest cowboy in all the land, and be my wife?"

Abbie was about to answer, but thought it'd be better if she were…more on his level. At once, she plunked onto both knees.

Mud squished and splattered beneath her, and Thatcher chuckled and shook his head.

"Yes," Abbie cheered happily. "I absolutely will!"

At once, his hand was in her hair and his mouth was on hers in a kiss that almost made Abbie forget all about the mud. She tipped her head back as the kisses slowed, enjoying the dreamy haze of his affections.

A quick glance downward said Thatcher was on both knees now too. He had just as much mud on him as she did. Still, Thatcher secured the ring, held it out for her, and Abbie moved in to make it easier so it didn't fall in the mud. Once the beautiful engagement ring was solidly on her finger, she squared a challenging look at him.

"True or false: you have an extra pair of pants waiting for you in the picnic basket."

He grinned and shook his head. "True."

She nodded, absolutely loving that about him. "Okay," she said. "You've proven yourself by playing in the mud long enough." She glanced down at her own pants. "I wonder if Taja would mind—"

"I've got you covered there, too," Thatcher said.

"No way."

He nodded, his grin so wide and triumphant she wanted to kiss the expression right off his face.

"I knew you couldn't resist a chance to play in the mud."

She looked down at the sloshy stuff, then lifted her gaze back to Thatcher as she sank one hand into the depths. She curled her fingers around a big, oozy clump, enjoying the feel of it in her palm. "You knew I'd like to play in the mud, did you?"

"Don't even," he warned.

"Why not? We haven't even really played in it yet." Abbie lifted the handful in the air, knowing she wouldn't smear it on his face like she was threatening to. But it sure was fun teasing him.

But suddenly Thatcher beat her to it by releasing a glob he'd been hiding behind his back. It splatted against her jacket, mainly, but it also coated the tips of her hair where it dangled in front of her shoulder.

"You did *not* just do that," she said, too stunned to retaliate just yet.

"Oh yeah?" He smeared a muddy fingertip down the bridge of her nose, assuring her he could take whatever she wanted to dish out. So dish out she did, with a hearty hurl of mud that splattered on his neck and shoulder.

The two of them struggled to their feet at once, each grabbing more mud and working to fling it at the other. Abbie ran, slipped, and fell right on her rear end with a plop. When Thatcher joined her, leaning his face close to hers, Abbie gave him warrior mud marks on his cheeks with her thumbs.

"You must really love me to do this."

Thatcher grinned. "You read my mind."

EPILOGUE

Abbie couldn't get the grin off her face. Behind a dual set of chapel doors, loved ones filled chairs and waited for the bride to walk down the aisle. Little did they know, Thatcher wasn't facing the pastor at the front like guests thought. That was Wyatt in his spot.

Thatcher gave Abbie's hand a squeeze. "You ready for this?"

To say he looked good in a tux was a complete understatement. He'd look even better as the two of them shuffled their way down the aisle while lip-syncing the popular radio tune about getting hitched in boots.

"I'm ready," she said, squeezing his hand in return. They had a few minutes until the song would come on. It was important, Nash suggested, to build up the suspense. Which had her recalling the weeks leading up to the wedding, and the moment Thatcher had called Wyatt and Wade to tell them the good news. It was only after they'd hung up that Abbie suggested asking Wyatt to stand in front to take his place. *"He's close in size, and now that you cut your hair, it looks like his too,"* she'd told him.

"I'm glad Wyatt said yes to this plan. Him being here will be a wonderful surprise to your parents too."

Thatcher grinned. "Me too. And you're right. It was probably mean of us to have him stay with Rem until the wedding, but it'll be worth it when they figure out that he not only flew out for the wedding, but he also agreed to pose as me so I could dance down the aisle with you."

Abbie could hardly wait to see the surprise on their faces. It would make their special moment all the sweeter. Family, she'd learned, was never just about one person. And a wedding wasn't just about two. This day was a celebration for all of them, Lloyd had said, and boy had Abbie liked hearing that. Liked knowing that the Copelands truly cared about her. That they were excited for her to officially join the family and carry their name.

Her parents had declined the invitation, but Abbie hadn't dwelled on that. She was where she belonged, with people who loved and cherished her.

Spring weddings weren't terribly warm in Montana, but today was warm enough to have a decent celebration outside, complete with food, dancing, and an open mic for anyone who wanted to say a few words or even bravely sing a song or two. So far, only Rosie had volunteered for that. But the day was young.

"Psst," Thatcher said. "What are you thinking inside?"

She took in his handsome face, warmed by the

sunlight, and felt as if her heart was melting like wax. "I'm thinking about how happy I am, here with you."

That killer grin of his filled his face. "Good," he said, "because I've never been so happy."

She smiled and blushed. "Save it for the vows."

"We were supposed to write vows?" His eyes went wide, but then he patted the pocket at his chest. "Just kidding. Mine are right here."

He leaned in then, pulled Abbie into his arms, and kissed her in a way that made her very glad their honeymoon was starting tonight. "I love you."

"I love you too."

The wedding song started, the one usually played for brides to walk down the aisle. That was their cue.

"All rise," she heard the pastor say from the other side of the doors.

"Let's go get married," Thatcher said.

Together they stood at the closed doors, holding hands in the center, gripping a handle with the other hand. Suddenly the wedding march cut off. Whispers broke out through the crowd, audible from the other side of the doors.

"Wonder what's wrong."

"Audio problems," one guest surmised.

"Or maybe she's changing her mind," another said.

Thatcher shot her an *as-if-that-would-ever-happen* look and puffed his chest.

Suddenly, the upbeat song blasted through the speakers, and Thatcher and Abbie flung open the doors. Together, they broke into the popular dance moves that went with the song. Laughter bubbled up Abbie's throat as the group cheered and clapped along. When Grandma C feigned looping a lasso over her head, Abbie only hoped the videographer was catching that too.

One thing she was certain they'd caught on video was Rosie, their sweet little flower girl, as she spread petals over the runner. Abbie had made a special note about recording that since they wouldn't be there to see it themselves.

Her eyes shot to Lloyd and Jacki who, until that moment, believed Wyatt was too sore at Thatcher to show up for the wedding. She saw them look back and forth between Wyatt and Thatcher, wiping tears and wearing grins as wide as their faces. Jacki wagged a scolding *you-tricked-me* finger at Wyatt before rushing over to squish him with a hug and plant a kiss to his face. The exuberant woman turned her gaze back on Thatcher and Abbie, clapping to the beat as she hurried back to Lloyd's side.

The entire chapel buzzed with excitement by the time they reached the front and the song died down. Wyatt started to make his way to the bench, but Thatcher stopped the guy and gave him a hug. "Thanks, man."

"Any time." Wyatt joined the family on the front seat. All but Nash, who was Thatcher's best man, and Taja, who was Abbie's maid of honor.

Thatcher shared his vows first, balancing each tender promise with enough humor to make her laugh and cry at the same time. When she shared her vows, causing Thatcher to laugh through watery eyes of his own, Abbie knew deep in her heart that he was meant to be hers all along.

"Dang springtime allergies," he griped as Abbie folded her note and handed it back to Taja.

The rings came next, the heavenly kiss followed—their first kiss as bride and groom—and then the pastor said what they'd all been waiting for.

"Say hello to the new Mr. and Mrs. Copeland!"

Cheers erupted throughout the chapel. Their song came on once more as Abbie and Thatcher shuffled their way back down the aisle and out front where they'd greet their guests.

"Let's skip the reception and head straight to the honeymoon," Thatcher said in her ear before giving her lobe a nibble. Chills surfaced over her skin.

"Too late. They're already coming." And so they were. A large group of happy guests with wide smiles and open hearts. Abbie lifted a prayer to the heavens as she greeted them in turn. She took a moment to bring her bouquet to her nose and breathe in the blend of lavender and mint. *I know you were here for the wedding,* she told Grandma Dottie mindfully. *Thank you for showing me the life that would bring me joy.* Already, Abbie mused, leaning over to kiss her new groom, she was well on her way to living the dream.

"I cannot believe we've got this whole place to ourselves," Thatcher said as he carried Abbie over the threshold and into the castle-like structure in Ireland. "We are the freaking queen and king of this castle for the next ten days?!"

Abbie chuckled. "I told you marrying me would have its perks."

"I'll say." He never had been one for dreaming of money or visualizing extravagant vacations. But one look at the castle Abbie's Benedict family owned, and he was starting to see what all the fuss was about.

"Remind me to give your folks a proper thank you."

"I will."

"But let's not talk about them right now." After all, his bride was soft and warm in his arms, and there had to be a big bed with their names on it.

What Thatcher would also shelve was the disturbing news he'd learned shortly after the wedding—Scott had asked Belle for a divorce. Turns out their struggle to have a baby was more than he could handle. In a way, the moment had reminded Thatcher of Wes's wedding, and the disturbing call he'd received from Abbie.

One day, when Belle was ready to hear it, Thatcher would mention the common thread, hoping it would give Belle hope for a future beyond the marriage she was leaving behind. Hope that one day she'd have and hold a baby of her own. At least Belle had the best family a person could have, and all the support—outside of Scott—that she could ask for.

Thatcher spun in place as he took in the massive stone arch over the fireplace, statues hunched at either side, and the many short hallways and doors in the distance.

"Which way?" he asked.

Abbie shrugged. "I've never been here. But you can let me dow—"

"Hush, love," he said in an Irish accent. "I'll not let ye down 'til I have me way with ye."

Abbie giggled. "Then pick a room. Any room. They're all empty, and I'm sure most of them have beds."

He hurried to the nearest door which—like the others—extended at least twelve feet tall. With Abbie cradled firmly against him, Thatcher twisted the knob enough to open the latch, then stepped back to make a show of rather kicking the door open.

"Quite the manly lad, ye are," Abbie said.

"Right, me lady." He set Abbie gently to her feet, moved to close the door behind them, and nearly lost his breath when he turned back around to see Abbie shimmying out of her dress. Sure, he'd playfully helped her unbutton it during the limo ride from the airport, and he'd not so playfully nibbled at her shoulders and neck as his patience slipped away with the setting sun, but he had not expected Abbie to be as ready as he was for this part of their getaway.

Abbie glided the silky dress off her curvy hips, a lacy camisole and thigh highs setting Thatcher's blood ablaze, and flung the dress at him with the flick of her foot.

Abbie-scented silk covered his face as he struggled to pull it away and look at his bride, who was now slipping out of her heels. His pulse spiked with desire as she tossed them aside.

"Catch me if you can," Abbie said, scurrying behind the bed.

Oh, he'd catch her all right. And the best part about it was that he didn't have to clutch onto her to make her stay. He'd chosen her, and Abbie had chosen him. God willing, they had a lifetime ahead of them to hold onto each other on nights like this.

Thatcher had lived enough life to know it wouldn't always be easy. They'd go through times of heartache together, of difficulty, mourning, and trial.

But if there was one thing his family had shown him over the years, it was that of all the locations around the globe, be it Ireland, New Hampshire, or the great state of Blue Sky Montana, *together was the best place in the world to be.*

Stay tuned for the next book in the Sweet Montana Bride Series, Belle's Cowboy Cradle, coming 2024.

FREE BILLIONAIRES IN HIDING BOOK

Thank you so much for taking the time to read Taja's Cowboy Caress and the bonus books included.

If you enjoyed this book, I hope you'll consider leaving a review on Amazon and or Goodreads.

Check out the other books in the Sweet Montana Bride Series here.

Want more romantic suspense?

How about a family of billionaires who've been forced into hiding to start a new not-so-luxurious life? It's called my Billionaires in Hiding Series and you can get the first book, *Springtime Love at The Homestead Inn*—by Kimberly Krey for FREE here when you sign up for my newsletter.

As a bonus, you'll also get book 1 in my Benton Brothers Series.

Each of theses series has five complete novels packed with sweet and swoon romance.

Those subscribed to my newsletter hear about my next releases, free books, and flash sales. I also share sweet romance deals by authors like me.

ALSO BY KIMBERLY KREY

Billionaires In Hiding Romance Series

Springtime Love at The Homestead Inn: Country Boy & City Girl

Summer Nights at The Homestead Inn: While He Was Sleeping

Autumn Romance at The Homestead Inn: Do Nice Guys Finish Last?

Winter Kisses at The Homestead Inn: Flirting With the Enemy

Cabin Fever at The Homestead Inn: Despite the Odds

The Sweet Montana Bride Series

Reese's Cowboy Kiss

Jade's Cowboy Crush

Cassie's Cowboy Crave

Taja's Cowboy Caress

Abbie's Cowboy Care

Belle's Cowboy Cradle (Coming Soon)

More Cowboy Romance:

The Cowboy's Catch

Unlikely Cowgirl Series

Her Gun-shy Cowboy

Her Kismet Cowboy

Her Dream Cowboy

Small Town Romance:

Cobble Creek Small Town Romance

The Unlikely Bride

The Hopeful Bride

The Determined Bride

Second Chances Series

Rough Edges

Mending Hearts

Fresh Starts

Benton Brothers Romance

28 days with a Billionaire

Her Best Friend Fake Fiancé

Stepping In For The Billionaire Groom

The Billionaire's Second Chance

The Billionaire's (Not So) Fake Engagement

Single in Forties Series

Sting Op Fun at Forty-One

Romantic Comedies

Five Days With My Super Hot Ex

Five Days With My Kinda Evil Ex

Six Days With My Celebrity Ex

My Grumpy Christmas Companion

Getting Kole for Christmas

Getting Micah under the Mistletoe

Beach Romance

Catching Waves: A Sweet Beach Romance (The Royal Palm Resort Book 2)

28 days with a Billionaire

Young Adult Novellas

Getting Kole for Christmas

Getting Micah under the Mistletoe

Chemistry of a Kiss

Novella

Ranch Hand for Auction

The Cowboy's Catch

Navy SEALs Romance

The Honorable Warrior

The Fearless Warrior

Christmas Romance

Her TV Bachelor Fake Fiancé

Her Best Friend Fake Fiancé

The Billionaire's (Not So) Fake Engagement

Snowed In For Christmas

Getting Kole for Christmas

Getting Micah under the Mistletoe

Dashing Through the Tropes

Collections

All's Fair in Love & Tropes

Benton Brothers Billionaire Romance Collection

Broncos & Billionaires

Cowboys & Billionaires

Dashing Through the Tropes

Falling for Her Bodyguard: Four Full-length Romance Novels

Cobble Creek Romance Collection: Three small-town Romances

Heartthrobs, Cowboys & Old Flames

It All Starts Here: Sweet Romance Collection

More Cowboys & Billionaires

Never Fall in Love with the Rich and Famous

The Sweet Montana Bride Series: Three Witness Protection Cowboy Romances

Second Chance Romance Series: Three Sweet Romances Featuring Second Chances

ACKNOWLEDGMENTS FOR ABBIE'S COWBOY CARE

I must give my incredible story editor, Valerie Bybee, a huge thanks. Your awesome insight sheds light on issues that might have gone unnoticed. You make each of my books better, and I thank you for that.

I'd also like to give a big thanks to my copy editor, Jeigh Meredith. I so appreciate your hard work and flexibility, and I look forward to reading your book.

Also, thanks to my ARC team. What a great crew! I appreciate your willingness to read, review, and also send messages that encouraged me along the way. You guys are awesome. Thank you!

ABOUT THE AUTHOR

Writing Romance That's Clean Without Losing the Steam!

USA Today Bestselling Author Kimberly Krey specializes in writing 'Romance That's Clean without Losing the Steam'. She's a fervent lover of Jesus, family, and cheese platters, as well as the ultimate hater of laundry.

Subscribe to her newsletter and follow her on any of the sites below for updates on new releases and or giveaways.

amazon.com/Kimberly-Krey/e/B009A0350I
facebook.com/kimberlykreyauthor
instagram.com/romance_is_write
bookbub.com/profile/kimberly-krey
tiktok.com/@kimberlykreyauthor
x.com/KimberlyKrey

Made in the USA
Columbia, SC
08 August 2024

40157621R00171